D1547322

THE BORDER BETWEEN US

BOOKS BY RUDY RUIZ

FICTION

Seven for the Revolution

The Resurrection of Fulgencio Ramirez

Valley of Shadows

The Border Between Us

NONFICTION

¡Adelante!

ANTHOLOGIES

Dillydoun Prize Anthology (contributing author)

Going Hungry (contributing author)

THE BORDER BETWEEN US

RUDY RUIZ

BLACK
STONE
PUBLISHING

Printed in the United States of America

First edition: 2024
ISBN 979-8-212-54526-6
Fiction / Literary

Version 1

Blackstone Publishing
31 Mistletoe Rd.
Ashland, OR 97520

www.BlackstonePublishing.com

To mi familia

PORTS OF ENTRY

"I don't see why you can't take him today," she protested.

"It's cold outside. He might get sick," my father replied, pulling on his boots in the dark. "Our godson, Carlitos, died of the flu when he was nine."

"It was cold last week and you took him. Besides, that's not why Carlitos died."

"Today's not a good day."

"Why?" my mother asked.

Silence.

"Are you seeing someone?" she pressed.

"What are you talking about?"

"¿Otra mujer?"

I listened quietly outside the door to their bedroom, my boots in my hands, bare feet shivering on the cold floor. I thought of my cousin, Primo Carlitos. We had learned to swim together. We had slept in the same bed at our grandmother's house, giggling under the sheets. Then, I'd been told I'd never see him again.

"Another woman? Are you going to start with that again?" His voice turned dark and tense.

"Why won't you take him then? If you're not doing anything you're not supposed to be doing?"

I peeked around the corner, watched him glower at her in the shadows, his thick eyebrows knitting together, a disapproving awning brooding over menacing windows. "Fine. I'll take him. But if something goes wrong, Marisol, you're to blame."

"What do you mean?" Sheets rustled as she sat up in bed, clutching her pregnant stomach.

"Never mind." The rocking chair creaked as he rose.

I scurried into the kitchen so he wouldn't discover me spying.

"Buenos días, Ramón." His voice softened as he discerned my silhouette in the blue glow of dawn. "Ponte tus botas. Grab a blanket so you don't get sick. Vámonos."

As our boots crunched over the yellow winter grass, I peered at my dad's faded red '67 Ford pickup. It was only a decade old, a year more than me, but it already belonged to a distant era, patches of brown rust consuming it like a rapidly spreading cancer. Once within its creaky doors, I was grateful for the sarape, unfurling vibrant stripes in burgundy, green, and blue. The colors emanated a magical heat. I wrapped myself tightly in it, but the truck still felt cold as a metal coffin on wheels, squeaking and rattling as we cruised the abandoned streets. The only signs of life percolated at the donut shop near the bridge. Señor Donut. Side by side, a portly woman served glazed donuts and pan dulce. Coffee and café. Gringos and Mexicanos.

"Everybody loves something sweet now and then." My dad patted my head, ordering a dozen chocolate donuts, a coffee for himself, and a hot chocolate for me.

Behind the counter, stuffed into a pink polyester dress, a white apron stretched taut across her bulging belly, the woman plundered the display case with long metal tongs, then poured coffee and chocolate without spilling a drop, a cross between a cursed sea monster with dexterous tentacles and a landlubber blessed with unfettered access to baked goods.

"¿Que cuentas, Perla?" My dad smiled, sliding a twenty across the Formica counter.

"Nada nuevo, Señor López. Working. Always working."

The collection of men hunched over the counter nodded their heads in somber agreement, their Brownsville Heralds rustling like the wings of restless crows as they slurped noisily from their mugs.

"You still have room at the boardinghouse, like we talked about the other day?" my dad asked as she handed him his change.

"Sí," she answered slowly, her eyes falling on me. Why was she looking at me? I didn't need a room at a boardinghouse. I already had a room.

"Bueno. I'll see you there, after your morning shift."

Why would my father want to meet Perla there? Was she the "otra mujer" my mother worried about?

Hesitantly, she held a steaming pot of swirling brown liquid in each hand, her eyes shifting again from my father to me. "¿Y el niño?"

"He's with me," he answered, touching the tip of his hat and retreating into the parking lot.

As we shed the stuffy warmth of the donut shop, the moist cold air stung my cheeks. Glancing back, I saw Perla place the coffeepots down and make the sign of the cross.

———

The rising sun illuminated the river as we crossed the Gateway Bridge into México. The streets were empty as we cruised through Matamoros, the inhabitants of its colorful houses—a blur of hibiscus, aqua, lime, mango—slumbering still.

Soon we were out on the open road, hurtling toward the ranch as the wind whipped noisily against the truck. When the weather was good, my dad rolled down the windows and sang Mexican songs, bringing an instinctive smile to my face. But today it was too cold. He remained silent, crouched over the steering wheel in his tan overcoat, his eyes burrowing holes through the windshield, his Stetson casting a shadow over his face.

Instead of his usual barrage of stories and advice, he turned and assessed me, pensively stroking his thick mustache. "You haven't touched the donuts. When we get to the ranch, they'll be gone in an instant."

I thought of the hungry mouths to feed out at the ranch. Whenever I accompanied my father, I was perplexed by the abundance of children the ranch hand and his wife had brought into the world despite their circumstances. When I asked my father, all he said was that El Primo Fernandez was a brave man.

Staring at the glossy orange box filled with pristine wheels of mouth-watering air-puffed flour and sugar, I mumbled half-heartedly, "I'm not hungry today." The donuts reminded me of the tires my dad baked in his retread shop. Except these tires weren't dirty and stinky. These were fragrant and perfect. "Primo Carlitos liked donuts."

My dad stared at the road ahead, his eyes glazing over.

When we spotted the row of elms on the left side of the road, we knew we had reached our destination. Five trees lined the dirt road from the highway to the humble ranch house. In their teens, my dad and his brothers had planted the trees amid bouts of nausea and vomiting, the labor a punishment for stumbling home drunk from the Fourth of July fireworks.

The pickup truck rattled along the bumpy road, kicking up a cloud of dust that enveloped us. When we reached the rusted gate, I descended to push the creaky behemoth open. Once the truck passed, I closed it and climbed back into the cabin. This was my weekly job, and I was proud to do it well. Rolling beneath the elms' sprawling branches, we reached a clearing. There, stood an obstinate cinder-block house. Two crumbling but defiant rooms. An explosion of children streamed toward the truck, laughing giddily at the prospect of donuts. Their faces were streaked with mud and soot, their hair matted and disheveled, their feet caked in dirt, but their smiles radiant. As my dad handed El Primo Fernandez the box, I was glad I hadn't eaten any.

While the children feasted, the men spoke beneath the nearest elm. "¿Y el bebé, Primo?" my father asked.

The haggard ranch hand shook his downcast head and frowned. As he did so, the cracks in his sunbaked skin deepened. "No better, Primo. The clinic won't help. Hijos de puta. They sent us home. For her to die."

"I talked to a doctor I know on The Other Side. She said she would help, but we need to bring the baby across. Like we discussed over the phone," my dad explained. "Did you look into the permiso?"

"Yes, but they won't give it to us. Chinga su madre. They think I want to go work over there. Pendejos."

My dad shook his head and spat onto the ground. "Chingados. Pues a la mala then. Is your wife ready to try?"

"Sí." Primo Fernandez summoned up a guttural wad of phlegm from his emaciated torso and spat on the ground as well. I wasn't sure if it was a macho competition or a country tradition, but the men always did this. They loaded their phrases with curses, spitting from their foul mouths as if their salivary glands were determined to cleanse them.

The men turned, their troubled eyes settling on the house. The children had scurried back inside because the breeze was too frigid and humid this time of year for their scantily clad bodies, even with the extra sugar to burn.

I was accustomed to tagging along with my dad and quietly listening to everything he said. Usually, his conversations revolved around selling tires and scraping together enough money to make the house payments or keep the lights turned on at the plant. At the ranch, his ramblings typically entailed talk of Primo Fernandez's tasks for the coming week: mending fences, breeding cattle, or planting sorghum to feed the scattered livestock grazing on the anemic pastures. Today's conversation, however, was different. Their words fell from their lips like stones, heavy with worry.

I followed as they sauntered toward the rustic wooden door. My grandparents had once lived in that insignificant home. Before that, on the same foundation, my great-grandfather had once burned down a wooden house by falling asleep with a hand-rolled cigarillo in one hand and a bottle of tequila spilled all over the sheets. The family had survived, but all their possessions had been destroyed.

As we entered, the children huddled around a rough-hewn table, the empty donut box dismantled at its center. We paused as Primo Fernandez ducked behind a sheet that hung across the opening to the back room.

Murmuring. Tattered, musty cotton. His weathered hand waving us through. The room shadowy, cold, and dank. Señora Fernandez—her dark skin leathery and gaunt, her hair frayed—cradled a frail infant in her arms, her piercing gray eyes glowing with fear.

They spoke in hushed tones as my dad leaned over the baby. I strained to make out what they were saying, but all I could decipher was the woman whimpering softly that she did not want her baby to die.

"Bueno," my dad feigned a confident tone as he told them we would wait outside.

I followed him to the pickup.

Moments later, Primo Fernandez escorted his wife to the truck. She required his support to remain upright as she shuffled barefoot across the packed dirt, the mass of children trailing behind her. I could never count how many of them there were because of their incessant motion.

"No, Mamá," a girl about my age cried. "No vayas."

My father gestured for me to open the passenger door and slide into the middle to make room for her. As Fernandez helped her up, I caught a whiff of a pungent odor. There was no running water out here on the ranch, only an outhouse and a pond that collected rain. They bathed in metal washtubs behind the house, and I reckoned they didn't bathe very often during the cold season. She shivered with cold, the baby's eyes remaining tightly shut. I marveled at its smooth skin. It looked as perfect as a doll. How could it face imminent death?

Primo Fernandez closed the door and gazed through the window like a man trapped behind bars. The children swirled about him like a churning dust devil, pressing their cheeks and lips against the cold glass, their breath fogging it up.

Setting his jaw, my dad nodded at him, something unspoken transmitted between their eyes.

As we rumbled into town, the woman and my father did not speak at all. Their lips did not move, but their eyes did. I observed as they glanced at each other and then at the infant cradled in her lap. There was something I could not interpret in their gaze. Was it fear, regret, or something altogether unknown to me? The cabin was awkwardly silent, the air tensed with anticipation. The woman was a dry husk, rustling like withered cornstalks as the truck jostled over the bumpy streets of Matamoros. She looked like the life had been sucked out of her, drained by her never-ending stream of children.

I had seen her during our weekly trips to the ranch. I knew she and her husband tended to the ranch in exchange for living quarters. They grew vegetables, subsisting off the land. When I asked my dad why he called Fernandez "primo," he had told me they shared the same ancestors that had originally settled those lands. He'd known both El Primo Fernandez and his wife since the days they'd all played out in the fields as children. I knew we were poor, but we seemed far more fortunate than our distant cousins south of the border.

In town, we stopped at a trucking compound. Every Sunday after our visit to the ranch, we swung by here to load tires. Two lanky men heaved the tires into the back, the vehicle shaking and bobbing as their weight dropped into the bed. As the truck rocked, the baby's eyes fluttered open and she began to cry, the woman fruitlessly shushing her. The men asked no questions of my father, and he offered no explanations. When the loading was finished, we creaked slowly back toward the bridge, the baby protesting loudly. A few blocks from the tollbooth, my dad veered off course, parking in an abandoned lot. There, he and the woman got down. Grunting, he pushed and pulled on the tractor-trailer casings, creating a nook between four towers of tires. He motioned for the woman to climb onto the tailgate and crawl into the hiding space, but she struggled to board the truck with the baby in her arms.

As she balked, my father instructed, "Déle el bebé a Ramón."

The moment she placed the baby in my arms, the clamorous bundle fell eerily silent, peering quizzically at me through outsized black eyes, her body weightless even to me.

My father helped the woman scale the tailgate, where she backed into the crevice. She reached out and I gently transferred the baby into her arms. As they retreated deep into their rubber refuge, I helped my father push the tires back together and shut the tailgate.

He circled the truck, examining his work. "Can you see anything, Ramón?"

I hopped up and down, peeking past the tires, but all I detected were smooth casings eager to receive a new lease on life at the retread shop.

My dad dusted his hands off, which was pointless because the soot wouldn't come off until we washed them with Lava soap back at the house. This was the life of a tire man, he often declared. Dirty but honest. Humble yet proud.

We clattered toward the bridge, the tollbooth sliding into view as a light rain drizzled across the windshield. The wipers squeaked, sweeping back and forth across the glass. Beggars lined the street, shambling in grimy rags, shaking rusted cups jingling with loose change. Cars snaked toward the crossing. The queue would swell throughout the day. At the right instant, crossing could take merely five minutes, but during busy times it might consume an hour. Radiators would rebel. Steam would hiss. Tempers would flare.

As we joined the line, a sudden cry pierced the cabin. My dad and I turned to look at each other as the line inched along, bumper to bumper. Surely the baby would stop. Wouldn't it? On the other hand, what did the innocent know about immigration officials and drug-sniffing German shepherds salivating over the slope of the bridge? What did the baby comprehend about being discreet while breaking the law? My heart pounded as I wondered what might happen to my father if he was caught smuggling humans beneath his tires. And what of the baby and her mother?

"What's wrong with the baby?" I asked.

"Not its lungs, that's for sure."

"What then?"

"They think it's her heart. In Brownsville the doctors can fix these problems . . . sometimes."

"Do you think she'll stop crying before we get on the bridge?"

"Hopefully her mother can make her stop. Maybe she'll feed her."

But the crying persisted, growing increasingly shrill as we neared the tollbooth. My father stroked his mustache, peering over his shoulder through the small window to the truck bed. "We can't do this with the baby crying."

"Maybe it's getting wet and cold," I wondered, wallowing guiltily in the warm cocoon of the sarape.

My dad glanced back at the tires again. The rain was coming down harder now. The baby screamed. We rolled another car length forward. Only two cars remained between us and the tollbooth, the point of no return. He looked at me again, then down at the blanket that enveloped me.

My eyes followed his gaze down to the stripes, the folds, the excess fabric spilling onto the floor, white tassels dangling in the shadows beneath my feet.

"What if . . ." I mustered. "I hold the baby beneath the blanket?"

Wipers squeaked. Tires rolled. Brakes squealed. Baby cried. One car left. Red light. Green light. Water sloshing. Baby screaming.

At the last moment, my dad jerked the steering wheel to the right and made a U-turn, backtracking along the road by the levee. A few blocks away, he turned into a side street and parked beneath the canopy of an evergreen tree.

He left the truck running as we got down and separated the tires.

Slowly, the woman crawled forth with the baby clasped to her chest.

"Lo siento," she said. "No deja de llorar."

The baby sneezed, wriggling in her arms, as if she were trying to free herself and escape this horrid, unwelcoming world, her face scrunched up, her skin fiery red.

"Maybe she doesn't like the fumes." I coughed in the putrid cloud rising from the rusted muffler.

"The doctors said that it's not good for the baby to cry so much. It puts too much strain on her heart," my father fretted, running his dirty hands through his tangled black hair.

The mother began to weep, in unison with her child.

My dad extended his arms. "Pásamela, María."

It was the first time I heard the woman's name. She did as she was told, but once in my father's arms the baby struggled and twisted, her cries growing stronger. He turned to me, a rare flicker of desperation in his eyes as I held out my hands. When he deposited the feather-like bundle into my arms, she opened her big, black eyes again and fell silent, her limbs relaxing as she ceased kicking.

The woman smiled feebly, wiping away her tears. "Ramón es una alma tierna."

His eyes trained on me, my father did not acknowledge María's compliment. Hurriedly, sensing even my so-called gentle soul could only buy us so much time, he explained to her that we would hide the baby up front. Waving his finger menacingly, he urged her not to move or make a peep until he removed the tires again.

María nodded anxiously, disappearing behind the tires. After he shoved them back into place, my dad opened the door and positioned the sarape over us.

"Scoot down on the seat," he said. "Suck in your stomach."

I followed his instructions.

"Hmm," he studied me. "Put your feet on the edge of the seat so the baby can lie between your knees and chest."

I contorted into the position. "It's kind of uncomfortable."

"Suck in your stomach again. Pretend you're sick."

I closed my eyes and let my head angle down to my shoulder.

"Act like you're trying to get permission to stay home from school."

I moaned.

"That's more like it."

I peeked at the baby beneath the blanket only to find it sound asleep.

When we returned to the bridge, the queue had doubled in length. Shaking his head, my dad muttered obscenities in Spanish as he followed the levee back to the front of the line.

My parents always said it was not proper to skip the line. They said it was unfair and that everybody should wait their turn, but clearly this situation was unusual. My dad gestured for a chance to cut into the line. After two rejections, an elderly lady consented.

Minutes later, we ascended the bridge's slope. At the summit, I gazed through the rain-streaked window at the river winding toward the horizon.

"Too bad we couldn't have brought them across the river near the ranch," I whispered.

"Too dangerous."

And this wasn't?

What if the baby woke up? What if she got hungry? What if she started suffocating beneath the blanket? Delicately, I raised it and softly blew air over the baby's face. She looked pale now, even in the pink light filtering through the sarape's fibers. Weak. Maybe the crying had drained her. What if she died in my arms?

The brakes squealed as we started and stopped, crawling toward the customs inspector. Sometimes, my dad knew the agent. He'd been crossing back and forth his whole life, ferrying tires across for years. He'd gone to high school with some of them, their parents knew each other. Other times, there might be a gringo inspector transferred from a northern city. More than once, those interlopers had sent him to the secondary inspection area, a covered parking lot where more officers and dogs searched vehicles for drugs and undocumented passengers. If that happened, we'd be finished. They'd order us out of the truck and the baby would be revealed. Wielding flashlights, they'd examine the tires and discover her mother cowering in fear.

My dad strained to see which agent was working each lane. But the rain made it impossible. The last thing he said to me before we proceeded was, "Ramón, remember. You're trying to avoid school. Sick as a dog."

As we reached the checkpoint and my dad rolled down his window, I moaned and let my head slump over my left shoulder. I couldn't read the agent's face in my weakened state, so I listened intently, pulling the blanket up around my chin, my arms wrapped tightly around the baby beneath the colorful woven fabric.

"López!" I nearly jumped out of my seat as the officer bellowed my dad's name.

"Treviño!" My dad replied as they shook hands vigorously.

"¿Que hay de nuevo?" the customs agent asked.

"Lo mismo, bringing tires back for recapping. But this time my boy got sick out on the ranch. I've got to get him home."

The man peeked in. At that instant the baby rustled and sneezed. Instinctively, I coughed and pretended to sneeze. Then I moaned for extra effect. *Just don't cry. Don't cry, baby.*

"It's this weather. Muy frio. You should've left him home with his mother."

"Tell me about it."

"Bueno." His eyes hovered over the tires. "I'll see you next week."

"Ándale, Treviño. Say hi to your parents for me."

The agent patted the truck bed and flashed the green light.

As we rolled down the slick ramp, we sat in silence, listening to our heartbeats slow.

———

Perla stood on the porch to her boardinghouse. It was a dilapidated wooden structure, once painted pink, now faded and peeling. A barbecue grill rusted in the front yard; a mangy dog lay chained to a scraggly tree.

As we parked in the cracked driveway, Perla descended the rickety steps. I couldn't help but wonder if she had donuts stashed in her apron pockets. All this stress had whipped up my appetite.

She helped my dad part the tires and held the woman's hands as she climbed down from the tailgate. Then I handed the sleeping baby back to her mother.

"Que Dios te bendiga siempre," the mother whispered to me.

"You're a hero," Perla remarked, shaking her head in disbelief. "A free donut for you next time you come to the shop. Cherry-filled."

I smiled. "I'm just glad we made it."

"Wait here, son." My dad patted me on the head.

I watched them walk through the light drizzle, up the stairs, and into the house.

On the way home, I asked him, "What will happen to the baby?"

"We called the doctor I know, and she is going to come this afternoon to examine the baby. Then she'll decide. Maybe she'll take her to the hospital."

"You think the baby will be okay?"

"I don't know, Son. Remember, todo lo que nace muere. Everything that is born dies. It is not for us to decide when, where, or why."

"But she's just a baby." My voice quivered as a surge of anguish rose in my chest.

"Tonight, include her in your prayers."

"I don't even know her name."

"Emilia."

"Okay," I said, wiping away the droplet of moisture that had condensed like morning dew at the corner of my left eye.

As we approached our house in Southmost, a collapsing heap of wood on a narrow lot behind a sagging chain-link fence, my dad cautioned me. "Not a word to your mother. Or she'll never let you go with me to the ranch again."

——

Their arguing had been worse than usual, rousing me several nights in a row. Then one morning, as I was about to walk into the kitchen, I overheard my mom on the phone. She was talking to my Abuelita Carmela. Between sobs, she cried, "Mamá, they say he has another family."

Another family? Impossible. My dad worked all day and came straight home from the tire shop every night. When would he have time for a whole other family?

"They say he keeps them in a boardinghouse. But he denies it. Can you imagine? We have a baby on the way. And we can barely pay our bills. What am I to do, Mamá?"

She had it all wrong. Why wouldn't Dad explain? I couldn't bear to hear her crying and badmouthing my father to Abuelita Carmela. He was just trying to help a family in need, greater need than us.

When my dad came home that night, I intercepted him outside.

"Dad, why don't you tell Mom about the woman and the baby?"

"It's none of her business."

"But she has the wrong idea," I said.

"Son, you let me take care of things. Go play."

As he entered the house, the yelling began. *Play?* I sat on the front steps, staring at the weeds choking out the grass, listening to the incessant buzzing of the cicadas vibrating in the trees. As I sulked, neighbors popped their heads out of windows to eavesdrop on the racket.

The next day, when I returned home from school, I found my mother standing behind the door next to a collection of tattered suitcases assembled at her feet. Her belly loomed over them menacingly as she dabbed her eyes with balls of tissue paper.

"What's happening?" I asked, eyeing the suitcases suspiciously.

"I'm going to my mother's house. You can come with me, if you like."

"To visit?"

"No. To stay."

"Why?"

"Someday, when you're old enough, you'll understand these things. But for now, you are too young."

I stared at the faded blue Samsonites, queasiness turning my stomach. I didn't want her to leave. I wanted her to understand that my dad wasn't as bad as she thought. But he had forbidden me from saying anything. What was I to do? I thought of the baby, Emilia, wondered how she was doing, thought of that day crossing the bridge with two stowaways. Didn't you have to break the rules sometimes simply to do what was right? What would be worse, betraying my father's trust and not getting to go to the ranch anymore, or allowing my parents' marriage to fall apart when I could do something to help save it?

"Is someone coming to pick you up?" I asked.

"I called a taxi. It's on its way."

I took her hand and gazed up at her. "Mamá, there's something I have to tell you."

"What is it?"

"I know the woman and the baby at the boardinghouse."

"What?" she exclaimed, clutching her heaving stomach.

"Dad is just helping them. The baby is sick. The woman's husband

and kids are on El Otro Lado at the ranch. They're the family that works and lives there, Dad's relative, El Primo Fernandez."

"I . . . but . . . people said . . ." She seemed to lose her balance but I hung on, steadying her until she placed her hand on the doorframe. "This is the problem with these macho López men!" she yelled at no one in particular. "He keeps me in the dark. He never tells me anything, what he is doing or where he is going or who he is with. He thinks it's a sign of weakness. Why is he like this? ¿Dios mio, porqué?"

Sobbing, she slid into a rickety chair next to the front door. As her crying subsided, the house fell strangely silent. Only the sound of our breathing filled the room as we stared at each other. Why was the person we both loved so incomprehensible? Was this our secret burden to bear? Was this what bound us, even more than our tie as mother and son?

Outside, the sound of an engine approaching. Through the window, a yellow car pulling up to the curb, brakes squeaking. On the wall in our meager front room, a clock ticking loudly.

She grunted as fluid streamed down her calves and splashed at her feet.

A frightened expression gripped her eyes. "Help me to the taxi," she said, reaching for the doorknob.

"What's happening? Are you still going to Abuelita Carmela's house? Didn't you hear me?"

"I heard you. The baby is coming. I'm going to the hospital."

I glanced back at the suitcases as I chased after her. "Do you want to bring something?"

"Just lock the door. Hurry," she huffed, waddling to the cab.

————

It was a long night at the hospital. The waiting room overflowed with family chattering over the din of crackling intercom announcements. My grandmothers. My dad's brothers. My mom's sister. Uniformed nurses drifted in and out like restless moths, white shoes squeaking across shiny linoleum. At first, it was a festive gathering, an enthusiastic welcome party for the newest addition to the López clan. But as the hours dragged on, everybody grew tired, worry lines etched across their foreheads, their dark features drooping like shadows at sunset.

My dad had been summoned behind the ominous swinging doors that held visitors at bay. I heard murmurs about a breech birth. What was that? Feet first. Pain. Blood loss. Then there were the screams. Shrill. Piercing. Savage. Everybody could hear them emanating from the long gleaming hallway. How many sets of those heavy doors stood between us and whatever table my mother's life balanced upon? How could her tormented shrieks still reach us all the way out here in the waiting area?

My uncles darted outside, anxiously igniting cigarettes, blowing clouds of smoke at the full moon. Abuelita Carmela wrung her hands around her rosary, pleading for her daughter as my paternal grandmother, Fina, comforted her.

My stomach growling despite the unfolding drama, I gravitated toward the vending machines, marveling at how the press of a button could mechanically transport shiny packages and tasty morsels into a person's eager hands, as long as said person was loaded with quarters. Over the cool hum of the soda machine, I discerned a familiar voice, turning to catch a fleeting glimpse of a pink puffball floating down the corridor. Others may have seen just another visitor checking on a loved one, but I recognized a free jelly-filled donut when I saw one.

"Miss Perla," I scurried after her.

She stopped. "Ramón. What are you doing here?"

"My mom's having the baby."

"Good God," she made the sign of the cross just as she had that morning at Señor Donut. "May everything go well for them."

"What are you doing here?"

"I'm checking on Emilia."

"She's here?"

"Yes, hasn't your father told you? She had her surgery earlier today. I took her mother home to rest because she hasn't slept in days."

"No, my father hasn't told me. But I've barely seen him. It's been a crazy day."

"Yes, I can imagine. Well, come with me. Do you want to see her?"

I followed Perla through a maze of corridors, ending up at a panoramic window. Beyond the glass, rows of babies rested in plastic baskets, swaddled in white blankets adorned with pink and blue stripes. On the sides of the baskets, cards hung with names written in black marker. Rodriguez. Gomez. Cross.

"Are those plastic cribs?" I peered curiously at the tiny beings lying on their backs, some sleeping, others jerking their limbs aimlessly in the air like dying cockroaches.

"Those are incubators. They keep the babies warm."

My eyes opened in awe. "I wouldn't mind having one of those myself. Our house gets cold in the winter."

Perla chuckled. "Yes. I wouldn't mind starting over in one of those incubators either. I'd do a lot of things differently, that's for sure."

I gazed up at Perla. Her life didn't seem half bad. She owned a boardinghouse and worked at a donut shop. She'd never go homeless or hungry. What could she regret?

She gazed at me placidly, as if she could read my thoughts. "Look over there in the corner, that's where the really sick babies are. They call it the NICU."

Sitting in the far corner of the room was a lonely incubator with a tiny, defenseless Emilia in it. The card read, "Fernandez." A fleet of machines surrounded the incubator. Tubes and wires ran into it, swarming the baby.

"Will she be okay?"

"There was a hole in her heart and they had to close it. She is a strong baby. But you never know. All we can do is pray."

"I prayed for her like my dad told me to."

"Good. So did I."

As we stared at the lone crib in the NICU, a nurse backed into the room through a set of white doors. She wheeled an incubator into the corner next to Emilia.

"Who's that?" I asked.

"I don't know."

I strained to read the card hanging from the side of the fresh arrival's incubator. It remained blank as the nurse connected hoses and tubes. We watched the nurse methodically conduct her work. When she finished, she extracted a black marker from her pocket and leaned over the name card. As she stepped out of the way, I gawked at the card hanging from the side.

"López," I whispered.

Perla gasped, covering her mouth as if she wished she could take it back.

"It's your brother," I heard my dad say from behind us. "It's Rubén."

As we turned around, my father looked like he'd aged ten years since that morning.

———

That night after the family left, my dad and I stayed as late as we could. Around 1 a.m. we finally drove home. It was the only night we had ever spent alone in the house. The place seemed strangely alien without my mother. He tucked me into my bed and dragged in the rocking chair from his room. Sitting in the corner, he swayed gently, the creaking lulling us hypnotically. We drifted in and out of sleep, his snoring occasionally stirring us.

"Dad," I asked. "What's wrong with Mom and Rubén?"

He rocked for a while. "Your mother lost a lot of blood. It was a very difficult delivery, but she will be okay."

"And my brother?"

He rocked some more, shutting his eyes, snoring and then finally answering, "Rubén came out feet first. They say he might not have gotten enough oxygen to his brain. We won't know for some time what it might mean. He also needs surgery for his neck."

I stared at the ceiling. This was all rather unexpected. Babies were supposed to be born healthy and happy. And here the only two babies I knew were fighting for their lives in the NICU.

"And Emilia?"

"Her surgery went well. The doctor says if she continues to improve, she could be out of the hospital in a couple of weeks. But she is still in critical condition, which means nothing is certain." He sighed deeply. "Even if she makes it, the doctors say she might have problems for years to come."

"Did I have problems as a baby?"

"No."

"I guess I was lucky."

"You are blessed. Now you have to work hard to make more luck and earn more blessings. Life is like the river. It has many twists and turns. You never know what is coming around the bend," he said, slipping back into sleep, the creaking of the rocking chair slowing until it stopped.

I thought of the Rio Grande carving its groove in the land beyond the levee we passed each day. Climbing that levee, I could see the river, the banks on the other side. I knew the river flowed east and emptied into the Gulf near our ranch, winding through the lands our ancestors had settled long ago. The river was dangerous and unpredictable. Sometimes it ran dry and people and livestock went thirsty. Other times it flooded and swept away entire neighborhoods like an angry god wreaking havoc on his inadequate followers. Was that what life was like?

When I dozed off, I dreamed of being out on the ranch. I saw Emilia and Rubén. But they weren't babies anymore. They were four or five years old. They ran through the fields, vanishing into tall reeds of swaying grass. I was surprised to find myself not chasing them, but rather waking within the confines of a giant incubator. Tubes and wires ensnared me as I gawked desperately through the plastic walls. I lurched and tugged at my restraints. Then a tenuous sense of calm washed over me as I caught sight of Emilia and Rubén. They held hands as they gazed back at me. Their eyes loomed large and vacant, like windows to an abandoned house. But there they stood, alive, slowly raising their hands to wave weakly at me. My fear subsided as I slipped back into the darkness of untroubled sleep.

We headed out the next morning, stopping briefly at Señor Donut. The shop was empty and silent except for the beeps that issued from the coffee machines. My dad had a distant look in his eyes. He stirred his coffee as Perla handed me the free donut she'd promised. I saw her pull it out of the bin marked "cherry-filled," but when I bit into it during the bumpy ride to the hospital, it turned out to be lemon. It was sweet and powdered on the outside, sour and bitter on the inside, but I ate it anyhow.

BENDING THE LAWS
OF MOTION

The shiny bicycle in the storefront window had my name written all over it. Not for real, but that's the way I saw it. Centered beneath my favorite words in the world—"Mac's Toys"—the Evel Knievel motocross bike was totally groovy. It gleamed white with blue stars, red stripes, and chrome highlights on the handlebars, wheels, and spokes. Evel Knievel was the epitome of cool. I pictured him jumping a long string of cars or the Grand Canyon, his cape fluttering behind him, his body a heroic streak of red, white, and blue.

"¡Ándale!" my mom snapped, tugging at me sharply as Rubén screamed in her arms. "We still have to go grocery shopping and your baby brother's already losing it!"

"Mom," I sputtered as she towed me away reluctantly, "you think maybe for Christmas? The Evel Knievel bike? The store clerk said they have only one in stock. I asked if he could save it for me, but he told me we'd have to pay a deposit to place it on layaway."

"Not now, Ramón. We can't afford it. We'll see what happens by Christmas. Maybe if things go better for your father . . ." She sighed as we walked into the old downtown H-E-B store, the smell of raw meat and garlic searing my nostrils.

Despite the difficult road, my dad remained a devoted tire man. He crossed the bridge to México every day, searching for worn tractor-trailer casings and delivering freshly recapped tires to his customers. He brought the cascos, the shells, back to his little vulcanizing plant by the railroad tracks. From the outside it looked no different from any of the small wooden houses that flanked the rail yards and the old cemetery on the corner. The exterior paint had once been white with red trim, but now it was peeling and run-down. A splintered sign dangled from a solitary chain near the front door, proclaiming, "Joe's Tire Shop."

Inside, the space was cramped and stank of burned rubber and sweat, but I loved it. Every day after school, I would beg him to take me to the shop rather than drop me off at home with my nagging mom and drooling brother. Usually, he didn't mind. He'd let me answer the phone and file papers while he talked to the plant engineer, Pedro. Pedro was a short, round man with spectacles. He looked like he'd been molded out of molten rubber himself. His overalls were always covered in soot, his hands and face dark with the black powder that constantly rubbed off the tires. Despite his weight, he rolled nimbly between the silver tire molds, checking gauges and adjusting levers and wheels. He reminded me of a pinball bouncing around inside an industrial-themed arcade machine. Through the hissing steam, he barked commands to his two helpers. It always seemed urgent to me, like he was maintaining a delicate balance and if he let it get out of hand, the whole place could blow.

My favorite part of the day was when the bell rang, and Pedro would call for help, spinning one of the wheels that crowned the molds. A miniature crane would swing over the steaming tire as he lifted the lid. With a crowbar, he'd pry around the tire's edges, ensuring its clean separation from the steel mold inside. Then he'd attach the hook hanging from the crane and give the order to pull. Out would pop a big old tire that now looked brand-spanking new, deep patterns grooved into its once smooth and useless surface.

My father would beam as if he'd just witnessed his own child being born. "Another one hundred dollars." He'd smile, winking at me.

When times were good, my dad's wallet would be stuffed full of hundred-dollar bills. But when times were bad, it would be crammed only with wrinkled little pieces of white paper. Receipts, he called them, as he instructed me to file them away for the taxes.

Even though tires emerged from the molds every day, they were piling up in the storage room at the rear of the tire shop. Dad's big worry was always how to keep the lights turned on at home and at the shop, the men paid every Friday, and enough money to pay for the boxes of rubber he ordered from Akron, Ohio. Accomplishing this always seemed like a delicate juggling act.

On the TV in our eat-in kitchen at home, President Carter had used the word "malaise" to describe our economy. When Mom asked what it meant, my dad said it sounded a lot like malo, which meant "bad."

Luckily for me, the nuns at St. Mary's Elementary School were merciful enough to let him run behind on the tuition. They knew eventually he would pay up, as always. I was in fifth grade and hoped to get the Evel Knievel bike for my eleventh birthday at the start of the school year, but sadly, the malaise had been contagious and turned my cumpleaños into more of a pity party than anything else. Christmas was my last hope for the bike.

"Not that I want to go back, Dad, but if I was still at public school instead of St. Mary's," I asked as we rode home in his rattletrap pickup truck, "could you afford to get me the bike?"

"Son, the best thing I can give you," he replied somberly, his thick mustache rising and falling with his words as he kept his dark eyes on the road, "is an education. A bike can be stolen. But your education? No one can ever take that away from you. Besides, you have a bike."

I thought of the pink girl's bike that had been handed down to me from one of my female cousins. It collected dust in the backyard because I didn't dare ride it in the street. Was he serious? Riding that contraption was sure to end up in a one-way trip to the hospital.

"How bad would public school really be? Maybe they finished building the new classrooms and I could have a desk of my own? It's less strict and it's free!" I envisioned riding my sparkly Evel Knievel bike to the public school, performing stunts for the awed kids in the parking lot, popping wheelies and jumping parked cars like the daredevil himself did on TV.

"Son," my dad replied, his eyes glowering beneath the brim of his tan Stetson hat, "you are a very smart boy. More than half of the kids that go to public school here in town don't even graduate. They drop out. Now, I know that wouldn't happen to you, but I want you with the nuns, where you get books and discipline."

I rested my chin on the open window and gazed out at the passing houses as dusk fell. We lived in Southmost, a neighborhood of tiny wooden shacks crammed behind leaning chain-link fences, smashed between the railroad tracks and the river levee. It was the southernmost neighborhood in the United States. All I had to do was walk across the street and climb the grassy hill in order to see the Rio Grande and México beyond.

When I'd started at St. Mary's the year before, I'd told a kid at school what part of town I lived in, and his jaw had dropped. He'd backed away slowly and then turned and run. So, the next day, when the class bully was about to pounce on me, I decided to try it again.

Staring at his shiny penny loafers, his pressed and pleated navy-blue slacks and white shirt, I had stalled, "Jimmy?"

"What is it, punk? Talk fast because I'm ready to smack you. It's your initiation," the biggest boy in our class snarled, droplets of saliva flinging down on my face.

"I live in Southmost," I stated flatly, searching his cold blue eyes for a response.

Jimmy lowered his fist. He reassessed me. I was short and scrawny, holes in my grayish white guayabera, patches on my secondhand faded blue pants, scuffs on my shoes.

"Southmost, huh?" Jimmy frowned.

"Yup."

"You ever get in a fight down there?" Jimmy asked.

"Sure, all the time," I lied.

Jimmy nodded.

"You carry a knife?" he asked.

I'd seen the teenagers in the barrio playing with switchblades while hanging out on the street corners, doing tricks, trying to impress the girls without slicing their fingers open. That was the closest I had ever been to owning a knife.

"Nah," I said. "My dad makes me leave it in a drawer in my room."

I could hear the gears turning in Jimmy's head.

"Okay, you follow me, kid," Jimmy said. "Don't tick me off and I won't mess with you. Understand?"

"Yeah, sure. No problem," I replied.

After that, I never had any problems at St. Mary's. I didn't always hang out with Jimmy, but the other kids knew he respected me and that was protection enough.

I liked the nuns' school better than the public school. At the public school, there were so many kids the building couldn't fit them. So they'd started bringing these portable trailers and parking them in the playground. The trailers were supposed to be temporary classrooms, but since they couldn't build fast enough to keep up with the growth in students, they never went away. Some teachers even tried landscaping around their trailers, but the kids would pick the flowers and trample on the plants just to be mean.

One day, while I was still at the public school, my dad had to come pick me up early because my mom was at the hospital with my baby brother, who was undergoing yet another one of his countless surgeries. When my father found my classroom, his bushy eyebrows knit together like they did when he was about to hit somebody.

"Mrs. Ochoa?" he asked my teacher, a wispy spinster in perpetual mourning who always dressed in black.

"Yes, Mr. López?" she answered, her gloomy voice quivering in fear.

"Why is my son sitting on the floor back there?" he asked, pointing at me, sitting with my legs crossed in the back row between two desks.

"Well, we just can't fit enough desks in here, sir," she answered as if it was a perfectly acceptable answer.

My dad scanned the room. It was hot and muggy because the air conditioning units in the portable classrooms weren't very good. There must have been a dozen of us sitting along the aisles.

"How come some kids have books and others don't?" my dad asked

Mrs. Ochoa, refusing to let her off the hook too easily. "My son is sitting down there on the floor, and he doesn't have a book in his lap."

"Well . . ." Mrs. Ochoa coughed nervously. "We . . . uh . . . share books, Mr. López." She forced a hopeful smile at him.

Sharing was good, wasn't it? They taught us that in kindergarten.

"Mrs. Ochoa," my dad replied, "how can he 'share' if he can't even see the page of the person sitting next to him because he's three feet lower?"

Mrs. Ochoa pursed her lips.

"C'mon, Ramón," my father commanded.

Cautiously, I climbed over my classmates, struggling to avoid stepping on anyone's fingers.

"Mrs. Ochoa, don't expect my boy back here. My orphaned father didn't come all the way from Yucatán to the United States of America for his grandson to go to school in a trailer and sit on the floor without a book. We could do that back in México if we wanted to."

So I got a few days off from school. Rubén was brought home from the hospital. And the next week, my dad took me to St. Mary's for the first time.

"Son, this is going to be a sacrifice," he explained in the parking lot. "But you're smart. You're going to take what you learn here and someday do great things with it. Maybe you'll even be the first López to go to college."

At St. Mary's, I devoured books and checked out magazines and biographies from the library. I liked reading about the American presidents, like Abe Lincoln and Teddy Roosevelt. I relished learning big words and impressing my teachers. The day after President Carter used the word "malaise," I had eagerly darted to the giant dictionary on the counter at the front of my spacious classroom to find the definition. My dad had been pretty close. It was malo. The dictionary said it was a general feeling of illness or sickness. Well, it had certainly infected my birthday proceedings, but I was determined to stop the malaise from killing my Christmas dream.

St. Mary's was not a very big school. There were only two fifth-grade classrooms. One was the A class, which were mostly the Anglo kids and the smartest of the Mexican American kids. The other was the B class, which consisted of the rich kids that came in carpools from México every day and the underperforming gringos.

At first, the nuns had put me in the B class. But after a few days, the teacher walked me to the principal's office and said something about me being too smart for her to feel right about holding me back. So I joined the A class. I would have been a little scared, but Jimmy was in that class and he made sure no one gave me any trouble. One of his best friends was a boy named Sergio Aranda. Even though we all had to wear uniforms, Sergio's somehow seemed nicer. His hair always looked sharply cut and shiny. And the girls always giggled when Sergio walked by. Even though he was a real Mexican, and I was Mexican American, he was lighter-skinned than I was. Jimmy, Sergio, and I hung out together during lunch. When the kids played games, we were always picked first. Jimmy was the strongest kid in class. He could beat anyone at arm wrestling. Sergio was the most athletic. When we played kickball, he always sent the ball sailing over the fence. And I was the fastest, the wind whipping through my long black hair as I zipped by everyone else in the races.

In the parking lot after school, the parents would circle through a half-moon driveway to pick up their children. I religiously hoped Sergio and Jimmy's parents would come before mine because I didn't want them to see my dad's beat-up pickup truck. Jimmy's mother drove a silver Mercedes-Benz. His family owned a chain of gentlemen's clothing stores. Sergio's father picked him up in a gleaming white Cadillac Eldorado convertible. Luckily, my dad always ran late.

One day, Sergio invited me to visit his house.

"I don't know if my parents will let me go across the border with you," I replied.

"Well, we can go to my house here," he said.

"What do you mean?"

"We have two, one on each side," he explained casually, as if everyone else did too.

"Of course," I shrugged, forcing a grin.

After much haranguing, my parents granted me permission to go home one day with Sergio. I'd never ridden in a Cadillac before.

"Your seats are so nice and soft, Mr. Aranda," I swooned as the cold air from the vents blasted my face. This vehicle could double as a refrigerator, I thought.

"Those are leather, Ramoncito," he replied, smiling at me warmly.

"Of course," I replied, petting them as if they were my long-lost puppy.

I felt so comfortable around Mr. Aranda. It was like I'd known him my whole life. Unlike my dad, who was always sweaty and covered in tire dust, Mr. Aranda looked like he'd stepped out of that fancy magazine I'd seen in the library, *GQ*. He wore a gold Rolex watch, lizard-skin shoes and belt, a European-looking shirt, and a gold chain around his neck. His eyes were shielded by Porsche Carrera sunglasses, which were all the rage.

Sergio's house was a paradise. In the backyard, a free-form swimming pool surrounded by palm trees overlooked a peaceful resaca flanked by real, live flamingos, just like the ones at the zoo. And his bedroom was bigger than my parents' and mine combined. Actually, it was probably the size of my whole house.

I ran my fingers over the switches and buttons on Sergio's stereo, the lava lamp and touch-tone phone, allowing my eyes to float over the posters of beautiful women in bikinis and shiny red Ferraris that he had pinned up on his walls.

"Wanna go for a swim?" Sergio shouted, jumping up and down on his bed.

"¡Vamos!" I yelled.

We changed quickly and cannonballed into the pool with glee. This was the life. This was the dream. I knew exactly what I wanted to be when I grew up: Mr. Aranda!

During the ride back to my house, as Mr. Aranda drove, I worked up the nerve to ask, "Mr. Aranda, what do you do for a living?"

Seeming a bit surprised, he answered nonchalantly, "Oh, I'm in the . . . import-export business."

I'd heard of that. I nodded my head, smiling. Import-Export. It sounded good. In fact, I'd heard it quite often, living on the border. Maybe I could get into that line of work too.

Later, back at home, I saw everything in a different light. My dad was a savage beast compared to Mr. Aranda. My mom appeared tired and old next to Mrs. Aranda, who always had her highlighted hair professionally styled and her makeup done at the Dillard's cosmetics counter. Our creaky, faded hardwood floors seemed primitive compared to the wall-to-wall carpet at the Arandas' house. And when Christmas finally came, while Sergio was swallowed whole by mounds of crumpled gift-wrapping paper, I found only a paltry red envelope and a slender rectangular gift wrapped in metallic gold paper beneath the plastic Christmas tree that teetered in the corner of our spartan living room.

"I'm sorry, mi hijito." My mom smiled faintly, running her fingers through my hair. "It was all Santa could afford."

I opened the envelope to find a wrinkled five-dollar bill and an American Greetings card with Rudolph the Red-Nosed Reindeer on it. American Greetings? They hadn't even cared enough to give the very best.

"And what's this?" I stared glumly at the light present clasped in my hands. The wrapping paper was so cheap that gold glitter had already stuck to my fingers.

"Open it," she said.

Inside was a blank spiral-bound notebook. It was similar to the memo pads the nuns gave us to list our homework assignments. I stared at it as blankly as its pages stared back.

Sensing my confusion, my mother explained the gift, always a bad sign, "It's a journal, Ramón."

"A journal?"

"Yes, I read in the newspaper that it is a good habit for people to write things down in a journal. Your dreams, your ideas, your thoughts. They said it helps turn goals into actions."

I fought off the knot growing in my throat. I knew times were tougher than ever. My dad had been forced to lay off Pedro's helpers at the plant. Weeks went by with nothing to do at the tire shop but hope for the phone to ring. My dad had run out of money, and credit to buy rubber. And the warehouse was still filled with tires he couldn't sell. At night, I'd hear my parents argue through the paper-thin walls. My dad blamed the hard times on the peso devaluation and the new radial tires that were flooding the market. My mom blamed him for not giving up on being self-employed and just getting a regular nine-to-five job like everybody else. They were hiring out at the Union Carbide plant by the port. She'd also read about that in the newspaper.

That Christmas, I went to bed in tears, thinking of the Evel Knievel bike in the store window at Mac's Toys, wondering if some other lucky boy had gotten it from a Santa Claus richer than mine.

I whispered my prayers as I drifted to sleep: "Help me, God. Help me figure out a way to get my bike. And help me grow up to be rich like Mr. Aranda, not poor like my dad. I'll study hard. I'll go to college. But help me now if you can! I don't want to wait forever and be an old man riding the Evel Knievel bike. It just wouldn't be the same."

I dreamed of riding my bicycle freely down the street, but then when I got a clear look at myself, I realized that I was wrinkled and rickety in my dream, sporting thick glasses. Worst of all, my wavy black hair was completely gone, just a few scraggly white strands clinging to my shiny head.

The very next morning, driven by the sheer terror of that nightmare, I picked up my new journal and scribbled a list of possible moneymaking ideas so that I could reach for my goal, all on my own. No longer would I rely on elves from the North Pole or wait in vain for the peso's value to rise. Sadly, my list was short and unimaginative.

Wash cars. This was pointless because pretty high school girls always put on car washes at gas stations to raise money for their extracurricular activities. There was no way I could compete. I crossed it out.

Mow lawns. But no one in my neighborhood would pay to have someone else mow their lawn. They'd either do it themselves or, more likely, allow the weeds to infest their yard and the grass to grow waist high. I put an angry slash through it.

Deliver newspapers. I'd need a bike, and I was not about to ride the pink one rusting in the backyard.

None of the options harbored any hope. In frustration, I tossed the journal against my bedroom wall.

Hopefully, something would come to me.

"Please, Virgencita," I added to my prayers, appealing to the Virgen de Guadalupe tapestry hanging in my parents' room. "Please remind God and Jesus to help me out with a great idea."

The following Sunday morning, after our weekly visit to the ranch, my dad invited me to go with him to the mercado across the border to buy avocados, calabacitas, and chile peppers. For some reason, the ones at the H-E-B could never measure up to the ones sold across the border.

The mercado bustled with activity, vendors hawking their goods loudly as crowds milled tightly amid the dizzying array of stalls. Every fruit and vegetable imaginable could be found, displayed in angled crates within the covered, open-air marketplace. Scattered between the stalls were small counters where people could sit and order freshly made tortillas and tacos al pastor as a smorgasbord of appetizing fragrances stimulated the senses.

At the avocado stand, my father chatted with the vendor as if he'd known him since childhood. The wizened old man deftly split the avocados open with one fluid flick of his blade, removing the pit at the same time. He then inserted a green chile serrano in the groove, clapped the two halves together, and placed them in a bag.

"Why does he take out the pit?" I asked in fascination.

"Because it's against the law to take the avocados to El Otro Lado with the seed still in them," my father replied, counting out the colorful peso bills that shared his wallet with dull green dollars.

"Why?"

"Well, because they're afraid that the seeds could carry diseases that might harm the crops in El Otro Lado," my dad explained.

"But they don't make you take the pits out of the peaches, or the mangoes or the plums," I observed. "And you couldn't take all the seeds out of the tomatoes or the chiles or the guayabas."

My dad smiled as he paid the avocado man. "You're right. I wonder why they pick on the avocados. Maybe they don't like guacamole."

"And why does he put the chile serrano in the middle where the pit was?" I wondered aloud.

"It helps keep the avocado fresh and green until we eat it," my dad said, guiding me toward the chile stall. "Speaking of chiles, I need to get some."

My eyes swept across the vivid display of peppers. Red, green, crimson, orange, yellow, brown, they came from all parts of México and in all shapes, textures, and colors. Long and gnarled, short and smooth. Fresh, dried, smoked, pickled. Big and small, round and oblong. As my dad picked out what he wanted, my eyes landed on my favorite treat from the mercado, the chile powder. It was a speckled orange and white blend of fine chile powder, salt, sugar, and crystallized lime, a taste-bud-tingling sensation with a spicy punch. It came packed in little plastic bags that were one inch wide and five inches long. All for only one peso, five American cents. And I loved it.

"*Papá*," I dared, tugging at his sleeve. "Could I get some chile powder?"

My dad glanced dismissively at me. "Not today, Ramón. Every peso counts right now."

I stared glumly at my tattered weekend sandals. Then I remembered the five-dollar Christmas bill smoldering in my pocket, and my face brightened.

"Papá!" I exclaimed. "I can pay for it myself. Look!" Digging through my loose jeans, I produced the wrinkled likeness of Abraham Lincoln. He was one of my favorites, after the biography I had read in the library. You could count on Honest Abe. Now he would help me in my time of need.

Reluctantly, my dad relented. "Okay, get your chile."

With the five-dollar bill in my hand, I felt empowered. Why get one pack of chile, when I could buy . . . a hundred? Well, no, that would be crazy . . . but it felt good knowing I could if I wanted to. Instead, I grabbed a fistful of the soft, squishy packets and laid them on the tiny counter for the chile vendor to count.

"Veinticinco pesos," he mumbled.

I handed him the bill, and he gave me back my change: four one-dollar bills and three quarters.

Giddily, I scooped up my Christmas chile and cradled it all the way home. During lunch the following school day, I tore open one of the packets, pouring a generous heap of the powder into the palm of my hand and licking it up straight from there.

In moments, a small crowd had gathered around me, asking for a taste of the chile. Jimmy and Sergio were the first. I poured a slightly smaller heap into each of their outstretched palms. But then there were more. My whole packet of chile would be gone. Luckily, I still had four more at home. I distributed a little bit to each of the kids, trying to save some for myself. But it wasn't enough. They wanted more.

"Please, Ramón," one Anglo girl whined, twisting her blond curls. "It's so good. I've never tasted anything like it. I need some more."

"I don't have more," I explained, throwing my hands up in the air.

"Can you bring me a pack tomorrow?" she cried. "I'll buy it from you."

Suddenly, I thought of Mr. Aranda and his import-export business. It was as if a choir of angels was singing in harmony and only I could hear it.

"Sure." I shrugged nonchalantly as I felt my pulse quicken.

At home, I sat on my bed and stared at the packets of chile I had left. There were four of them, costing me twenty cents. I wondered for how much I could sell them to the kids at school. A dime a piece? A quarter? Tomorrow I would find out. I figured I should aim high.

"You can always come down on your price," I had heard my father say, based on his tire-selling experience. "It's a lot harder to go up."

At school, Jimmy and Sergio were the first at my side during recess. Then, the blond girl from the day before, and three of her friends. Five customers, but only four bags of chile. And what about me?

"How much are you selling it for?" Sergio asked.

"I was thinking a quarter," I replied casually. In seconds, the bags were all gone and I strolled away with a rewarding jingle in my pocket. I had spent a quarter on chile two days earlier, and today I had a dollar. And I'd gotten to eat a bag of chile for myself. Not bad.

At home I lined up my quarters and stacked my bills, retrieving my journal from its leafy heap in my bedroom corner. Starting a fresh page, I wrote down my business plan.

The Evel Knievel bike was seventy dollars and worth every penny. How many bags of chile would I have to sell to reach my goal and cross the finish line in stars, stripes, steel, and chrome? At a profit of twenty cents per bag, I calculated that I'd need to sell 350 bags of chile to buy the bicycle. In math class, I would never look at a word problem the same way again.

I ran to the phone and called the tire shop.

"Dad," I panted. "Are you going to México tonight?"

"Yes, I have to drop off some tires. Why?"

"Can I come with you, please . . . please . . .?" I begged.

"Sure, I'll swing by the house on the way," he replied.

As we rumbled across the bridge with a pile of recapped tires bouncing around in the truck bed, my dad asked, "So why the big interest in coming with me?"

"Well, I was hoping you would do me a big favor," I said slowly, lacing my response with suspense.

"Really? What favor is that?" he asked, raising an eyebrow in curiosity.

"Could we stop by the mercado so I can get some more chile," I blurted out quickly, my words running together. "I'm gonna sell it at school to make money for my bike."

A smile spread slowly across my dad's sun-beaten face. "Sure, son. I'll take you to the mercado."

My dad joked with the chile vendor as I gambled my savings away. If I used all of my money, I could buy one hundred and fifteen bags. I decided to round it to a hundred and keep some change, just in case I needed it.

" Te vas a enfermar si te comes todo ese chile," the vendor warned from behind his stall.

My dad laughed, "No, señor, el niño va a vender el chile en El Otro Lado, a sus amigos."

The vendor grinned, "Ha! Es comerciante. ¡Buena suerte, mi hijito!"

My dad glanced at me out of the corner of his eye as we drove back home over the Rio Grande. I was running my hands through the bags the vendor had placed in a medium-sized cardboard box, which now sat between us. I inhaled the rich, tangy aroma. *Mmmm. So spicy and sweet at the same time.*

"I'm proud of you, son," he said. "There's a dicho that goes: Con paciencia y un ganchito, hasta una fortuna se alcanza."

With patience and a little hook, even a fortune could be attained. I had my hook. And I knew I had patience. If I could put up with my crybaby brother, I could surely work toward my dream.

Day after day, I stuffed my backpack full of chile and headed off to school. And every day, the lunchtime crowd that gathered around me grew larger. I would stand beneath a big mesquite tree in the schoolyard and dispense my imported treat in the shade. From there, I could see the concession stand, the only other alternative to bringing your lunch to school. It was a small grill from which the nuns sold hamburgers and hot dogs. Usually, the lunch line wound its way around the small building. But as time passed and my customer base grew, I noticed the grill line was shrinking. I couldn't help but think of Isaac Newton's Laws of Motion, which we'd been studying in class: For every action there was an equal and opposite reaction. Maybe that old British dude had been on to something, after all. And, if that was the case, I'd do everything in my power to be on the positive side of the equation.

Every weekend, I pooled my earnings and went to the mercado with my father to replenish my inventory. At home, I kept two containers under my bed. The smaller one was an old cookie tin stuffed with dollar bills and quarters. The larger one was a cardboard box overflowing with bags of chile powder. Next to them sat my journal, in which I kept a running tab of my progress. If my calculations proved correct, in a couple of months, I'd have more than enough money to buy my Evel Knievel bike, which still gleamed like a beacon in the store window at Mac's Toys. I began a weekly pilgrimage to pay homage to it. And I took pride in buying a growing number of bags of chile every Sunday at the mercado.

One Friday, at lunch, Mrs. Barrera, the elderly lady who ran the concession stand in the schoolyard, stuck her head out through her open window and looked both ways as if she was expecting a bus to run her over. Not only were there no oncoming vehicles plowing across the playground toward her, but there was also a conspicuous absence of customers for her hamburgers and hot dogs. At that moment it struck me like a *metate* crushing corn: she should expand her menu to include tacos and burritos. I watched as she waved her fist in the air, her eyes burning straight through me like an overdose of chile.

"Ramón López!" she declared bitterly. "Stop selling that chile. You're taking away all my business!"

Instinctively, I burst into laughter. I tried to cover my mouth to avoid angering her further, but it was too late. She slammed her fist onto the wooden countertop.

The crowd in line for my bags of chile jeered at her. And Sergio Aranda began a chant: "The nuns are going broke! The nuns are going broke!"

I blushed with embarrassment, somehow knowing this was going to hurt more than help. Mrs. Barrera closed her window and drew her blinds to shut out the noise.

Later that day, I was thrilled to put business aside and join Jimmy and Sergio at the Arandas' house for my first-ever sleepover.

Earlier that week, I'd battled my parents for the chance to spend the night at Sergio's house.

"Sleepover?" my dad had fumed. "What's that? Another gringo tradition we're supposed to adopt?"

"All the kids do it, Dad, come on, please . . . just this once?" I pleaded, looking to my mom for support.

She ignored me, pretending to be completely immersed in washing the dishes. She knew how to pick her battles and was not about to get her sudsy hands dirty on this one.

"It's not natural," my dad said. I'd heard the argument a hundred times before. "A child belongs at home with his parents. How else are we supposed to make sure you're safe? What do I know about the Arandas?"

I wondered if he was secretly jealous of Mr. Aranda, if he knew how much cooler Sergio's dad was, if he was afraid I wouldn't want to come back home after a night in the lap of luxury. I wondered if he was hiding his true sentiments behind his usual protests: "How do I know the Arandas are not child molesters? Perverts? Psycho killers?"

"They're nice people," I said. "Mr. Aranda is a businessman, like you, Dad! He's in import-export, just like us."

My dad fought back a chuckle. Luckily, he'd sold a handful of tires that day and he was in an unusually generous mood. "Import-export, eh? Okay, just this once," he relented. "But you better not 'import' any bad habits."

I nearly cried as I hugged him. "Thank you, Papá. It's going to be so much fun!"

At the Arandas' palatial home, Jimmy, Sergio and I splashed around in the pool while blaring "We Are The Champions" on the outdoor stereo speakers. As I lounged on an inflatable raft and watched the palms sway in the warm gusts of the Gulf's evening breeze, I couldn't help but call out to Mr. Aranda, who sat in white linen behind his thatched roof tiki bar: "Mr. Aranda, this is the life, sir!"

He smiled weakly and raised his glass in response. Afterward, we all sprawled on giant leather couches and watched movies on the giant projection TV in their entertainment room. Venturing into the kitchen for a new batch of popcorn, I ran into Mr. Aranda, who was sitting at the kitchen table poring over numbers. He punched at a calculator, and a roll of paper trailed onto the floor.

"How's your chile business going, Ramoncito?" he asked absent-mindedly, never raising his eyes from the figures.

"Well, it's been going well, sir," I replied, eager for advice from a successful importer-exporter, "but I am a bit worried."

He clicked away at his calculations. "Why's that?" he asked politely.

"It's the lunch lady, Mrs. Barrera. She's angry because I've taken all her business. I'm worried she and the nuns might shut me down."

"Yes, that would only be natural." He paused and finally looked up, furrowing his brow and running his hands through his hair. For the first time, I noticed the worry lines around his eyes and the streaks of silver through his wavy locks. "Success brings envy. You may need to give them a cut of your profits but, sometimes, even that's not enough. Greed is the root of all business, but it's also the root of all evil."

"The nuns aren't very easy to talk to," I said, refilling the bowl with popcorn Mrs. Aranda had made in a skillet topped with foil. "Maybe I could talk to Mrs. Barrera . . . although she is pretty scary herself. So, offer them a cut?" I asked, backing out of the room with the red bowl heaped with popcorn clasped in my hands. I was eager to get back to the movie.

"I'd say so," he replied, frowning at his calculator. "And hope it's not too late."

As I headed back to the entertainment room, I felt somewhat dispirited. The Arandas' house was pretty incredible, but Mr. Aranda didn't seem to be enjoying it half as much as everybody else.

The next morning, I awoke with a jolt. I thought I'd heard a popping noise outside the window. Rubbing at my bleary eyes, I wondered if I'd been dreaming of the popcorn Mrs. Aranda had made the night before. Dawn was barely breaking and we'd stayed up so late, I thought I'd sleep till noon. I glanced over to see Sergio and Jimmy snoring lightly in the sleeping bags spread out on the thick beige carpet in Sergio's room. I heard tires squealing on the street. My heartbeat quickened as I peered out the window, glimpsing a pair of taillights vanishing around the corner. I *had* heard something.

I knew I should ignore it and crawl back into my sleeping bag, but something compelled me to tiptoe into the dark hallway.

"I'll get a drink of water," I whispered to myself.

I crept silently over the cool white marble floors, drifting past the shadowy shapes of the modern furniture in the living room. Entering the kitchen, I surveyed the table Mr. Aranda had worked at the night before. There was no trace of his papers and calculations. The table was wiped clean. That's when I noticed the door to the carport was ajar.

"That's weird," I muttered. Reaching for the doorknob, I peeked outside. In the rising blue light of dawn, I could make out the white convertible sitting in the driveway with the engine running and the driver side door wide open. There was no sign of Sergio's dad.

My throat tightened as I walked slowly toward the idling Cadillac. Then I saw a dark trickle of crimson fluid on the cement. Mr. Aranda's Rolex-clad wrist and bejeweled hand rested motionless on the ground, peeking out beneath the car door.

Without hesitating or daring to look any further, I scrambled back into the house, calling out, "Mrs. Aranda! Sergio! Mrs. Aranda!"

The ambulances were there in minutes, but there was nothing the paramedics could do to put the blood back in Mr. Aranda's body, or to plug the numerous holes I overheard the sheriff attribute to a semi-automatic weapon.

Jimmy and I hovered uncomfortably near Sergio, who cried in his dazed mother's arms.

When my dad picked me up, he parked across the street, traversing a wide arc around the crime scene. He glowered at me beneath the brim of his Stetson, like somehow this was all my fault.

With a tip of his hat and a solemn nod, he acknowledged Mrs. Aranda and escorted me away.

It was my first and last sleepover.

Sergio didn't come to school the next week, nor the week after that. When I asked my teacher, Miss Oak, she replied that Sergio had moved back to México, to be closer to family. Then she added that she needed to talk to me about my chile business.

With all the sadness and distraction, I'd never gotten around to implementing Mr. Aranda's final advice. The truth was, I'd been too intimidated by the wiry Mrs. Barrera, seething in her lonely concession stand. And the nuns seemed so remote and untouchable in their giant habits, waddling awkwardly about the hot, dusty campus like penguins dropped into a desert by some bizarre accident of nature.

"Ramón," Miss Oak explained, sitting with me on the curb outside the classroom. "I think it's very creative of you to try to make some money. It's . . . enterprising."

Miss Oak was an ample, friendly woman. Even though she was Anglo, she always wore colorful, flowing Mexican dresses. I wondered why she hadn't joined the convent, like most of the other teachers at the school. Maybe she shied away from the discomfort of the habits. Maybe cotton, embroidered dresses from the tourist shops across the border were too comfortable to sacrifice for a life as a bride of Jesus.

"However, the sisters have asked me to talk to you about this chile business," she continued. "They want you to stop selling chile on school grounds."

My thoughts jumped like Evel Knievel to the box full of chile bags stashed beneath my bed, the shiny bike waiting in the window at Mac's Toys, the funds that still fell short of bridging the chasm between me and my dream. I decided to try the late Mr. Aranda's proposed gambit as a last resort.

"What if I shared the profits with the sisters? Could I keep doing it?" I looked up at Miss Oak eagerly, but I could read the answer in her cold blue eyes.

"I'm sorry, Ramón," pity tinged her voice. "It's not the profits the sisters are concerned about. It's the nutrition and health of the children. The parents have been complaining that their kids are using their lunch money to buy your chile. And then they're going home with sick stomachs. It has to stop."

She patted me on the head and walked into the classroom. "C'mon," she said. "We have to get back to our schoolwork. Someday, if you stay in school, you'll have your chance to be a big entrepreneur."

I looked up the word in the dictionary the first chance I got. It read:

en·tre·pre·neur n

somebody who sets up and finances new commercial enterprises to make a profit

I thought of Mr. Aranda sprawled out next to his car, his perfectly pressed clothes soaked in blood. I envisioned my dad puttering about town in his rattling pickup, peddling recapped tires and praying the peso would stop deflating like a poorly patched spare. I thought of the earnings I'd sunk into my inventory of chile. It seemed like far too simple a definition for such a complex endeavor. What did Webster know about being an entrepreneur on the border? Maybe it should read: "somebody who risks his life and everything he owns for the chance to reach his dream." In that sense, wasn't everyone who dared cross the Rio Grande an entrepreneur in their own right?

At the dinner table, I commiserated with my dad. I waited patiently while he recounted his day's troubles, and then I heaped my own serving onto the platter, like an extra dollop of arroz mexicano from my mom's generous serving spoon.

After listening to my story, my dad cleared his throat, "Son, I'm proud of you. You can't break the nuns' rules, but you also can't give up on your dream. Never give up. Just remember, it's hard to tell the difference between taking a risk and taking a shortcut. You have to take risks to reach your dream, but you shouldn't take the shortcuts. It's about hard work and determination. There's a natural order and process and, when you try to speed things up too much, or take dangerous shortcuts, you're going to get hurt. Just look at Mr. Aranda."

With that, he got up and cleared his plate at the sink.

His silence spoke volumes. I understood. Dad was trying to tell me that Mr. Aranda had taken a shortcut to his dreams. His fast-found wealth was a mirage rippling in this desert parched for success stories. Whispers around town were that his money and death both flowed from his dubious dealings importing a powder far more treacherous than chile.

"The kind of success that lasts," my dad continued, scraping beans from his plate, "usually takes a long time to accomplish. But you can't give up. You have to stick with it. And here, unlike south of the river, you have a chance to make it. That's why we're here. That's why it's called the American Dream, not the Mexican Dream."

He was right, of course. This was bigger than the glittering prize in the store window. It was bigger than the nuns shutting me down. It was about what kind of person I wanted to be in life. Would I be one that succeeded or one that failed? Would I keep my bike on the high road or be tempted by the detours? I struggled to reconcile those questions with the very understanding of what defined success and failure. Just days earlier I had seen my dad as a disappointment and Mr. Aranda as a role model. Now Mr. Aranda was dead, his fleeting achievements an illusion created by border-world sleight of hand. And the sheer will and integrity of my dad's efforts was crystallizing solidly, like the lime and salt mixed into my powdered chile. Maybe my dad didn't make a fortune fast, but he kept food on the table and was putting me through private school in America. And he was his own boss. To him that was success, even if Mom disagreed.

Life was confusing. And living in a world of blurring boundaries, colliding cultures, and contrasting values didn't make it any simpler.

Before going to sleep, I counted my bags of chile and my savings. If only I hadn't recently doubled my inventory, I would have nearly enough for the bike. Instead, I had four hundred bags of chile. I was stumped. Maybe I didn't need a bike. Did I have to take it so personally? Did it have to be a symbol of my failure?

I went to school the next day. My eyes opened wide when I saw kids walking away from Mrs. Barrera's concession stand at lunch time with burgers, hot dogs . . . and packs of chile in their hands! The sisters were selling the same packets I had. And for a dollar a bag!

"It's an outrage, dude," Jimmy said, pouring some powder into the palm of his hand and taking a big lick. "But they're the only game in town now. Sorry."

My jaw dropped. The sisters had lied about their health concerns. I pulled out my private chile bag and took a tangy, tear-shedding wallop in my cheeks.

I yearned to show those sisters what I was made of. I vowed then to reach my goal, to sell every last packet of chile I possessed.

That night, when my dad got home, I scampered out to his pickup and pulled out the frayed city map he kept in the glove compartment.

"Dad," I asked as casually as possible at dinner. "Can I borrow your delivery map for school tomorrow?"

"Sure, son," he answered, cocking an eyebrow. "Are you working on your business plans?"

"As a matter of fact, I am," I replied with a restrained measure of self-satisfaction and steely determination.

At school, I polled my best customers, asking their addresses and placing a red dot on the map with a number for each of them. On the back, I copied the number, name, and exact address. It didn't take long for me to confirm my suspicions. Most of my frequent customers lived in the two fanciest neighborhoods: Rio Viejo and Hidden Valley. I knew most of the Anglo kids got what they called their "allowances," a foreign concept to my parents, on Fridays after school. So Saturday would be the perfect day to strike.

"Dad," I asked that night at the dinner table. "Do you think you'd have time to help me on Saturday?"

"What do you need, son?" he asked.

"I think I can sell most of my chile if I go door to door with my best customers. It might take several weeks, but it's my best bet. My prices are much better than the nuns'."

"Sure, I'll help you. I can't believe those Irish mobsters." He shook his head. "Don't repeat that or I might end up like . . ."

He trailed off but I knew what he was thinking.

On Friday, I took orders from my schoolmates, jotting directly into my journal. After paying the astronomical price charged by the nuns, my rates seemed like a bargain. They ordered large quantities and—with about thirty stops—it looked like I would sell half my inventory. In two weeks, I'd be home free.

Saturday morning, while most kids slept or watched cartoons, my dad and I climbed into his pickup truck. I carried my densely packed cookie tin to make change for the larger orders, while my dad hoisted the oversized cardboard box loaded with chile. We drove from Southmost across town to where the nice houses were. I had only seen them in passing, on the way to the Aranda home in Hidden Valley. Palm trees soared and giant manicured lawns stretched beyond wrought iron fences and tall stucco walls. The lush, grassy expanses in front of pristine homes were like pampered private parks, completely alien to my weed-choked neighborhood where tiny patches of dirt were boxed in by chain-link fences. My barrio's tiny public park was an asphalt jungle languishing in the shadows of a freeway overpass under constant construction.

By the time I reached the end of my list, I'd sold my entire inventory. I'd been paid in cash, and received a six-pack of Coke, a dozen freshly baked cookies, and a kiss on the cheek by the blond girl with the chile habit. Triumphantly, I drew a giant checkmark in my journal, next to the total of my earnings. My dad's truck could have run on my euphoria alone as we rumbled back home.

As I counted my money for a third time, my dad smiled. "You did it!"

"I can't believe it . . ." I mumbled in awe.

"Where there's a will, there's a way," my dad spouted, always able to deliver maxims as if he had personally coined them for the first time, again.

Glancing out the truck window, I suddenly didn't recognize the landscape. "Where are we going?"

"You have to ask?" He chuckled lightly. "Downtown."

"Mac's Toys!" we said in unison, grinning as if we were both kids.

The white Evel Knievel bike sparkled in the window just as it had the first time I'd seen it.

"Wow," I gasped. "There it is."

I saw my dad and me, smiling in our reflections on the broad pane of glass that separated me from my dream. Suddenly, I did a double take, whipping my head around to scan the sidewalk and street behind me.

"What is it, hijo?" my dad asked, putting his hand on my shoulder to calm my nerves.

"I . . . I could have sworn I just saw . . . Mr. Aranda, walking by in the crowd."

Saturday shoppers from both sides of the border bustled about in the midday heat. We both searched for a moment, but there was no sign of him.

"Anything's possible!" a voice boomed next to us, again startling me.

I turned to see a burly man with white hair, a matching beard, and tiny gold-rimmed glasses. He looked like Santa Claus, except he wore a light blue guayabera instead of the traditional red velvet suit, which would have been too warm for this environment.

"Mac!" My dad replied, his eyes brightening as the two hugged.

"You know Mac?" My eyes widened in awe. Maybe my dad was pretty cool after all. So what if he was grimy and reeking of tire rubber and sweat on most days? He knew Mac!

Mac opened the store, his copious key chain jingling against the glass like sleigh bells.

"Of course," my dad answered as if everyone should know Mac.

"Macario and I grew up together in the old neighborhood on Garfield Street."

I eyed Mac. *Macario?* I had always envisioned "the Mac" of Mac's Toys to be an Anglo man, a pillar of the local elite. He looked the part, but his name was Macario? He was . . . one of us?

Macario lightly ruffled my hair as he led the way through the aisles bursting with toys.

He chortled, channeling the spirit of Old Saint Nick again. "M'ijo, on the border things are rarely as they seem. Move a step and your whole perspective changes. Sometimes you don't even have to move, the world moves around you, or the ground shifts beneath you, or the river takes an unexpected twist and turn." His eyes darted to my dad as he added, "Remember El Chato?"

"How could I forget?" my dad replied.

I'd heard of El Chato. He had been one of the mafia kings across the border. A few years back, he'd been holed up for days in his house, under siege by both cops and rival gangsters. There was a huge gunfight and the house was blown up with a rocket launcher. When the dust cleared, they carried out a bunch of charred bodies, and it was declared that El Chato was dead. His wife and kids had been at their house on El Otro Lado at the time. After the siege, they all moved south, deep into México. Then rumors started surfacing that El Chato was not dead at all, but alive and well with his family, still directing traffic from an old hacienda near Guanajuato. It was said he'd had his face surgically altered and adopted a whole new identity, but everyone still knew he was El Chato. I couldn't help but wonder . . .

"But enough of that!" celebrated Mac in a jubilant tone. "I have a feeling anything's possible when it comes to you and that Evel Knievel bike! My store clerk told me about your quest."

"He did?" I couldn't believe it. I was almost famous.

"Yes, are you ready to ride?" His eyes twinkled like silver Christmas tree ornaments.

"Am I ever!" I proudly deposited my shoebox full of neatly stacked dollar bills and shiny quarters on the counter.

Mac merrily counted the money, like it was his first sale all over again. "He did this all by himself, huh?"

My dad nodded proudly.

"Well it looks like we have another empresario from the old barrio. Give me a call when you're old enough for a job!"

My smile stretched from ear to ear as he ambled over to the display shelf and lowered the bike, meticulously removing all of the tags, polishing it, and adjusting the seat to my height.

As my dad and I carried it out to load on the truck, Mac held the door open for us.

"Ten cuidado, m'ijo," he said. "Be careful. That Evel Knievel is a real crazy loco. Only gringos can afford the luxury of doing wild stunts and taking risks just for fun. We Mexicans face more than enough risk in our daily lives."

Mac and my dad shook hands and patted each other on the back. I watched my bike with an eagle eye to make sure it didn't fall off the truck bed as we rode home.

As my dad gently placed the bike on the asphalt in front of our dilapidated house, my mom and baby brother came out on the porch to watch.

"I'm happy for you, Ramoncito," my mom said, carrying my brother, who giggled and cooed in a rare moment of cuteness. "But please be careful. I don't want you to end up in the hospital."

I knew she was thinking of the time Evel Knievel had crashed, trying to jump thirteen Pepsi delivery trucks. And I remembered the time I'd read one of his entries to her from the Guinness Book of World Records. "Look, Mom," I had gawked. "It says here Evel Knievel has had four hundred and thirty-three broken bones and he's still alive. It's a world record!"

I wished now, as my mom clung to my brother like he was a lifesaver, that I hadn't read that out loud.

"Ándale, enjoy," my dad whispered as he helped me onto my new bike. "You've earned it."

I waved to them as I rode slowly down the street and around the

corner, my mom and brother watching from the porch, my dad standing in his guayabera at the chain-link gate to our overgrown front yard.

The bike felt good. It handled worlds better than the rusty old girl's
bike on which I'd learned to ride. I could feel the neighbors' eyes following me as I rode toward the levee, old couples watching from their
rockers on shady front porches and clusters of teenagers pointing from
street corners.

One kid whistled and called out: "Jump, Evel. Jump!"

I hit the pedals harder, my thighs burning. I rode up a narrow path
to the ridge of the grassy levee, skidding and kicking up a cloud of dust
as I turned and headed south along the trail.

As I rode, a panoramic view unfolded around me. To my left lay the
teeming shacks, broken streets, and tin roofs of Southmost. To my right,
the Rio Grande snaked mysteriously toward the horizon in the east. Beyond
that, I could see the vast sprawl of Matamoros, the spires of its cathedral
jutting up into the clear blue sky, then ranchlands stretching beyond the
fringes of the city. Somewhere out there, the river opened up and poured
into the ocean. My thoughts and emotions swirled like the treacherous
waters of the river below, with stories, memories, and conversations bubbling up like the remnants of a raft capsized and shattered on the rocks
beneath the surface.

Life on the border was truly mystifying. It was hard, at times, to tell
the difference between good and bad, failure and success, life and death,
Mexican and American, dreams and delusions, especially when the thin
dividing line often blurred and twisted in unexpected ways, and when
my instincts were to constantly cross that border back and forth rather
than stop at its edge. In my mind and heart, the border ran through
all things, including me. It was a wavering high wire I always balanced
upon, my center of gravity invariably and incessantly shifting from one
side to the other in an instinctive search for equilibrium. It was an invisible line I straddled, rather than an imaginary boundary at which I
felt compelled to stop. I saw it not as a constraint, but as an invitation.
Not an end, but a beginning, maybe the same way Evel viewed a ramp
pointed at a precipice.

I pumped hard at the pedals, yearning to leave the confusion behind and simply savor my moment. Riding fast along the crest of the levee, hugging the curves, I picked up speed in a flash, my knuckles tightening their grip on the chrome handlebars. I was just a kid riding my bike on a sunny day, trying not to notice the people wading across the waters below in search of a better life. The Gulf breeze whipped through my hair. The sun warmed my face. And the golden light bounced off the red stripes, the white paint, and the blue stars of my dream in motion.

THAT BOY COULD RUN

Uncle Bobby showed up barefoot on my grandmother's doorstep one night in late July.

The kitchen door was open so the balmy air could circulate through the screen, and she saw him standing there beneath the yellow porch light in a halo of madly fluttering moths.

Grandma Fina sat in a rocking chair. She said when she first noticed the lanky silhouette looming behind her screen door, she reached for the shotgun propped up in the corner. But as he remained motionless, gazing placidly through the wire mesh, enveloped in that hazy amber radiance, a calm washed over her. Slowly, she rose in her faded flower-print nightgown and coolly assessed the interloper.

He was gaunt and drawn, sporting a full mustache and beard, clad in a powder-blue polyester suit. Shiny white shoes would have made the perfect finishing touch, but instead her eyes landed on two bare feet. She knew it was him from the scars that pocked their surfaces since that fateful football game.

Bobby Rocket. His legendary exploits were López lore.

She threw the door open, flung her arms around him, and cooked breakfast at midnight.

Uncle Nick and Cousin David bumped into each other as they

emerged from the bedrooms Grandma had surrendered to them. Yelps of joy resounded through the rafters. Uncle Nick, burly as a bear, hugged Bobby, delivering thunderous slaps on his younger brother's back. When released from his grip, Bobby smiled sheepishly, shuffling back and forth on his bare feet, his crystalline eyes wobbling beneath the bright light.

Bobby avoided their expectant gazes, casting his eyes downward at those pitted feet squirming on the hardwood floor, at the faded patch before the stove where Grandma presided like the captain of a ship.

Aglow with excitement, Uncle Nick reached for the banana-colored phone hanging on the wall and raised it like a welcome torch. He yanked at the rotary dial impatiently. The tiny kitchen would soon teem with López men hovering around Bobby, just like the moths.

———

The phone rang once, startling me from sleep.

"Can't it wait until morning?" My mother groaned as my father strode out the front door, raising his Stetson toward his head.

I tiptoed into the living room. Spying from the corner, I saw him shoot a glowering look from those dark eyes of his which could sing with joy just as easily as they could seethe with rage. Then the shadow of his hat fell over his face.

I scooted back to bed. My parents could be tyrannical when they were in a bad mood. Tomorrow would be terrible. Or so I thought, until she announced the news at breakfast.

"Bobby's back." Her tone reminded me of when adults lamented someone's cancer coming out of remission.

My younger brother Rubén's eyes betrayed no flicker of recognition. At age three he was developing slowly. He struggled to keep his balance so he sat in a highchair to avoid tumbling to the floor. Cerebral palsy, the doctors had explained to my parents as they made the rounds seeking an elusive panacea. The medical bills had nearly bankrupted my father. It had always been tough surviving on the earnings from his tire shop. But rather than flatten him, Rubén's condition had driven him to: "*Diversify!*" He wielded the word like a happy toddler enchanted by a new toy. When speaking in Spanish, he shifted excitedly into English just to drop the D-bomb.

To me, on the way to school: "¡Ramón, todo va ser major, when we *Diversify!*"

To my anxious mom, as she served rice and beans to stretch the budget: "¡Marisol, el secreto al éxito es: *Diversify!*"

I wasn't sure where he gleaned this secret to success, but it sounded plausible. I knew from my experience selling powdered chile packets at school that when you offered only one product, it was pretty easy to be run out of business.

In his quest to take my brother to expensive specialists, he diversified by acquiring a gas station uptown. The owner was eager to retire, and my father happened to be *At The Right Place At The Right Time*, arranging monthly payments to take over the business.

The station was an ARCO. Its gleaming sign—a rectangular blue background, modern white letters, and a red "diamond spark"—soared majestically over the intersection. It seemed more dignified than the hand-painted "Joe's Tire Shop" sign dangling from a rusty chain by the weed-choked train tracks.

His hours were longer than ever as he shuttled back and forth between the tire plant, the station, and our house in Southmost. But it felt like we were making progress.

"It's never easy for immigrants to get ahead," he reminded me. "But each generation can go a little further."

At one point, Uncle Bobby had given the family hope he might just accelerate the process, hurdle the labor of generations. He had even made it look easy.

Bobby "The Rocket" López. I'd heard my father and uncles retell tales of his storied high school football career around Grandma Fina's kitchen table countless times.

Although all the López brothers had played football and were brawny, bold, and hard-hitting, Uncle Bobby was taller. Stronger. Faster. And, my dad told me more than once, there had always been a sliver

of something else different about his mercurial brother. He harbored
a certain recklessness that, when combined with speed, spelled either
danger or delight on the football field. They would shake their heads
and remember: that boy could run.

*Bobby Rocket cuts right. He scrambles to the sideline. The crowd's on its
feet. He breaks a tackle. He's flying down the field. The thirty. The twenty.
Touchdown! Bobby Rocket.*

There had been calls from college scouts on that banana-yellow telephone in Grandma's kitchen. Talk of athletic scholarships. He'd be the
first in the family to earn a degree. The first to escape our border town
for a reason other than getting shot at on foreign soil.

Glorious. Tragic. Wrapped in a puzzling package, Uncle Bobby was
home. The López brothers had been convening since the wee hours of
the morning. It was never too late for Bobby to turn the corner. He was
magic. Quicksilver. Anything was possible. He just needed time and
some good blocking by his stalwart brothers.

———

I cherished any break from the summer monotony. Since we couldn't
afford vacations, even funerals provided a welcome opportunity to re-
unite with visiting family. That's simply how boring life could be in
Brownsville.

So that very next morning, I couldn't wait to ask my mom, "When
can I go see Uncle Bobby?" as I piled up brownie points by helping her
pick up the dishes from the breakfast table.

"When your dad comes for you," she sighed.

"Should I hurry and get dressed?"

"Sure. Go on." She yawned, staring at the mountain of plates in
the sink.

From my room, I could hear her muttering something about how
those crazy López brothers would never learn. And also, how her brothers
never showed up barefoot anywhere, much less at their mother's house
in the middle of the night.

"They think Bobby's magic, but he's nothing but trouble," she vented to Abuelita Carmela on the kitchen phone. "They can't let go of their childhood dreams."

———

When my father ferried me over to Grandma Fina's, the López men clamored about the kitchen, satellites swinging clumsily around their prodigal sun.

"Hey, Big Money!" Uncle Bobby roared as his powerful arms crushed me. "You're growing!" Adults always seemed simultaneously astonished and dismayed by that incontrovertible fact.

"Why Big Money, Uncle Bobby?" I asked.

"Your dad told me about your entrepreneurial ways, selling chile, earning enough money to buy your own bike. Impressive."

My cheeks flushed. I liked this nickname. I hoped it would stick.

After a heap of bacon and egg tacos, a pot of coffee, a shower, and a clean set of clothes, Uncle Bobby was looking good. Much better than he had the night before, Grandma Fina asserted. Why, he was even wearing a pair of Uncle Nick's shoes.

"You gonna shave, Bobby?" my dad asked, stirring his coffee giddily.

"You'll look like back in the day, Bobby," Uncle Hernando assured. "Those mamacitas will come after you just like in high school."

The five López brothers had built somewhat of a reputation around town, apparently. And they were the first ones to revel in recounting the glories of their past conquests. They all sported matching mustaches and slicked-back, wavy locks. Nick was the eldest, his black hair already graying a bit. My dad was next in line, followed by Uncle Hernando, who was often mistaken as my father's twin, although to me they looked quite different. Less than a year apart in age, Uncle Hernando's skin was as fiery red as his legendary temper. My mother claimed his hue and hubris alike were fueled by a constant flow of tequila. As a result, he looked older than my dad, even though he was a bit younger. And, finally, after a long gap, Bobby and David had been born. Even now, their difference in age from their older siblings was evident. Bobby and David retained the lanky athleticism of young men, whereas Nick, my dad, and Hernando bore the brunt of their years in their thick, trunk-like midriffs. In their youth, before the harsh South Texas sun and hard knocks living had exacted their toll on their faces, their high school portraits reflected a posse of Pedro Infante impersonators with smooth olive skin and dreamy eyes that the ladies supposedly found impossible to resist. Anyway, that's how they liked to remember it, and who was I to argue if I carried some of the same genes?

"Now, now, boys," Grandma Fina clucked, stirring her arroz con pollo, the scent of garlic, onion, and oil permeating the kitchen. "That's the last thing your brother needs."

"No more ladies for me! I'm off that juice. And I'm definitely gonna shave." Uncle Bobby grinned, tousling my hair.

"What happened to your new wife, Uncle Bobby?" asked Cousin David.

Aunt Florida had been the first of his wives to mail us Christmas presents. I liked her even though we'd never met.

"She was Wife Number Three, right, Bobby? But who's counting?" Uncle Nick joked.

Bobby chuckled, shaking his head as he retorted glibly, "Well, everything was going just fine until Florida tried to run me over with her daddy's Cadillac."

The López brothers laughed and shook their heads. Somehow, Uncle Bobby—ever nimble and slippery—could turn a sorrowful tale into an outlandish joke, a near-death experience into a spectacular escape.

"So, is that it? You done with Florida?" my dad asked.

"You couldn't drag me back to Florida. Better suited for Anglos. Not very friendly to Mexicans."

I wasn't sure anymore if they were talking about the wife or the state.

"Why did Florida nearly kill you?" Cousin David asked.

"Boy, I'm gonna call you 'Pop Quiz.'"

"Why 'Pop Quiz?'"

"Yeah. Why?" I prodded.

"'Cuz you're full of questions!"

The room erupted into laughter as a football came flying through the open window into Uncle Bobby's hands. The unexpected missile would have probably knocked out a normal person's tooth, but this was Uncle Bobby. His reflexes were still as sharp as they'd been back on the field, back in Nam, back in the parking lot of that country club in Boca Raton where his estranged wife had nearly repaved the porte cochère with him.

"Hey vatos! Y'all hiding from the law? Or you gonna come outta that kitchen?"

"Dad!" Cousin David scrambled to the porch to greet his dad, who—recently divorced—resided in a bachelor pad downtown while Grandma Fina watched over his son. According to my dad, Cousin David's mom had run away. From what exactly, I was not quite sure, but I was getting the impression the López brothers were not the easiest men to be married to.

The party followed Cousin David onto the lawn, where it continued the rest of the day. Grandma Fina enlisted my cousin and me as servers ferrying food to the table beneath the oak tree. Uncle Bobby and Uncle David tossed the pigskin around until a pair of neighborhood chicas walked by and started chatting them up. At the table, the elder brothers conspired, stealing sideways glances at Uncle Bobby.

"There's still time," my dad insisted.

Nick sighed. "Not much I can do, Joe. I'm dead broke."

"That's obvious. You said you were moving in with Mom for a few weeks while your divorce got settled and it's been three years," Hernando quipped.

"You're one to talk," Nick replied. "It's bad enough to be broke and divorced. But broke and married to two women at the same time? Now that's disturbed."

"Touché." Hernando smiled, lighting up a cigarette and blowing rings into his older brother's face.

My dad shook his head and curled his hand into a fist, furrowing his brow. "We can't let him end up like you two. Not Bobby."

Dusk was falling. Across the street, in a shadowy park surrounded by a moat of stagnant river water, fires flickered in barbecue pits. Sable palms towered. Cicadas serenaded us as the stars poked through the inky sky.

"It's good to be home!" Uncle Bobby called from the curb, where the women twisted their long hair into makeshift braids and leaned toward him, hairbrushes jutting from back pockets.

Nick and Hernando gave him the thumbs-up, smiling wistfully while my dad hunched over a notebook scribbling numbers in the dark.

———

The very next day, my dad "hired" Uncle Bobby as his "assistant." At least that was the way my mother sarcastically relayed the news to Abuelita Carmela over the kitchen phone in hushed tones. My father and Uncle Bobby were "planning," she repeatedly carved quotation marks in the air with her free fingers, as she spied through the blinds onto the back porch where they schemed, papers and endless mathematical calculations in my dad's florid handwriting splayed out on the rusted wrought iron patio table that had once been white but now left a copper residue on anything that dared touch it. I lived with a gnawing fear of tetanus.

I ate my breakfast as slowly as I could, pretending to watch the small black-and-white TV flickering in the corner, the volume down so my mom could eavesdrop through the screen door, the long green spiral cord of the kitchen phone snaking through the room.

"It's always the same with these López brothers," my mother whispered, her lips pressed to the handset's transmitter. "Talk and talk and talk, the grandest ideas to get rich quick, but the only one that ever really works is José and still we never see a dime come this way. The bills are always late, the house is falling apart. The electricity gets cut off . . ."

I could make out about every other word Abuelita Carmela was saying on the other end of the line in Matamoros, but there was no doubt in my mind she was not only agreeing but also adding chile to my mom's salsa. Then, Abuelita Carmela's tone rose to an alarming rate, cutting clearly across the room.

"Where does all the money go from all of his hard work?" Abuelita Carmela pressed. "I still hear people say he supports another family here on this side of the river. He wouldn't be the first man to do so. Why do you think he's any better than the others?"

My mom stared at me silently for a moment. She'd never brought this topic up again since the day she'd gone into labor with Rubén. I had been lulled into thinking the suspicions had been lain to rest.

In the living room, Rubén cried for her from his playpen.

"I have to go. I can't talk about this again, Mamá. I have to take care of Rubén. And I can't do it alone." She slammed the phone back onto the receiver clinging perilously to the wall. Sometimes she hung it up so assertively that it crashed to the floor. But that did not happen today, as she scrambled to tend to Rubén's needs.

My appetite had taken about as much of a beating as my dad's reputation, but instead of putting down my tortilla, I loaded it up with more chorizo con huevo, hoping it would miraculously make me feel better.

On the TV, the local news played. I raised the volume, searching for a distraction from the unsettling topics of my mom's conversation, which still lingered in the air, like the aroma of the spicy Mexican sausage that had been fried on the range minutes earlier.

The Channel 4 anchorman, a stately silver-haired elder, declared a Luby's Cafeteria had been robbed at gunpoint in Harlingen two days earlier. A $5,000 reward was offered for tips leading to an arrest. A police sketch flashed across the screen. I almost choked on my breakfast taco. It looked like Uncle Bobby with the beard and mustache. A phone number crawled across the screen. The segment concluded with a geezer proclaiming, "I wooda chased that Mezcun and wrassled him to the ground, but he wuz faster than Speedy Gonzalez. Hell, that boy could run!"

Before cutting to commercials, the anchorman concluded that they would keep the phone number for the reward up on the screen for the rest of the broadcast.

Placing the remnants of my taco down on the plate, I took my mom's position listening at the screen door. I could hear my father and uncle plotting, but as the conversation dragged on, I could also make out the sound of worry creeping into my dad's voice. He was explaining to his younger brother how important it was that he avoid falling into his past destructive patterns. There was mention of drinking and womanizing and gambling. Uncle Bobby shook his head vigorously, insisting that those days were over, that he was "off all those juices," that he could be trusted this time. My dad insisted that Uncle Bobby not only work but also go back to school to finish his degree so someday he could be more than his assistant.

As Uncle Bobby nodded reluctantly, I rifled through the kitchen junk drawer, searching for a pen and something to write on. Glancing from my dad and uncle outside to the television screen inside, I copied down the phone number for the police tip hotline. Stuffing the scrap of paper into my pocket, I turned the TV off and peered out through the blinds. My dad was hugging Uncle Bobby. Neither of them noticed me, but I saw a single tear rolling down my uncle's weathered cheek.

———

Running wasn't Uncle Bobby's only specialty. It turned out he also knew a thing or two about cars. So during the day, Bobby worked at the ARCO, and at night, he attended community college.

There wasn't enough room at Grandma Fina's house, so Dad set up a cot in the back room of the gas station. I posited that it was meant to serve as the restroom, on account of the urinals clinging to the grimy tile wall. But perched on the edge of his cot, Uncle Bobby waved me off, claiming he'd slept in worse places.

I asked him where, 'Nam?

He stared back mournfully for a good, long while. I shifted uncomfortably from side to side, unsure if he was mulling his response or completely lost in his memories of the war. Eventually, he answered with a long list of towns scattered through Texas and the South, ending with a ditch outside the Florida country club where his eponymously named wife had almost turned him into a hood ornament. He said his roommate that night had been a gator. If he could survive that, this wouldn't kill him either.

The filling station reeked of gasoline, tire rubber, and cleaning fluids. When drivers rolled over the hose stretched across the carport, a bell rang. In a flash, Uncle Bobby was at their window. Sometimes, his speed startled the customers. But now clean-shaven, he quickly charmed them.

"Where'd *you* come from? Did you fall outta the sky?" A blond lady cooed in her convertible, staring at his sinuous arms.

Uncle Bobby chuckled and gave her the Full Service. Or so he later recounted to his brothers, who all laughed except for my dad.

"Bobby, you've got to be serious. Respect the customers."

"Okay, Joe. I get it," said Uncle Bobby. "Don't worry. Your customers love me."

Based on the station's increased profits, my dad couldn't argue.

"You run the place, Bobby," he said one night as they closed the station. "I need to spend more time at home. Remember to make the monthly payments and we'll split the profits."

Uncle Bobby looked up at the ceiling, doing numbers in his head. "Why not? Thanks, Bro." He winked. "I'm gonna make you rich. You wait and see."

Bobby Rocket scores again.

He made it sound easy. Things were going so well that I managed to put aside the fears triggered by the news report about the robbery in Harlingen. I chided myself for suspecting my own flesh and blood of committing such a crime. I even felt guilty for having thought such things about Uncle Bobby as he worked tirelessly to rebuild his life. So what if the police sketch had resembled him? After all, nearly every Mexican American man in the Rio Grande Valley had dark hair and a mustache. It was the macho look preferred in México and popularized in America by the Valley's own musical star, Freddy Fender. How could I have been so stupid to doubt the most beloved and most promising of the López brothers?

Disgusted with myself and my runaway imagination, I crumpled up the piece of paper with the hotline and flushed it down the toilet.

———

One weekend after school resumed, Uncle Bobby asked my dad for permission to take Cousin David and me to visit his son in the nearby town of San Benito.

"C'mon, Joe, it'll help me break the ice with my son. The boys will have a blast with Little Bobby. We'll head out to the beach. I can show them that some of that marine biology I'm studying. It'll be educational."

He sure knew how to work my dad, who sacrificed a great deal to pay for my education. David and I jumped up and down when my dad agreed.

"I'm curious to learn about marine biology, Uncle Bobby." I smiled, sliding into the backseat.

Cousin David proudly piped up, "My dad was a marine!"

"This is different, Pop Quiz." Uncle Bobby smiled, winking at David in the rearview mirror.

Aunt Irma couldn't tolerate the sight of her ex-husband, so we found Little Bobby sitting by himself on the curb as we pulled up to his modest wooden house.

Our first stop was a corner store. The elderly man at the register smiled as we entered. "I remember you." His cloudy eyes twinkled as he wagged a finger at my uncle.

Bobby Rocket strikes again.

Uncle Bobby flashed his pearly whites and shook his finger back at the man.

"Some things you don't forget," the old man rambled as Uncle Bobby pulled a tall boy from the fridge, swept up three pairs of sunglasses resembling his black wayfarers, and collected three bags of Hershey's Kisses. "Don't ask me to tell ya what I dun yesterday, but I remember that game between Brownsville and Mac Memorial like it wuz yesterday."

Uncle Bobby extracted a wad of cash as the man punched keys on his antique machine. "Everyone thought McAllen wuz gonna steamroll ya boys. They wuz huge. And here you were, a bunch of scrawny Mezcuns marching into their big ol' stadium with 15,000 fans screaming their heads off."

And Number Seven takes the field, Bobby "The Rocket" López. He's shattered every rushing record in the state, but how will he fare against this championship-caliber defense?

The register chimed. Uncle Bobby lay down a crisp twenty. As the cashier made change, he let out a sudden whoop, like he'd just caught an instant replay on the TV flickering inside his head. "You ran by 'em and around 'em and through 'em. They wuz chasing the wind. I talked to one of 'em boys years later, and he said he reached out for your jersey, but all he came away with was a cool mist through his fingers. The Galloping Ghost! That's what you were like. Didn't they call you that too?"

Uncle Bobby slipped his sunglasses back on and nudged the bill closer to the man's age-spotted hands. "I've been called a lot of names over the years," he said, sounding like a gunslinger in a Western.

The man counted out the change, picking up his pace. "Well, thanks for the memories. You boys have a great day."

Uncle Bobby brandished a pistol-like gesture with his right hand and smiled slyly. "No. Thank *you* for the memories, sir."

Outside, he distributed the goods. Piling into the white '66 Mustang he'd borrowed from the gas station garage, we'd never felt so cool.

And Bobby Rocket scores again! Brownsville beats Mac Memorial. What an upset!

He cracked open his beer, rolled down his window, turned the radio up, and gunned the engine as we shot toward the Laguna Madre.

———

I'd never snorkeled before. Or seen a grown man naked. I guess those kinds of things make an impression on you.

After traversing the causeway, Uncle Bobby drove to a cinder-block building at the tip of Padre Island. He jingled a set of keys, and we waltzed right into the vacant place. It smelled like fish as we drifted silently through a cold laboratory into a locker room where he instructed us to change into our swimming trunks and handed us snorkels and masks.

We shuffled barefoot over the sandy parking lot, through knee-high reeds to a tranquil beach. The waves lapped gently onto the sand, furrowing undulating grooves that echoed the outline of the bay. A cluster of sandpipers stood stiffly in the shallows, cocking their heads in jerky movements, staring at us impassively with flat, round eyes. Seagulls hovered overhead, cawing mournfully. The water was cool on our feet as we waded in behind Uncle Bobby.

"Wrap your lips tight around the snorkel." Uncle Bobby demonstrated, his voice turning nasal as the mask covered his face. "Then let yourself float in the water. Hold the snorkel so it points toward the sky."

At first, all I could discern were swirls of sand churning like miniature, underwater dust devils. But as the particles settled, Uncle Bobby pointed out curiosities. Crabs scurrying sideways. Fish darting between us. Streaks of silver light chasing each other through fields of oscillating seagrass. As my breathing relaxed, I noticed tiny colorless granules moving in unison, like rivulets of sand winding through underwater dunes. I opened my eyes wide and inched closer. They weren't particles of sand at all, but impossibly small creatures, like underwater ants. I became so immersed in watching their movements I completely lost track of time, drifting in absolute peace.

Startled by a firm tap on the shoulder, I jumped out of the water.

"Big Money." Uncle Bobby smiled. "You like that sea life?"

"Incredible!"

"We better get back inside, your shoulders are getting red, and I don't want the fishermen to think you're a lobster and haul you in for dinner."

As we walked back to the lab, I couldn't stop talking about what I'd seen: "It's like a different universe down there."

Little Bobby and David ran ahead.

"Yeah," he said, "that's what I enjoy about it. It's like an escape. It's why, after I came back from 'Nam, I started studying marine biology, but it's been hard for me to stay in school . . ." His eyes glazed over as he stared back at the bay. "When I'm with the sea creatures, I find that it is . . . What's that word my second wife loved to use? Therapeutic."

"It's like this other world, and you can watch its inhabitants, and they don't even know you exist."

"Yeah, they don't expect anything from you," Uncle Bobby agreed, sounding envious. "Going with the flow. Living as nature intended."

Inside, Uncle Bobby led us to the showers. He stripped off his trunks and turned the faucets. Snickering, we lingered at the entrance. He was rinsing the saltwater out of his hair when he noticed us.

"Don't be shy, boys. Ain't nothing here you haven't already seen."

Giggling, we undressed and ran into the steaming water.

"Uncle Bobby, you look like a wet caveman!" Cousin David laughed.

"You will too someday, Pop Quiz. You wait and see."

Glancing at Uncle Bobby, it wasn't his hair or his private parts that caught my attention. It was his scars. Similar to the ones on his feet, but larger. One on his right thigh. One on his stomach. Yet another on his left flank.

Sensing my stare, he looked down at his body. "You have a sharp eye, Big Money. You noticed my souvenirs."

"Souvenirs?" I answered, reaching for a towel.

"Parting gifts from Vietnam." He pointed at his lean belly. "This one nearly sent me home in a box."

We all gaped. I imagined blood instead of water pooling around his feet, a stunned caveman punctured by incomprehensible steel projectiles.

"Tell us war stories, Uncle Bobby!" David implored.

"Yeah, Dad!" Bobby pleaded, wriggling into his tattered jeans. "Tell us."

"Nah, boys. All I can say about war is that you'd best avoid it. Don't believe what anyone says about how great it is to be a hero. Let's not ruin a fine day. Let's enjoy some more marine biology."

From the lab we walked to a nearby pavilion overlooking the jetties where the Gulf of México met the bay. Waves crashed, spraying white jets over a long pier of rocks crowned by fishermen, surfers, and pelicans.

Families huddled at picnic tables beneath a corrugated metal roof. At the concession stand, Uncle Bobby bought us chocolate ice cream cones and got himself a beer. Then we followed him to a bench overlooking the beach. We sat there and stared at the sea as the breeze bit into our sunbaked skin.

"There it is. Marine biology. My favorite kind." Uncle Bobby smiled mischievously, taking a long swig of his beer as he gazed ahead.

We followed his sightline to a bikini-clad woman emerging from the sea, water dripping from her long hair.

"Marine biology, boys. I found my calling a long time ago. I just didn't know its name."

"I thought you were *off that juice*," David recalled verbatim.

"Pop Quiz, some things never change."

———

With business booming at the gas station, my dad took a gamble. He placed a bid on a massive lot of used tractor-trailer tires being auctioned by the State.

"I haven't won anything since third place in the potato sack race in high school," he remarked, staring at the official notice bearing the seal of the great State of Texas. "It's my lucky day!"

My mom hugged him joyfully. What she didn't realize was that to amass the funds to fulfill the bargain, my dad would have to skip the house payments. As he later explained to me: *No Risk, No Reward.* I added this latest teaching to the growing list in my notebook:

Diversify!

At The Right Place At The Right Time.

No Risk, No Reward.

"The dates line up like dominoes." My dad pointed at the calendar in his soot-streaked office. It would take three months to raise the capital required for the bid. That coincided with the ninety days the great State of Texas decreed available to collect his bounty. The mortgage installment for that month, which happened to be December, was due five days after his tire deadline. And he already had a buyer for a load of used tires to be culled from the first load. My dad clapped his hands triumphantly: "As soon as I have that cash, I catch up on the house payments, and we're in business."

"What if the timing goes wrong?"

He shot me one of his silencing glares.

After a month, the school principal called me into her office.

"Ramón, can you remind your father about the tuition," she asked in her Irish accent. "He's several months behind."

My gaze dropped to my scuffed shoes, which had developed a hole, exposing my big toe.

"Yes, Sister. I'll remind him."

"Will he get upset? Does he hit you?" she asked, her moonlike face expressing concern.

"No, Sister. My father doesn't hit me."

"Good. Then tell him for me, please."

I recalled how the nuns had banned my chile business and it angered me. I could be paying my own tuition or at least wearing a new pair of shoes. Instead, I felt doubly humiliated.

When I relayed the message at dinner, my dad fumed, setting down his fork and furrowing his brow. "Jesus wouldn't hound people for money."

My mother boldly differed. "Yes, but Jesus wasn't running a school. Think of all the bills those poor women must pay."

Before my father could reply, my brother spilled his milk.

"Ay no." My mother scrambled for paper towels to sop up the mess.

"I'll call that sister and tell her to stop bothering my son. I'm good for it. I always pay my bills, eventually."

My dad adhered to his own warped perception of the American financial system. He believed as long as the bill was paid then the debtor's honor was preserved. The timeline for such payment was irrelevant. I wasn't wholly convinced this pillar of his philosophy should be added to my evolving mantra for success.

————

The first orange envelope arrived on a Friday. I was home alone because on Fridays my mother took Rubén to visit Abuelita Carmela across the border. Sitting at the kitchen table, I eyed the ominous notice. It reminded me of a ticking time bomb.

I called my dad.

"What does it say?" He hollered over the hissing steam of the tire shop. I envisioned his foreman, Pedro, rolling around like a pinball in his machine, bouncing from mold to mold checking gauges and adjusting knobs as he cooked tractor-trailer tires for the eighteen-wheelers lined up at the bridge to México.

"I don't know."

"Well, ándale, open it!"

I read the contents slowly, stumbling over the legalese.

"What does it mean?"

"If you don't make the house payment soon, they're going to take the house away."

A string of colorful expletives followed in Spanish. "Don't worry. I'll call the bank, tell them I'm good for it. Just throw that letter away before your mom sees it. She's got enough on her hands."

"Yes, sir."

I hung up and deposited the orange letter in the kitchen trashcan. Just as I sat back down, the phone rang.

"Put it in the garbage can in the alleyway. And lay something on top of it."

"Yes, sir."

———

A black-and-white photo of Uncle Bobby graced the hallway that bisected Grandma Fina's house. In the picture, he wore his football uniform, the number 7 emblazoned on it. He knelt on one knee, and his helmet sat on the grass. His smooth face turned dreamily toward a distant horizon, his dark hair slick and shiny like glistening tar. In that cobwebbed hall of fame, the photo hung heavy between the Virgen de Guadalupe and an array of military portraits. Nick had served in Korea. Hernando and Bobby had fought in 'Nam. David was in the Marines. Only my dad had not attained a place on the wall, due to a medical exemption, a ruptured ulcer. The shame haunted him eternally. It was probably why he always tried to help his brothers.

I was standing in the hallway admiring the pictures when Cousin

David brushed past me on the way to his bedroom. "David, why do you think Uncle Bobby didn't play college ball?"

He paused and gazed up at the photo of our uncle, "When you live here, as I do, you hear a lot of things you probably shouldn't."

"Such as?"

"I overheard Uncle Bobby and Uncle Nick talking about it one night," he said. "Uncle Bobby was making out with his girlfriend before a big football game . . ."

———

As the story went, an agitated Aunt Irma told a flustered Uncle Bobby that everybody was waiting for him in the football stadium, that he was a hero. But Bobby didn't want to be a hero, all he wanted was her. So while they rounded the bases in the back seat of a car in a pitch-black alleyway behind the school, the crowd, the cheerleaders, the home team in crisp red-and-white uniforms, and the coach all anxiously waited beneath the bright lights.

The marching band performed the national anthem. The refs huddled, arguing with the coaches. Then the head referee blew his whistle, announcing that the kickoff could be delayed no longer, despite the fact it was a pivotal playoff game. Despite the college scouts up in the bleachers with their binoculars, all there to see the only missing player. Despite the legend of Bobby Rocket.

The visitors kicked off to start the game. Instead of Bobby receiving, his backup fumbled the ball, and the opposing team scored. They kicked off again, and Bobby's backup caught it and kneeled. Right as the home team's offense took the field for the first time, Bobby emerged from the locker room at full sprint, helmet and cleats in hand. The coach rejoiced, throwing his clipboard into the air.

The crowd goes wild.

In his haste, though, Bobby did a piss-poor job of tying his shoes. And, on the first play from scrimmage, the mishap that doomed his future befell him.

Bobby Rocket gets the ball. He finds a hole in the line and punches through. He spins. One of his shoes flies off as he bolts up the middle of the field. Defenders collide as he zooms through them like a gust of wind. He kicks off the other shoe and hits the jets. He's at the fifty. The forty. The crowd is on its feet! The thirty. The twenty. He's gonna go . . . all . . . the . . . Wait a minute, Bobby hits a slick patch and slips! He fumbles. Bobby's crushed beneath a dog pile battling for the loose ball. The refs pull the players apart. Bobby Rocket lies motionless face down on the field, right at the goal line. His white pants are splattered red. The crowd gasps. The college scouts drop their binoculars and shake their heads. Bobby Rocket's feet have been trampled and punctured by the other players' spikes. He's carried off the field. Brownsville loses 52-0.

Bobby never played football again. He dropped out before graduation. Married Aunt Irma in a shotgun wedding. Shipped off to 'Nam before the baby was born.

———

The second and third notices also came on Fridays. Both times I read them to my dad and disposed of them in the alleyway.

The house would be seized if payment was not delivered in full by December 15th. The deadline for picking up the tractor-trailer tires at the State's lot in Kingsville was December 10th. As the day drew near, my dad had nearly accumulated the total. The piles of cash were stashed in his safe at the tire shop. His plan remained clear as dominoes lined up, ready to fall. When I read him the third notice, he picked me up and we visited Uncle Bobby at the ARCO.

"We've got a couple days left, Bobby," my dad said. The veins on his forehead throbbed in sync with his heartbeat. "How much do you have?"

Uncle Bobby produced a crumpled brown bag that looked like it should contain stale popcorn. Instead, he extricated wads of cash.

"Between this and what I have at the tire shop, it's almost the five thousand dollars we need to make good on the bid," my dad said.

"There's some folks that owe us some money," Uncle Bobby added. "All I've gotta do is go collect and we'll make it."

"Owe us? I told you to never sell on credit," my dad complained.

"Well you should've seen these ladies, Joe. Any single man in his right mind would give them credit just to see them again when they come back to pay."

"I'm not single. And technically, neither are you. When are you going to grow up, Bobby? C'mon. It's now or never." My dad's eyes bulged. His face flushed red.

"Let's not scare the boy," Uncle Bobby glanced at me like I was the only thing standing between him and his brother's fury. "I have their addresses here. Let me go out and do some collections."

"And who's gonna watch the station while you're doing that?"

Uncle Bobby's gaze fell on me. "How about Big Money?"

"Yeah, Dad! Let me."

"Fine. It's the weekend. You'll work here while your uncle does the rounds." My dad had agreed. I couldn't believe my luck.

"By Monday we'll have the mula, Bro. You'll be home free."

Bobby Rocket scores.

———

Everything was going smoothly. I knew how to pump gas, wipe windshields, make change. Then up prowled a sheriff's cruiser.

The officer stepped out slowly. He wore a Stetson, Ray-Bans, and a shiny star over his heart. My eyes drifted to the gun at his hip as he approached.

"Howdy, son. Where's the manager?"

I could hear my heart drumming in my ears. "You're looking at him, sir. My dad owns the place."

"Is that right?" The deputy grinned. "Well, whomever said them Mezcuns are lazy wasn't talking about you, wuz they?"

"No sir, they weren't."

"You speak good English too." He seemed surprised.

"I study with the nuns."

"I see. Well that explains it then."

He reached into his shirt pocket and fished out a piece of paper. "Have you seen this man?"

It was the police sketch from Channel 4.

And he's scrambling right. The defense penetrates into the backfield.

For a moment all I could think of was the $5,000 cash reward. All my dad's problems could be solved with the sale of Uncle Bobby. But what if the resemblance was a mere coincidence? What if Uncle Bobby was truly innocent and reformed of his past ways? On the other hand, what if a big chunk of the money in Uncle Bobby's mysterious brown paper bag had truly come from Luby's and not from the gas station?

I froze, the sketch blurring.

"Son? Have you seen this man?" the officer repeated.

I shook my head, swallowing hard. "No, sir."

He cuts back the other way and picks up a blocker.

"We got a tip from some lady that she'd seen someone 'round these parts resembling this man. You sure ya ain't seen him?"

I hesitated, wondering what my mom would have me do. Save my uncle or save our house? What if I could help do both without betraying my father's brother?

"Yes, sir. I'm sure," I heard myself answer.

He eyed the station suspiciously. "Mind if I look around?"

"Go ahead."

I followed him as he sauntered through the garage, the small office with the cash register. Stood behind him as he peered into the room where Uncle Bobby slept. My heart raced as I prayed there were no clues lingering there. But as the officer stepped out of the way and I stuck my head in, I was surprised to find the cot folded and propped up against a corner. The rest of the room was completely empty. Gone were Uncle Bobby's clothes and personal effects. I watched as the cop slid the vertical cot aside, revealing a couple of empty bottles of whiskey. I surmised Uncle Bobby had never truly been "off all those juices."

There was evidence of drinking and womanizing. What if he was also reckoning with gambling debts?

The officer strolled back to his tan-colored patrol vehicle. He reached in for a poster, which he handed me. "You mind asking your dad to put this up?"

"Yes, sir."

"You do mind?"

"I mean no, sir. I don't mind," I fumbled, struggling to conceal my fraying nerves.

"All right, muchacho. As you were. Don't grow up too fast, now, ya hear?" The deputy climbed back into his cruiser and drove off, flashing his lights as cars swerved out of the way.

I took the poster inside and placed it on the counter for Uncle Bobby to see. I supposed it was important for him to know the law might be onto him, if that was really him, which I truly hoped it wasn't. I didn't want to be an accessory to a crime. But I also didn't want to be a liar or—worse even—a traitor to my own kin. I wondered if I should confess my suspicions to my father. How would he react? Would he become enraged at me for doubting his beloved brother? Would he condemn me, dismiss me, or confront Uncle Bobby? The last thing I wanted to do was put another obstacle in the way of their already precarious plan. Yearning to drive the confusing thoughts from my mind, I shook my head like a wet dog drying himself and carried on with my duties.

By Monday, the funds were gathered. Dad and Uncle Bobby drove me to school. "From here, Uncle Bobby's leaving me at the gas station so I can cover for today," my dad said. "Then he's driving up to Kingsville to make good on the bid. He'll bring back the receipt, and we'll head up tomorrow for the first shipment of tires."

"Too bad I can't take some of that money to the nuns right now." I eyed the bag full of cash on the floor.

"Don't worry, son." My dad smiled. "Soon we'll be caught up on the house and the school. The nuns will sing to the heavens."

Uncle Bobby stared at me pensively as I got down. "Don't let those

nuns or anyone else ruffle you, Big Money. Stay cool, like that day floating in the bay."

"You got it, Uncle Bobby. Go with the flow." I smiled and waved
goodbye.

———

That afternoon, nobody picked me up after school. When the other kids
had all left, I walked to the gas station. Standing in the doorway, my
dad appeared unusually disheveled. His sky blue guayabera was stained
with soot from servicing the cars. His usually slick hair hung sloppily
over his eyes.

As I approached, I asked, "Where's Uncle Bobby?"

He frowned. "I don't know." He sat behind the cash register and
lowered his forehead onto the keys, exhaling slowly.

I scanned the surroundings, which appeared oddly barren. The posters
bearing the ARCO brand were gone. I peered into Uncle Bobby's bedroom; it was as empty as the day the sheriff had visited. Inside the garage,
all the tires and air filters and fan belts were missing. That's when I noticed the pumps were garnished with handwritten "Out of Service" signs.

"What's going on here?"

"Son, you don't want to know," he answered without lifting his head.

"But I do want to know." I thought of the journal sitting under my
bed, wondered what sage learnings I might be jotting into it that night.
"What happened?"

"The man I bought the gas station from came by today."

"Why?"

"Because your Uncle Bobby never made the monthly payments to
him as we had agreed. He also never sent the checks to ARCO for the
franchise fee, like he was supposed to."

"And?"

"ARCO canceled the franchise, and the man repossessed his gas station. He doesn't know if he's going to close it or sell it to someone else.
But he took everything that was here."

I looked about mournfully, my eyes ascending to the glorious ARCO sign high above, the colors of the flag flying in the clear blue sky. Had Uncle Bobby seen the poster I'd placed on the counter and decided it was time to go? That would make this all my fault. It simply couldn't be, I tried to convince myself as my gaze landed on my crestfallen father.

"The only reason I'm still here is because I don't have a way to get home," my dad confessed, finally raising his head. The keys from the register had creased grooves into his face. He looked like he was suffering from the mumps.

"Maybe there was an accident," I said, my voice catching. "Uncle Bobby wouldn't just run."

"Son, running's what your Uncle Bobby does best."

———

Right before five o'clock, my dad called the great State of Texas' used tire depot. A lady informed him his bid was canceled. Nobody had showed up with the payment. Grandma Fina gave us a ride home in her VW Beetle.

Five days later, a sheriff's patrol car pulled up to our house. It was the same deputy who'd come sniffing around the gas station. He recognized me and shook his head.

"Sometimes, no matter how hard you work, you just can't catch a break." He grimaced as he nailed a red notice to our front door.

"What's this?" my mom asked.

"I'm sorry, señora. This is your eviction notice. The bank has foreclosed on your house."

My mom steadied herself against the doorframe. Rubén crawled over the officer's boots and plunged off the porch into the bushes, crying.

Neighbors poked their heads out windows and stood at sagging chain-link fences, pointing in our direction.

While my mom yelled at my dad on the phone, I shuffled slowly toward the officer, who stood watch on the sidewalk.

As I stood there looking up at him expectantly, he removed his sunglasses. Squinting at me in the late afternoon sun, he prodded, "What is it, son?"

"Did you ever find that robber?" I asked, hoping they had so that either Uncle Bobby could be absolved of one crime or apprehended for both.

"No." He shook his head. "Strange case, that one."

"Why?"

"All we ever found were his shoes," the deputy replied. "Apparently, he ran so fast that they flew off his feet. Found them in a nearby parking lot."

My dad pulled up in his delivery van, a decrepit bakery truck he had repurposed to ferry tires. Once painted white, it was now smeared with soot and grease and stank of sweat, rubber, and exhaust fumes. It was a monstrous machine with only the driver's seat, springs jutting from the torn cushion.

Gloomily, he signed a document the sheriff held for him. He then carried out our belongings and loaded them into the van. Along with the rubbernecking neighbors, the sheriff watched indifferently, leaning on the hood of his cruiser. Silently, I helped my dad convey our meager possessions across the yard to the truck as my mom sat on the withered grass removing thorns and splinters from my brother's tender skin.

The last item we hoisted into the truck was my Evel Knievel bike. For some reason, I felt sorry for it, as if it were a cherished friend who had come to visit from faraway only to find disillusionment, strife, and homelessness.

When we finished loading, we rattled slowly away from the only house my brother and I had ever known. The muffler let out a single shot, ringing defiantly through the falling night. I pictured the neighbors laughing at our misfortune. A pair of figures skulked away with the scrawny Christmas tree my dad had tossed on the curb, tinsel still clinging to its branches like forgotten tears.

Driving along the levee, my dad muttered that maybe we would have all been better off if his parents had never crossed the river to America. His smoldering eyes burrowed holes through the windshield as the rest of us jostled about on the floor.

My mom wept in hushed tones, cradling my sleeping brother in her arms as she sat on the floor where the front passenger seat should have been. About halfway to Grandma Fina's house, she whispered hoarsely, "Why? Why did you have to trust him?"

My dad waited until Grandma's house materialized out of the shadows to reply, "Because he's my brother."

I eyed Rubén, dozing serenely amid the chaos. What would I write about brothers in my journal? One thing was certain. I would tear my dad's business teachings into shreds.

"I knew he was no good," my mother cried.

"He had good in him," my dad insisted, gripping the steering wheel so tightly his knuckles turned white.

"A person can have good in them but still be no good," she stated defiantly, wiping her tears.

Even though they sat a couple of feet from each other, my parents seemed miles apart. The magnetic pull of the chasm between them threatened to suck me in and drown me. It was like a black hole from which no light could escape. I considered blurting out what I knew about Uncle Bobby, but I figured it could only make matters worse. Even though I resented him for his poor decision-making, I felt sorry for my dad. He loved his brothers and that would never change, no matter how much they hurt him. This was one family secret that would have to die with me.

The van rattled onto the front lawn, its squealing brakes announcing our arrival as the roof scraped against the oak's limbs, scattering severed branches and leaves like confetti at a parade.

When we stood on her porch beneath the yellow light, enveloped by frenzied moths in mute rebellion, Grandma Fina saw us from her rocking chair in the kitchen. She didn't reach for the rifle. She didn't bother standing up. She just murmured, "Come in. I'm glad you've got shoes on."

ALLEGIANCE

"We're moving back to México," my dad proclaimed as we crowded around the tiny table in my Grandma Fina's perpetually stuffy kitchen.

"Back? That implies we've lived there before," I retorted, stunned by his cavalier announcement. "What about our old house? Aren't we getting *that* back?"

My father furrowed his forehead in his characteristic fashion, his thick eyebrows gathering like storm clouds. He didn't appreciate my budding sense of sarcasm, which he also struggled to differentiate from my obstinate naivete. "The house is gone for good."

My mother slumped, wiping a tear away.

"And your mamá lived in México," he continued. "She was born and raised there. She'll be very happy to be closer to her mother. Won't you?" He searched her eyes for affirmation as she sullenly stared at the plate of steaming huevos a la mexicana Grandma Fina slid before her.

The kitchen burst with the fragrance of fried onions, tomatoes, and chile serrano as Grandma Fina reigned over the stove in her flowery house robe, her gray hair dotted with pink curlers. Through the screen door, I could hear my cousin David playing fetch with Golden, a retriever that had unexpectedly materialized one recent evening at the front door and never left.

It was fun bunking with David, but I missed our home. I frequently awoke in the middle of the night—in the sweltering heat trapped beneath the creaky ceiling fan—and struggled to fall back asleep, fretfully reliving the shame as the sheriff's deputy posted the eviction notice on our front door.

What my father had claimed would be a short stay at his mother's house had turned into weeks and then months. In the cramped quarters, everyone—Grandma Fina, Uncle Nick, Cousin David, and I—could overhear my parents arguing in hushed tones night after night. My uncle, who had been living there since his divorce, had moved out onto the back porch, relinquishing his room to my mom, dad, and little brother. Every day, my dad left at the crack of dawn to toil at his tire plant, but no matter how many tires he vulcanized and sold, the money couldn't stretch like the rubber with which he recapped them. It was simply not sufficient to even rent another home while keeping up with my school tuition, and my brother Rubén's mounting medical bills from the trips to the children's hospital for tests and the varying and infinite opinions regarding his confounding condition. Was it cerebral palsy? Was it Dandy Walker Syndrome? My father wouldn't even repeat the words "mental retardation," which is what most of the doctors diagnosed him with at the time. I had a sinking suspicion he suffered from all three, and with every medical appointment it seemed like—instead of answers—all that my parents received were more vexing questions, more bad news, and more hefty invoices.

"México is the answer." My dad's eyes gleamed with the insouciant excitement he usually reserved for one of his new business schemes. I expected him to start scribbling numbers on a napkin, as he usually did when detailing his business plans. "Everything costs less there. We can rent a house dirt-cheap while we get back on our feet. And your Abuela Carmela can help your poor mom with Rubén."

"I can help her too, you know," Grandma Fina interjected from her well-worn spot at the stove. She was after all . . . a full-fledged abuela, a Mexican grandmother, a woman who'd proven her mettle by raising not just her own children, but also a grandchild or two for good measure.

"You have your hands full here already. Besides, a woman needs her mother in times like these. Isn't that so?" He once again sought my mom's support, but she was busy spooning her breakfast into Rubén's mouth. Although he barely fit in the highchair, he required its rigid structure to support his stubbornly flaccid and uncoordinated body.

"And what about the tire plant?" I asked, picturing the wooden structure imploding by the railroad tracks.

"I'll move it too," he replied. "I'll put it out on the ranch in México. Rent free! Our profits will soar."

Stubbornly, I frowned, "But we're American."

They stared at me as if I'd just descended from the moon with Neil Armstrong's star-spangled banner in hand.

"We were Mexican first," he schooled me. "Anyway, it doesn't matter. We're Mexican American. We're both. We can live here. We can live there. It doesn't change who we are. What matters is that we provide for ourselves and that I can put a roof over our heads. We can't stay here forever, like your Uncle Nick."

"I heard that!" Uncle Nick bellowed from the back porch. "I'll be back on my feet soon. You'll see."

"Yeah, to go to the liquor store," my dad muttered as he drained his coffee.

———

Every morning at school, the nuns lined us all up in rows like soldiers about to march into battle. There in the parking lot, we placed our right hands over our hearts and recited the Pledge of Allegiance.

It was no different on the last day of school. After the pledge, we filed neatly into our air-conditioned classrooms, our blue-and-white uniforms drenched in morning sweat. That day, however, instead of Sister Claire Veronica launching into the routine class schedule, the Mother Superior visited our classroom, delivering a speech specifically aimed at the eighth grade.

I'd attended St. Mary's for nearly five years, and now that my final semester was winding to an end, it was widely assumed my classmates and I would transfer seamlessly to high school at the crosstown Marist Academy. The Mother Superior pontificated at great lengths—in her Irish accent—about how well-prepared we would be for the challenges the Marist brothers would thrust in our faces. And then she ceremoniously paced up and down the aisles handing each student a bloodred envelope. As my classmates opened their missives, they extricated creamy cards bearing elaborate script, smiling proudly and exchanging exuberant high-fives. This, she said, was our exclusive invitation to an excellent Catholic school education, our prestigious ticket toward an eventual college acceptance and a life of unprecedented productivity, prosperity, and privilege. She only hoped and prayed that we would be so kind as to learn from Jesus and share that aforementioned prosperity with the church and those in need.

I glanced across the room at my best friend Jimmy, who admired his pass to greatness.

As she swept by my desk, the Mother Superior hesitated, a red envelope trembling in her hand. I reached out for it, but she hastily withdrew it.

"Mr. López, please accompany me to my office when we're done here," she clipped tersely, the corners of her shriveled lips turning unmistakably downward.

A communal "ooh" rose from the class as I flushed red with embarrassment. How could this be? I had earned straight A's. I had not been disciplined in years.

I followed her down the long hall, her stubby heels clicking on the shiny marble floor, her navy-blue cloak swirling behind her. In her office, she motioned for me to sit across from her. Taking her seat, she placed the red envelope bearing my name on her desk, her hands folding over it as if she were about to pray. My eyes gravitated toward the cross hanging on the wall over her head.

"Mr. López, it is my solemn duty to address your special situation," she explained.

My eyes widened expectantly. Maybe my stellar grades had earned me a scholarship to the Marist Academy. Maybe the nuns were about to waive my unpaid tuition. Or better yet, maybe I'd been recruited to attend one of the fancier Marist boarding schools up in the Northeast. The future was wide open. This was my chance.

"I'm afraid the brothers at the Academy are hesitant to grant you a seat at their school due to your parents' . . ." She paused, searching for the appropriate phrase. ". . .lack of financial responsibility."

I'd known for years my father struggled to keep pace with the tuition, not to mention the utilities and, obviously, the mortgage payments, but he worked so diligently I'd never once considered him irresponsible.

Wondering what then—if not a letter of admission—lurked within the red envelope, I spoke, a tremor in my voice startling me. "So what happens now, Sister?"

Sliding the red envelope toward me across her desk, she croaked, "This is how much your parents owe our school. And if you wish to attend high school at the Marist Academy, the diocese demands that you not only fulfill your obligation to us here at St. Mary's, but that you also prepay the entire year of tuition before you commence at the Academy."

I grasped the envelope, but I didn't bother opening it. I was naturally good at numbers. I had witnessed the tuition bills piling up on my dad's grimy metal desk in the back room of the tire shop. I knew that, added together with a whole year of fees at the Academy, the total would be exorbitant, in the four digits, more than we could ever dream of affording.

I was as surprised to find my view of Sister Marie Antoinette wobbling and wavering as I had been by my voice faltering. *Don't cry*, I urged myself. *Be strong. Imagine what Jesus must have felt like dying on that cross. Now that was pain. This is nothing.* I fixed my eyes on the crucifix, hoping that by gazing upward the threatening tears would be contained within my eyelids.

"We enjoyed having you here as a student, Ramón," her tone softened. "You possess great promise."

I yearned to ask her if I'd ever see my friends again. Was this the end of the road for my education? I wanted to confess to her that I'd truly come to believe this private schooling would be my ticket out of this place, out of poverty really. My father had sold me on this fantasy since the day he'd plucked me from that makeshift, doublewide public-school classroom back in fifth grade and fortuitously planted me among the rich kids and the nuns. And the Sisters of Holy Charity had egged him on, hadn't they? He had never provided comprehensive details, but he had spurred me to study harder, convincing me the sisters insisted that I contained the potential to be "number one," that I was some sort of López Chosen One—like Uncle Bobby had once been—destined to hoist our family upward and forward in our grand pursuit of the American Dream.

Were there no scholarships available? Should I ask? Should I swallow whatever remnants of pride I might still cling to and beg, like the crippled mendicants that littered the church steps on Sundays, hoping for alms to fall from the hands of guilt-ridden churchgoers?

But I couldn't bear to hear my voice crack and break again. I could not allow the tears to stream down my cheeks, rendering me helpless. Instead, I clenched my jaw and rose swiftly to my feet, the red envelope clasped tightly in my right hand. I nodded awkwardly as I held my head up high in a vain attempt to keep my tears from spilling. And I raced to the boys' bathroom, where I locked myself in a stall and collapsed into uncontrollable sobs.

———

The red envelope lay crumpled into a ball on the greasy tire shop floor. The statement of insurmountable tuition charges shuddered like the portent of an earthquake in my father's calloused and soot-streaked hand.

"I thought the nuns and the brothers were supposed to help people in need." I squinted through the steam rising from the scalding iron tire molds.

"We're not in need," my dad asserted proudly. "It's just a temporary cash flow situation."

How many times had I heard that? It seemed that in the vocabulary of the López men, "temporary" could apply to the entirety of our transitory existence on this Earth.

"People who are sick. People who are disabled. People whose bodies or brains don't work as they should. They are the ones in need."

"Like Rubén?"

The paper floated in the air as his massive open hand flashed through the shadows and struck my cheek. Then I could not stop the tears. I fled the tire shop, frantically streaking into the bright summer light.

"Ramón!" he shouted over the hiss of the steam rising from the tire molds. "Come back here."

Dashing along the tracks, all I could think of was escaping the sweat and the stench of the baking rubber, the grime, and the sting of the vaporized, synthetically enhanced dust in my eyes, mirror images of his own dark and brooding visage. His deluded dreams. Why had he sowed these bitter seeds of disappointment in my heart?

At a bend in the tracks, I veered off into the old graveyard. There, I searched for a familiar spot beneath a giant cottonwood tree. The name "López" was chiseled into an unremarkable gray stone. I'd come here with my Grandma Fina on Día de los Muertos plenty of times. Every year, she religiously brought pan dulce, sugar skulls, and bright, orange-colored paper marigolds to dutifully adorn her departed husband's tomb. I'd never met him, my abuelo. He was nothing more to me than a quarter of my DNA and a cryptic face in a handful of tattered black-and-white photographs, a foreign stranger in a white guayabera, straw hat, and horn-rimmed glasses. Sitting on the grass, I wondered if he had ever slapped my dad. Whipped him with the belt. Exhorted him to accomplish the impossible tasks that he himself could not master. Generation after generation, these López men passed down the wisdom that our people had come here to America to make a better life, to make progress that was impossible south of the border. But generation after generation, it seemed we remained stuck in a cycle. Now my father was determined to turn back the clock, to literally go backward and retrace the steps of his father in retrograde. It was sheer madness. I glared at my grandfather's name on the tombstone. I was angry at him. I hated him for dying before finishing his job. Maybe it was his fault my father seemed so incomplete.

———

When I walked into the kitchen, Grandma Fina stood at her usual spot, stirring a pot of menudo boiling on the stove as she gazed out the window. The spicy scent mingled with the cloud of steam instantly made me sweat. I was about to ask if I could open the window when I noticed she was not looking through the glass, but rather staring blankly at an invisible point in front of it. Her eyes glazed over, a faint smile graced her lips.

"Grandma?" I whispered, fearful of startling her.

Slowly, her eyes refocused as she turned to look at me, "Oh, Ramón. It's you."

"Yes . . ." I answered. "What were you looking at?"

She pursed her lips and pointed at the kitchen table with her wooden stirring spoon. "Sit," she commanded.

Grandma Fina was not to be trifled with, so I did as she said, staring up expectantly at her. Was something wrong with her? Should I be worried? Maybe the heat was getting to her.

"Should I open the window?" I asked.

"No . . . I like it steamy in here," she answered.

"I can tell." I wiped my brow.

"Ramón . . . do you know why I like to cook?"

"Because there's so many of us to feed?"

"No. That's not why I like it. I like it because it reminds me of my mother."

I had never met her mother, who had died many years before my birth somewhere down in México.

I nodded patiently, waiting for her to continue her story in the same haltingly suspenseful fashion that my father had inherited.

"You and your father remind me of me and my mother," she continued. "We did not always see eye to eye. She did not approve of my choices."

"Which choices?"

"Marrying who I did, coming to America . . . you name it," Grandma Fina said, tasting her menudo and closing her eyes to savor its nuances. Licking her lips, she continued, "but the one thing we enjoyed doing together was cooking. She taught me everything she knew. In a way, you know her, through the food I make."

"So you argued and fought, like my dad and I do sometimes?" I asked.

"Yes, we did," Grandma Fina answered, leaning back against the counter as she looked down at me. Her spoon was a scepter and her pink curlers a crown. "Before I left home to come to America, I said some things I wish I could take back."

"You never apologized?"

"Oh, yes I have, many times over, but not until long after she died."

"How could you do that?" I asked.

"I talk to her still."

I shifted uncomfortably in the hard wooden chair. Maybe the heat was indeed getting to her. "How?"

"When I cook, and the kitchen gets steamy, and the smells of the spices fill the hot air . . . I sense her presence . . . I see her standing in front of the window . . . I talk to her in my mind and she listens."

"And does she talk back?"

"Yes, I hear her words."

"What does she say?" I leaned in.

"She tells me she loves me and that none of our differences matter anymore, that they never truly did, that we only saw divisions that were not really there to begin with. From afar . . . through time and distance . . . none of those differences matter at all. We are together."

"That is beautiful," I said. And I meant it. I was moved. Even though it must have been nearly ninety degrees in that small room, I shivered with emotion. And even though I could see only the two of us, the room felt strangely crowded. "Is she here now . . . with us?"

"Yes, m'ijo. She is."

"Will you tell her something for me?"

"Sí. ¿Que es?"

"Tell her I say gracias."

"Gracias for what?"

"For you."

Grandma Fina nodded, glanced at the window, then back at me. I knew my message had been conveyed as she smiled broadly. "She likes you, Ramón."

I gazed through the steam out the window at the palm trees lining the resaca across the street. Their fronds reflected the sunlight like green mirrors.

"Do you think I should just do what my dad says? Keep quiet, go along with everything? Move to México?"

"I think you must speak what is in your heart, Ramón. Follow your own compass. In the end, your father will always be your father, but you must be you."

I followed her distracted gaze. For a fleeting instant, in the dust motes that swirled through the misty air, between us and the window blasting us with golden light, I could have sworn I'd seen the outline of a woman nodding in agreement.

———

The next time I saw my mother, I wasted no time in confronting her with my rebellious ideas. "I'll take no part in it," I said.

"What do you mean?" she replied, as always carrying her oversized baby in her arms. Did she ever put him down? He was seven and still hapless. How much longer could she keep carrying him? I stared at her bulging biceps.

"I will not be moving with you and Dad to México."

Finally, she placed Rubén in his playpen, where he began to writhe and cry. "But you have no choice."

"Of course I have a choice. We all have choices. We make them every day. Just like you choose to stay with Dad despite everything. I choose to make my own way."

"But you're still a child!" She began crying too.

"I'm no younger than my grandfather was when he was orphaned down in México during the Revolution and made his way up here to the border."

"You've been listening to too many of your Grandma Fina's stories."

"Well, they're true."

"Why are you doing this?"

"Because I'm an American. I belong here. My future is here. I'm not going backward."

"But you said the Academy won't take you because of the money we owe."

"I'll go to public school. I was born here. It's my right. I've learned a lot with the nuns and I'll do great. I'll be 'number one,' like Dad wants. And I'll get into college and make it out of this place."

"What's so wrong with this place?" she protested indignantly, acting like she'd created it.

"Are you kidding?" I scoffed. "It's basically México but with tap water you can drink. And even then, you don't want to because it's brown and smells bad."

Rubén screamed as my mother wept.

Finally, I picked him up and bounced him up and down against my chest. Immediately, he hushed and stared at me with his uniquely unnerving, vapidly vacant gaze.

"¡Que demonios!" my dad huffed, filling the room with his overwhelming presence. "What's going on in here?"

"He's not coming with us," my mother cried.

He looked at me as if I had just shot him in the gut. "What?"

"I'm staying here at Grandma Fina's. If I live here in Brownsville, I can at least go to the public high school, but if I move with you to Matamoros, they won't allow it."

"Your place is with us," he commanded. "You can study in México."

"No thanks. I belong here. My Spanish isn't even that good."

"Just think, our Sunday trips to the ranch will be much shorter," he tried to convince me. "And the tire plant will be right there too."

"I'm not interested in going to the ranch or the tire plant anymore," I snapped, sensing a shudder of pain rippling through him.

Our eyes clashed as my heart raced. I had never dared contradict him, much less confront him. I expected him to hit me again, to barrel toward me and mow me down, to toss me out the window onto the back porch and then kick me into the dusty yard where Golden might take mercy on me and lick my wounds. Instinctively, he raised his hand to strike me, but then he stopped, as if some invisible force had come between us in that moment and held his hand aloft, protecting me for an instant but dividing us for an eternity.

"This conversation isn't over," he snarled, storming out of the house with a slam of the front door.

When my mother opened her arms toward me, I thought she was going to give me a hug, but then I realized she simply wanted me to hand Rubén back to her. That's why he hadn't hit me. It hadn't been God or Jesus or the divine peace of the Holy Spirit restraining him. Rubén had been the invisible force shielding me from my father's wrath.

———

The house my father rented in Matamoros was a ten-minute drive across the river from Grandma Fina's. It was on the same block as my Abuela Carmela's house, where my mother had grown up. In México, there were no zoning laws, so the residences were crammed between bodegas and hardware stores. Most people ran one or more businesses out of their homes in these neighborhoods that teetered between the chaos of poverty and the somewhat sufferable stability of México's floundering middle class.

He rented the house without letting anyone else see it first. "It's close to your mother's place, so that's all that matters," he assured my mom as we traversed the river.

Once we wormed our way through the tangled traffic into the center of the densely populated city, she relaxed as she recognized the neighborhood of her youth. How bad could it be, returning home?

The structure was one story and made of cinder block somebody had forgotten to paint, both inside and out. Like most homes in Matamoros, there was no front lawn, just a wall with a door in it, right off the busy street. Within those clammy walls, the noises of the city reverberated exponentially, and the heat suffocated us as we ventured tentatively through its low-ceiling hallways like cautious explorers on a colonizing mission. Overhead, bald light bulbs illuminated the way. My mother put on a brave front, but I could tell she was devastated. This was not a home; it was a prison. At least our hovel in Southmost had been warm and soft, made of wood. But this was my nightmare vision of a Siberian gulag. In the back, there was a tiny kitchen with a rustic gas stove and a rusted fridge. It opened up to an even tinier patch of dirt, which was meant to serve as the backyard. Out there, a concrete sink was designed to wash clothes, and wires spanned the square of sky for drying clothes. The four of us filled the space to the point of discomfort as our tight shoulders rubbed against each other. We could hear the neighbor talking to his pig over the crest of the glass-spiked wall. In México, it was commonplace to shatter beer and soda bottles and encrust the tops of cement walls with the shards for security. On the other side, the elderly man was assuring his pig that its life had been worthwhile and that its impending death would serve a noble purpose, to feed his family. Soon, his sharp blade would slice its throat and spill its blood. And its final squeal would pierce the night.

Horrified, my mother scuttled back inside the house. I lingered on the patio with my father, wondering if the carnage would ensue immediately or if the man would wait, rousing his neighbors in the middle of the night with the dying animal's bloodcurdling shrieks.

"You'll spend most of your time at your mother's," my father consoled my mother during the ride back to Brownsville.

Not having uttered a word during the entire international trip, I harbored no desire to begin now, as we sat in congested traffic on the bridge. But then he had to goad me.

"And you, Ramón? What did you think?" He feigned unbridled optimism as only he could.

"There were no power outlets," was what came out of my mouth as I stared out the car window at paraplegic beggars scooting about on crudely made skateboards, palms outstretched for change.

"What do you mean?" my mother prodded.

"I mean just that," I explained. "Where there should be outlets, there were holes in the wall with wires sticking out."

"That's a simple fix," my dad waved his hand dismissively. "A trip to the hardware store."

"Which is conveniently located next door," I added sourly.

I could sense his eyes glowering at me via the rearview mirror. Next to me, Rubén hunched asleep in a child car seat three sizes too small for him.

The vehicles inched toward the summit of the bridge, hovering over the center of the Rio Grande. My mother stared somberly out her window toward the east. Out there, my dad often mentioned, the river flowed out to the Gulf of México.

I thought of the water channeling restrained within the banks, one to the south and another to the north, people teeming in the shoulder-high weeds at its edge yearning to cross, and I wondered if the river felt liberated when it met the sea.

"I can't do it," I whispered.

This time I sensed both sets of parental eyes on me, his boring disapprovingly through the mirror, hers peering knowingly at me over her shoulder.

The cars moved yet again. Starting and stopping. With each release of the brake and each subsequent depression, the car lurched and halted; Rubén's head slumped forward and rolled backward.

"What was that, Ramón?" my father dared me.

I looked out at that river carving its wound toward freedom. I shut my eyes tight. I imagined myself drawing energy and power from that water flowing, and I heard myself repeat, "I can't do it."

"Can't do what?" my mother insisted, even though she knew the answer to her question.

"Can't move with you to México."

Now the car lurched and halted more vigorously, violently even, as my father fumed at the wheel. I expected him to lash out at me, put me in my place, insist that I follow his commands and go wherever they went, even if it was the furthest corner of the world.

A few minutes passed. As my agitated pulse slowed, I saw his eyes shift in the mirror toward the silhouette of my mother leaning into her window-sill. Then I understood, perhaps for the first time, he was picking his battles.

"What did you think, amor?" he asked in a softer tone of voice, but he wasn't fooling either one of us.

She sniffled, dabbing her ruddy nose with a tissue.

"Amor?" he pressed, gritting his teeth.

"It will do," she assented.

Uncomfortably, our eyes met again in the mirror. Then the light flashed green, indicating we should advance toward the immigration officer.

——

On the last night my parents and Rubén stayed at Grandma Fina's house, Cousin David and I strung a pair of pink hammocks between palm trees in the backyard. Our elusive grandfather had brought them from the Yucatán decades earlier. Swaying in the Gulf breeze beneath the rustling palms, we gazed at constellations brightly puncturing the inky sky.

"What's public school like?" I asked my freckle-faced cousin, his curly locks tumbling down to his shoulders as he stared up at the stars.

"You've been there. You know. It's like mud instead of sand. It's like smoke instead of air."

I grimaced. It had been a while. "I'm not used to it anymore."

"You can do it. Everyone else does."

"Good point."

We swung silently for a while.

"It'll be cool to be in the same class finally," he said. "Too bad Little Bobby can't join us."

"Yeah," I thought of our cousin stranded in San Benito, his father, our ephemeral Uncle Bobby, still MIA, just like he'd been for six months back in 'Nam in '72. "Too bad."

"Don't worry, man. We'll look out for each other," David said, his eyes trained on the stars overhead.

I wondered what skills I could bring to that endeavor. After another long pause staring at the impenetrable sky, I ventured to plumb the depths of knowledge only he could fathom, "David?"

"Yeah?"

I glanced back from my hammock toward Grandma Fina's back

porch, a warm glow diffusing from the windows. "What's it like to live without your parents?"

I imagined him swimming through a tumult of indescribable emotion. I knew he missed his mom, who had resettled up north and was rumored to have started a new family. I'd heard him call for her in his sleep. He waited for a while before he answered, but when he finally spoke, all he said was, "Grandma Fina's all right."

I shifted onto my side and looked at him. He forced a grin, mischief lurking in his eyes like he was a Mexican jack-o'-lantern.

————

When they left, it was like surgery without anesthetic. Organs rudely removed from one's body.

The furniture we spirited from our Southmost shack had lingered all summer long in the delivery van, a rusting testament to my father's stagnant sales prospects. Surrounded by towering weeds, the vehicle squatted next to the disintegrating brick barbecue pit my grandfather mythically erected with his own hands when my dad was knee-high to a tlacuache.

After several attempts, my dad coaxed the van to life and maneuvered it clumsily onto the front yard. The driveway, which he treated as a suggestion, sloped down toward the Lincoln Park Resaca, two strips of cracked cement, grass sprouting between them like unkempt hair.

My mother embraced me, Rubén sandwiched between us, his mournful moans subsiding as his skin pressed against mine beneath the triple digit sun. Maybe for the first time, but certainly not for the last, I respected her. Why? Because she did not beg for me to accompany them across that violent, watery divide. Quite the opposite, as my father stared expectantly at me, she reinforced her stand, "Vámonos, José. Déjalo con tu mamá."

Defeated, he hung his head and slid behind the vast wheel of the "panadera," as we called it. It was a bakery truck after all, even if the baked goods it delivered in its second life were tires instead of bread or donuts.

He scowled reproachingly at me through the cracked windshield as they backed out of the driveway with our family's sparse goods. Many things had stumped and confounded him in life, but his son defying him had probably been the last contingency he would have ever imagined.

Probably to reassure her own son more than me, in that final instant of their departure, Grandma Fina wrapped her hefty arm around my narrow shoulders and smiled proudly. I knew then: No descendants of hers would ever find themselves without a place to call home, without a patch of dirt to pledge allegiance.

THE LIMES

I took to drawing limes the Sunday my father announced his latest business scheme at Grandma Fina's kitchen table. After my parents had retreated across the border to Matamoros, it was typically the only day of the week that I saw them and my little brother. I'd hoped my dad would toss the football around with me in the front yard, or take us out to Boca Chica Beach for a long, toasty afternoon of building sandcastles and pulling icy Coca-Cola bottles from his red Igloo chest, but instead he rambled incessantly about the incredible margin between the low cost of the limes he would purchase somewhere deep in the interior of México and the exorbitant price they would bring at market in Dallas.

"That's where the money's at," he exclaimed, scribbling unintelligible numbers on scattered napkins as the rest of us ate slowly, watching him with wide-eyed apprehension. "Dallas, te digo. The gringos up there are rolling in green. Oil money. Real estate development money. There's even a Federal Reserve Bank there where they print money! They'll pay top dollar at the market. That's where all the big supermarket chains buy their produce."

"Do you have a solid plan?" I asked, wary of his new venture given his track record of missteps.

"My plan is 'a la brava'!" He yelped exuberantly as my mother and grandmother winced in dismay. 'A la brava' meant he was—yet again—boldly flying by the seat of his pants.

My long-suffering mom sat quietly to his side, spoon-feeding Rubén, who was forcibly stuffed into his too-small highchair. I watched in disgust as he pointed at a bowl of ketchup. He couldn't speak yet, despite the fact most kids his age were already in first grade. But he could effectively point at the things he wanted, which created a lopsided family dynamic involving his complete self-absorption and everybody else's constant and herculean efforts to hastily respond to his ever-multiplying requests. Every couple of months he seemed to cycle through a random new obsession. He would point at the item and my parents would pour whatever scarce resources they could marshal into procuring said substances or objects for him. Typically, at this age, his requests involved various types of food, although our family had recently survived his fleeting flirtation with batteries. My parents had become unable to ferry Rubén anywhere that might sell batteries, lest he point hungrily at them from his undersized stroller, his feet dragging on the floor. Suspicious about how he managed to suck the life from so many batteries in so little time, I shadowed him one Sunday only to discover him sneakily crawling to Grandma Fina's trash can to dispose of a brand-new pair of double-A's. I'd hastily reported his abominable act, only to be chastised by my parents for snitching on my disabled brother. It was useless. So I drew limes. I was running out of pages in my tattered journal.

As my father rhapsodized about the tangy green morsels, I watched Rubén open his mouth wide for spoons heaped with ketchup and sketched circles in my spiral notebook.

"Does that count as a vegetable?" I asked, gesturing with my colored pencil toward the nearly vanquished bottle of Heinz at the center of the table.

"It's made from tomatoes," my mother answered, inserting another spoonful into Rubén's expectant orifice.

I frowned, scrutinizing the ingredients on the label. "There are a bunch of other ingredients too. What's high fructose corn syrup?"

"Limes are definitely not vegetables," my father asserted. "They grow on trees. Only fruit grows on trees."

Shrugging, I flipped the page and started a new sketch, this time quickly delineating a tree and populating its branches with limes surrounded by leaves shaped like dollar bills.

"How is school, Ramón?" my mother asked, as Grandma Fina paused her cooking to retrieve a fresh bottle of ketchup from the cupboard.

I couldn't help but wonder how my grandmother felt about her cumin-infused picadillo tacos being smothered beneath a thick red blanket of sweetly processed gringo flavor instead of being enlivened by her homemade salsa of chile piquín picked from a bush in the backyard. I watched her closely, but if she was in any way offended, she effectively concealed her feelings in deference to Rubén's special needs.

"I'm still alive," I replied dryly, but by then Rubén had begun fervently jabbing his finger toward the cucumber slices Grandma Fina set on the table and my mother forgot all about her question.

My father was visibly relieved by the distraction. It had been his dream to send me to private school, but now—due to his "cash flow" issues—I was nearly finished with my freshman year at Porter, which was widely considered one of the worst public schools in the country.

"Lime is good on cucumbers," he added for good measure, dousing the cucumber slices with juice from his favorite new fruit. "It's good in guacamole too."

I gazed down at my sketch, deciding to support the sole lime tree with parents and siblings, an entire orchard of dysfunctional citric promise. Sadly, I no longer harbored much hope in my father's entrepreneurial endeavors.

Wincing at the acrid flavor of the lime juice that my father overzealously squeezed onto the cucumber, Rubén spit out a sticky ball of masticated green mush which rolled down his ketchup-splattered shirt and plopped onto his highchair tray, its surface now resembling an abstract rendering of a crime scene.

I chuckled as he pointed decisively back at the gleaming new bottle of ketchup and grunted greedily.

"He didn't like the lime juice," my mother lamented.

"Some people have no taste," I retorted, grinning down at the ever-growing orchard in my fertile notebook.

I didn't look up from the page, but I could feel my parents' eyes drilling into me with pointed disapproval.

———

In Brownsville, it was rumored that the Porter Cowboys always won their football games because the players were cheered on by their wives and children. Fortunately for me, during the first few weeks of school I was befriended by one of those Cowboys.

Dante, a burly behemoth with a full beard and mustache, was an offensive lineman. And, contrary to the local stereotype, he assured me that he had never been married or fathered any children, at least not yet. In compliance, however, with another—more universal—high school trope, I served as Dante's tutor, which was how we met, and he served as my bodyguard, which was how I survived.

"I'm used to protecting the smart guy," he explained, referring to the team's quarterback. "That's what an offensive lineman does."

"Oh, I thought maybe you all just went around insulting people and beating them up."

"We do that too," he replied, unaware that I was being sarcastic.

Although we were an odd pair, me of average height and scrawny, him soaring and muscle-bound, the combination proved effective in ensuring Dante could keep playing sports by passing his classes and I could survive my journey through the new world I'd been thrust into by my father's financial misfortunes.

After school, during one of our tutoring sessions, we sat in the study hall. Dante hunched over a set of remedial math problems I had scrawled out for him as I worked on my sketches of the lime orchard where money grew on trees. Suddenly, I felt a presence over my shoulder. Turning, I was surprised to see a tall beanpole of a man crowned with floppy gray and white hair. It was Mr. Dean, the guidance counselor at our school.

"Hello, Mr. López," he said. It may have been the first time I'd been addressed in such a respectful manner. The nuns mostly spared me their words and struck me with the paddle, while the teachers at Porter generally ignored me on the off chance I might have brought more knowledge from private school than they'd gained at the community college where they earned their teaching certifications.

"Hello, Mr. Dean," I replied.

"That's a lovely sketch you're making." He pointed at my journal.

"Thanks. They're limes."

His crystalline blue eyes scanned the sorry assortment of stubby colored pencils splayed out before me on the table. "Your palette seems somewhat limited. When you have a chance, come by my office."

I smiled politely, nodded and returned to my work as he strolled away.

The following day, I visited his office during recess.

"Follow me," he instructed.

Through the labyrinth of long, sterile hallways I still barely understood, he led me to a room I had yet to encounter. Inside were several easels supporting half-painted canvases. A long worktable was covered with containers of paint and cans stuffed with brushes of all sizes. The smell of turpentine seared my nostrils, summoning tears to my eyes. In the far corner of the room, a curly-haired woman knelt on the floor. She appeared to be scrubbing the tiles, but as we approached it became clear she wielded a sponge to smear various shades of blue across a large sheet of butcher paper.

"This is Mrs. Martinez."

Her head jerked upward in surprise, curls bobbing. She'd been so immersed in her craft that she hadn't even noticed us entering the room.

"¡Dios mio! Señor Dean, casi me da un infarto."

"I'm not sure what an 'infarto' is, but I sincerely hope it's not what it sounds like." He grinned mischievously.

When Mrs. Martinez rose to her feet, the top of her head barely reached my shoulder. She was covered in blue paint, splotches of it on her face, splatters on her glasses, gobs in her hair. She looked like a Smurf, but there was only one female Smurf and she was blond, unlike Mrs. Martinez.

"It is much worse than what it sounds like, Señor Dean. An 'infarto' is a heart attack. You can't creep up on artists at work."

"My most sincere apologies, Mrs. Martinez. I hope that my discovery atones for my transgression."

She smirked at him. "I'm a painter, not a librarian, Señor Dean. Don't use those fancy words with me. What have you brought me that's worthy of disrupting my creative reverie?"

"This is Ramón López." Mr. Dean motioned toward me. "He came to us this year from St. Mary's. I'd like him to show you his sketches."

"I see." Mrs. Martinez lowered her purple, horn-rimmed spectacles to the tip of her nose, peering curiously at me. Without even asking, she plucked my weathered journal from my hands and leafed through the sketches I'd been making of my father's limes. When she reached the last drawing, which was forced onto the inside back cover, she arched her right eyebrow and leaned into it, squinting as if she might find some hidden meaning in the strokes of my pencil. She then flipped the notebook shut and handed it back to me, assessing me from head to toe. "What a handsome young man. You are very neatly dressed. I bet you're smart and well ahead of many of your classmates given your previous schooling."

I nodded shyly, smiling, "Thank you. It's nice to meet you, ma'am."

"Oh please, call me Marcela, m'ijo." She patted me on the shoulder and fanned her sinewy arms, drawing my attention to the art supplies and colorful pictures lining the walls. "So, what do you think of all this?"

"It's beautiful. I've really never seen anything like it."

"Have you ever been in an art museum?" she asked.

"No, ma'am." I hung my head. "I've never left Brownsville."

She nodded slowly. "Most students here haven't. That's okay. That's the wonder of art. It can take you places without you ever leaving the room, ever leaving your mind."

Mr. Dean tiptoed toward the door, smiling and waving as he buzzed along to his next task.

Mrs. Martinez reached into a drawer and pulled out a sketchpad and a small tin. "Ramón, fortunately for you, I can see by your drawings that you have something most people lack. You know what that is?"

I shook my head.

"Talent," she answered, handing me the sketchpad and pencils. "It's time to trade in your journal for a sketchbook. So keep drawing and start coming here every chance you get."

———

"What do you mean, 'impounded'?" My dad's troubled voice filtered through Grandma Fina's house as he spoke on the phone. "I thought it was just a routine inspection."

There was a pause as the person on the other end of the phone explained something to him.

When I entered the room, I had to duck under the long, coiled, banana-yellow phone cord, like when we played limbo at the nun's school.

I sat in my usual chair in the corner, setting down the wooden palette and the thick pad of paper Señora Martinez had most recently bestowed upon me like a fairy godmother. Every time I visited her class, she taught me a new technique and gave me a new tool to practice it. And, thanks to Mr. Dean's administrative wizardry, I had been allowed to transfer into her art class as an after-school elective.

"Several more days?" my father's voice cracked. "Pero . . . the heat has been brutal. It was over 100 degrees today. The limes are just sitting out there in the sun . . . cooking."

Now that I was in the same room, I could decipher some of the other person's words. He mentioned "customs being backed up" and not receiving "the usual advance notice of the shipment," and then something about a "customs broker."

"Customs broker?" My dad grimaced. "I can't afford a customs broker! Just do what you can. I'll be back there tomorrow."

When he returned the phone to its cradle on the wall, he found himself entangled in the cable. I stifled a snicker as I watched him struggle out of it.

"It's not funny, Ramón," he huffed, freeing himself and sitting back down, hunched over his figures and calculations. "Customs broker?" he muttered to himself.

I dipped my brush into one of the shades of green paint Mrs. Martinez had taught me how to mix and began applying color over the limes in my sketch.

"What's going on? Why are you even here?" I asked nonchalantly. "It's a weeknight. You're usually in Matamoros with Mom and Rubén."

"The limes have arrived and I had to use the phone. Calling from México costs a fortune."

"When did the limes get here?"

"The truck came in from Yucatán two days ago. By now, it should be in Dallas at the market."

"Is it going to be okay?"

He looked at me, his hazel eyes momentarily betraying a trace of doubt. Then he regained his composure, resuming his steely countenance and obstinate confidence. "Of course, it will be fine. Ya veras. Mañana, we'll fix everything."

He gathered his papers and stepped outside, speaking in an animated fashion with my chain-smoking Uncle Nick beneath the shade of the avocado tree.

I observed them through the screen door. Even as dusk settled, the heat pressed in from outside. It was like staring into a broiling oven. I pictured the eighteen-wheeler sitting all day in a dirt lot by the old railroad bridge, its long wooden trailer packed full of hard green nuggets slowly—but surely—softening and yellowing. Nothing but a grimy tarp tethered to the top by fraying rope shielded my father's investment from the blistering inferno.

As the days crawled by torturously, my father's phone conversations became increasingly heated. There was talk of the shipment being sent back to México. The words "total loss" were bandied about repeatedly. My dad's hair began to resemble a raven version of Albert Einstein's famously chaotic coif as he tugged at it in a futile effort to wring some brilliant idea from his exhausted brain to salvage his new business.

Eventually, a compromise was struck, thanks to the intercession of one of his childhood friends that worked at the border checkpoint. At my father's expense, the truck would be unloaded at a warehouse, where the limes would be sorted by hand, allowing only those still in tip-top condition to be reloaded and released from impound. In order to save money, our whole family, including my uncles and cousins, trudged to the warehouse, which must have been hotter than Hades, its corrugated metal roof and aluminum walls scalding to the touch. There, an endless cascade of limes rolled down a ramp from the trailer bed onto special manual sorting tables. I was confident I'd never seen so much of any one object in my entire life, nor would I ever again. Unfortunately, most of the fruit was already rotten. Flies swarmed around us, a sickly stench filling the oppressively hot air.

When all was said and done, there were only enough good limes to fill the bed of my dad's rickety red pickup truck, the heap rising precariously to the same height as the cabin.

"It's not worth it to haul them to Dallas," my dad bemoaned. "I'd spend more on gasoline than whatever they would fetch at wholesale."

As the spoiled limes were hauled away to the landfill and my mom and Grandma Fina headed home with blisters on their fingers, I loitered by the pickup truck.

"I'm sorry, Joe," lamented the border agent who had helped my father salvage what he could. "Next time, I recommend you work with a customs broker and follow the protocols. A little planning can go a long way. Maybe even spring for a refrigerated truck."

During the tense ride back to my grandmother's house, all I heard from my dad were those same words echoed once and only once: "Refrigerated truck." He nodded pensively as he murmured them.

———

The following day, when I came home from school, I was surprised to find my mother pounding graham crackers into smithereens on Grandma Fina's kitchen table. Cans of condensed milk and tubs of sour cream crowded the counter. My grandmother whisked ingredients vigorously in a bowl. Mesh sacks of my father's rescued limes lined the walls, some spilling out and rolling around rebelliously on the hardwood floors.

"What's up?" I asked, acting as if—at this point—nothing could truly startle me.

"Your mamá had a good idea," Grandma Fina said, using a silver lime press to squeeze juice into her bowl.

My mom demurred. "Oh, no. We came up with this together."

"What is it?" I asked, saving a graham cracker from my mother's threatening rolling pin and spiriting it into my mouth.

"We're turning as many of your father's limes as we can into pies," Grandma Fina elucidated.

My grandmother's key lime pie was renowned within the family. It was always fresh, sweet, and zingy, topped with a thick layer of her unequaled homemade meringue.

"We figured the limes can only be sold for a few pennies," my mom said, "but the pies could go for several dollars."

"That's the smartest business idea I've heard in a very long time," I surmised. "But how will you sell them?"

"I already did," Grandma Fina proudly proclaimed, whisking as if she had been robotically designed to do so. "I called my church group. I spoke to the Christian Lady's Lunch Club. I phoned the head of the Neighborhood Watch."

"We've got about one hundred orders to fill." My mother smiled, shooting me an unprecedented expression of self-satisfaction.

"That's awesome," I said. Who would have thought? After all of the misguided entrepreneurial efforts of the López men—including my own brief stint as a chile powder dealer—it took the ladies to get it right. "So, where's Dad?"

"He's selling what he can on the highway out to the Island," my mom answered.

This I had to see. Excusing myself, I rode my bike to the road leading out to South Padre. Sure enough, I spotted my dad's red truck parked at the corner of an empty field. It was a busy intersection, but he sat alone on the tailgate with the remainder of his limes. A crudely fashioned cardboard sign offered them at an ever-descending price. It had started out at ten cents a lime, then been crossed out and reduced to five cents. I considered buying a couple of bags and joining my mom and abuela in the kitchen.

The sun in his eyes, he didn't notice me from across the street, but I watched him for a long while, memorizing the haunting image. Then I pedaled home and spent the evening drawing the scene, envisioning it as a painting.

———

At the school's year-end art show, Señora Martinez forced us "artists" to stand by our work and answer any questions that might arise. We spent the morning in the school gym, which felt oddly alien as it was, populated by easels displaying canvases and tables topped by sculptures. The rest of the students were compelled to parade through the aisles and appreciate the artistic efforts of their creatively inclined schoolmates. The judges also strolled slowly through the gymnasium, conferring imperiously and taking copious notes.

When a cluster of jocks swung by my still life of a talavera bowl filled with verdant limes, one of them grinned and snidely commented, "Nice, López! You finally found your balls!"

The others broke out into laughter until Dante cleared his throat. "Hey, leave him alone. I like his limes. They look fresh and real."

I smiled gratefully at him as they shuffled sullenly along. I never would have taken Dante for an art connoisseur, but his critique came more naturally to him than his mathematical ability.

When Mr. Dean arrived at my easel, he lifted his hand to his chin and stared at the still life for a long time, assessing it from various angles. Then he leaned in close and examined how I had rendered the highlights and shadows, the tiny granular texture of the tough skins, the knobby brown bulbs at the tips, the sheen of the light illuminating them.

"This is good, Ramón," he concluded. "You must have worked very diligently. This shows real skill."

"I've learned a great deal from Mrs. Martinez," I answered.

"Have the judges come by yet?"

"No. I'm a bit nervous. I heard they give brutally honest feedback."

"This piece is very . . . safe," Mr. Dean assured me. "I doubt they'll find much fault with it."

I nodded, sensing a tinge of disappointment in his voice. "Were you expecting something different?"

He hesitated, scratching the white stubble on his cheeks, knitting together his bushy salt-and-pepper eyebrows. He resembled a human version of the lovable shaggy dog that starred in those movies about a canine DA.

"Forgive me for spying, but I saw some of your other works in Señora Martinez's studio. And, while I think this work is perfectly fine, I feel like some of the others were much more . . . insightful, powerful even."

"Really?"

"One in particular stood out to me. A red pickup truck. A man sitting on the tailgate wearing a cowboy hat. A mountain of limes behind him under a brilliant sun . . . but what really got to me was the cardboard sign at his feet, the price was cut and still his limes baked."

I stared at him, unsure which of the emotions swirling inside me should be allowed to supersede the others. Should I permit myself to feel fulfilled and exhilarated by his feedback, or should I wallow in the sorrow I felt for my muse?

"There's still time," I determined breathlessly, eyeing the judges one row away.

"I'll hold down the fort," he smiled, his eyes glimmering. "Go get it."

I bolted past the metal doors, hurtling through the concrete maze. In Señora Martinez's room, I pulled the painting from the storage shelves and hurried back.

As I entered the gym, the gaggle of judges was nearing my easel. Discretely, I swapped the paintings, handing Mr. Dean the still life.

"I'll put this in the art studio," he offered. "Good luck, Ramón."

The judges stood before my painting for what seemed like an excruciating length of time. They didn't say a word. They didn't offer a shred of feedback. I was overwhelmed by a sense of dread. Should I have stuck with the safe choice? Had they been repulsed by my work?

At the end of the day, when the judges handed the principal a list of prizes and winners, the elderly Anglo man stepped up to the podium and counted down the various runners-up, handing out a slew of consolation prizes. I slumped as I watched others march proudly to the stage to claim their certificates. Nothing for me. Just another López loser.

Then, finally, when the principal came to the Grand Prize for Best Painting, he had to say my name twice before I realized what was happening. The student next to me shook me by the shoulder and pointed toward the podium, urging me on.

In a daze, I received a golden trophy and a blue ribbon emblazoned with the number 1 as the audience applauded.

Mr. Dean was nowhere in sight, but Señora Martinez gleefully threw her arms around me, squeezing me tightly. She proclaimed, "This is the beginning of great things, Ramón!" She proceeded to tell me I could take the painting and easel home to display my accomplishment. A congratulatory throng of students and teachers formed around me.

Finally, as the crowd dissipated, Dante smiled smugly, reminding me, "I told them I liked your limes."

———

Grandma Fina insisted on displaying the painting in her small formal parlor. My cousin David and I called it the "No-No Room," because we were not permitted to sit on the furniture or touch the decor. The yellow sofa was shrouded in crunchy, transparent vinyl. The coffee table was adorned with plastic fruit. In the corner, dainty shelves displayed tiny porcelain figurines she'd collected over the years. And now, in front of those shelves stood the easel bearing my painting, the blue ribbon pinned to the top right corner.

Cousin David slapped me on the back. "You nailed it."

On Sunday when my parents and Rubén came for their weekly visit, they filed into the No-No Room to pay their respects. My mom spent her time trying to stop Rubén from knocking the easel over as he crawled beneath it, acting like it was a jungle gym brought in to amuse him. My dad, on the other hand, stared at it for a long time, and then—without a word—went out onto the back porch and sat in a rusted metal rocking chair. All through dinner, he remained taciturn. Afterward, he went back outside and resumed his position in the rocking chair, swaying gently in the cooling evening breeze. After a while, I joined him, sitting in the rocking chair next to his, nervously waiting for him to dispense his wisdom, or his criticism. If I was lucky, perhaps he would say nothing at all about the painting.

"I didn't know you liked to paint," he began.

"I just started this year. But my teacher says I have promise."

He nodded approvingly. "Promise is a good thing. This is the land of promise."

I smiled as the shadows lengthened, the gnarled mesquites spreading spidery echoes of their branches across the sun-dappled grass.

"So you liked it?"

He took too long to answer, squinting at the mesquites, listening to the breeze whisper mysteriously through their blue-green spindly leaves, losing himself in the shadows and sound.

"It is sad," he finally concluded.

After a long silence, the yard fell dark and the mesquites contorted into mournful, mangled ghosts on the lawn. Unsure what to say, I simply sat there, my innards twisting like the trunks of the trees.

When my mother called from inside that it was time to go, my father rose slowly and looked down at me with those dark yet glowing eyes of his.

"I am proud of you," he said.

———

Grandma Fina and I stood on the driveway as they backed out, their red taillights fading into the night like twin fireflies. After I helped her clean up, we each retired to our rooms. Mine was atypically quiet as my cousin

David was spending the night at his other abuelita's house. I lay there, staring at the dark ceiling, again wondering which of my conflicting feelings should be allowed to triumph. Happiness for winning at something? Guilt for doing so at my father's expense? Excitement for finally finding something I might be good at, for having what Señora Martinez called "promise"? Or sorrow for the glaring reality that while my potential lay untapped, my father's seemed drained. Amid the swirl of confusing emotions, a darker—but clearer—force emerged at the center. Anger. I was livid at being in this position. Why couldn't a much-needed victory be clean and neat? Why couldn't everyone be happy just once? Why did my inspiration have to be interpreted as an insult? When Grandma Fina and my mom turned my father's bitter lime juice into sweet key lime pies, the money had rolled in and everyone had been pleased. But, somehow, this was different. This was personal.

Enraged, I tore out of my bed and strode into the front room. I yanked the painting off the easel, blue ribbon and all, and I carried the whole lot into the backyard. At the crumbling brick barbecue pit, I smashed the easel over my knee, doused it with lighter fluid, and struck a match. The flames rose vindictively into the night sky, sparks dancing around me. I took one last look at the painting and—in a gut-wrenching motion—flung it onto the pyre and watched it burn.

COFFEE PORT ROAD

Reeser loved to shoot down Coffee Port at midnight on the wrong side of the road with his lights off.

I met him through art class, not because he was a particularly creative type or even enrolled in the course, but because he was Julia's boyfriend and Julia had won the top prize in the school's art festival two years in a row before I swiped it by surprise at the end of freshman year.

After my painting won Best in Show, I became somewhat of a celebrity within the severely limited art circles at Porter High. So much so, that in my sophomore year I was deigned worthy enough to consort with seniors like Julia and, by association, Reeser.

Reeser was a lanky surfer dude with dusty blond hair, pale blue eyes, and a seemingly endless supply of marijuana. Nobody could decipher what kind of academic schedule or calendar he adhered to, and he seemed to share no classes with anyone I knew. Everybody at Porter was required to participate in a certain number of electives or extracurricular activities, but Reeser was neither an athlete nor an artist, not a musician nor a member of the metal shop. He was a metalhead though, invariably sporting a black T-shirt emblazoned with album cover art by Iron Maiden or Judas Priest or Black Sabbath.

Reeser drove a souped-up 1983 Chevy Monte Carlo SS, black with darkly tinted windows. This act alone gave him a certain amount of street cred with a broad cross section of Porter's social classes. The gearheads accepted him, despite his gringo status, hovering over his open hood in the senior parking lot, pontificating about the benefits of nitro and turbo and eight cylinders versus six. The girls in general liked him even though he was a pothead because he had a cool set of wheels and he was a surfer to boot. Plus, there weren't too many blond guys in Brownsville, let alone Porter. And, of course, the stoners and the skaters hallowed him as one of their own, perhaps a shining beacon of what they might attain if only they could play their cards as well as he did.

Aside from the car, and the cool hair, and an uncanny ability to ride the waves while high, Reeser's most coveted claim to fame was—no doubt—his enduring relationship with Julia.

Julia was a rare cross between Goth artiste and smoldering Mexican mob boss' daughter. She wore a uniform of tight black jeans and black tank tops that showed off her curves. Her wavy black hair tumbled down to her waist. And, whenever she appeared, she was both preceded and followed by the delicate fragrance of gardenias in bloom.

The first time she spoke to me, my heart sped up and I thought I might hyperventilate. All she was trying to communicate was her sincere congratulations when I bested her in the art show, but judging by my metabolic response, one might have thought she had threatened my life. It wasn't like I never talked to girls, but Julia was different. She made the other girls look—well—like girls, while she seemed to inhabit a whole other level of womanhood. And it wasn't just about her looks, although they probably would have been enough to rob me of my breath. It was her throaty voice, her pout while she assessed her work on canvas, and the laser-focused fury with which she painted, completely engrossed in her work as she unwittingly entranced others.

When she casually invited me to join her and Reeser at their lunch table in the cafeteria, my status immediately skyrocketed, as did my blood pressure.

"Do you like to play games?" Julia asked, smiling mischievously.

"Sure. What kind of games?"

"Strategy? Role-playing?" Reeser probed.

"I like chess and Risk, but what do you mean by role-playing?"

"D&D?" asked Julia.

"Dungeons & Dragons?"

"Yeah," Reeser replied, leaning forward. "What about it?"

"I've heard of it, but never played."

"Wanna join our group?" Julia offered.

"Sure!" I couldn't believe my luck. "But why me?"

"Our paladin went and got himself killed," Reeser explained in terms only a seasoned D&D player could understand.

I balked. "You mean one of your group members . . . died?"

Julia giggled. "Not like for real, dork. Just in the game."

"Oh," I slumped back in relief. "Like I said, I've never played, but one hears things. My Grandma's church group calls it demonic."

My eyes hovered over Reeser's T-shirt, which sported a glowing orange demon head and the name of a band called DIO in Gothic script. Reeser had already shown me that when you flipped the logo upside down, the script spelled "devil."

"What's a paladin?" I asked, wishing to push thoughts of Satan worship out of my mind.

"A paladin is a holy warrior, someone who fights for what's right and what's honorable," Julia explained, her amber eyes swallowing me whole as she said it. "I think you'd make a good paladin. And, yes, there are evil monsters in the game, but it's all make-believe. Plus, as a paladin, you can fight those demons."

Reeser smiled slyly. "Yeah, my Grandma used to call it demonic too . . . till we converted her."

My eyes widened in apprehension.

Julia laughed. "Don't listen to him. His Grandma lives in Ohio and has no idea what goes on down here on the border."

Reeser chuckled. "Yeah, she probably thinks everything down here is Satan's work."

Julia planted a kiss on his mouth and acrobatically swung one of her legs into his lap. "Speaking of which, we've got time before next period."

Reeser cocked an eyebrow. "The Blaster?"

"C'mon."

As the two left with their arms around each other's waists, I watched them traverse the parking lot, making a beeline for Reeser's car. She had a way of swinging her hips as she walked, her long mane following in rhythm like a hypnotic pendulum. After they got in the car, the engine roared to life and their forms vanished behind the impenetrable windows. What went on in there, I wondered. Were they smoking pot? Doing drugs? Making out? Having sex? Summoning Beelzebub? All of the above?

My rumination was disrupted by a hard kick against the metal leg of my flimsy plastic chair, the impact nearly knocking me out of my seat.

"Hey, Ese, outside. Now!" A menacing figure towered over me, tattoos emblazoning his sinewy arms.

"Ándale," another guy shoved me, forcing me to scramble to my feet in order to avoid sprawling to the floor.

I immediately recognized them as a pair of senior bullies known as Juan Diego and Chuck Norris, not that those were their real names. Juan Diego had earned the pseudonym as a result of his Virgen de Guadalupe tattoo. And his goon-like follower had attained his moniker due to his obsession with martial arts and action movies.

Flanked by one of my assailants on either side, I was gruffly escorted out of the cafeteria and into a corner of the parking lot, my back pressed against the school wall.

"Who do you think you are, Fish, hanging out with seniors?" Juan Diego asked.

"Yeah, Ese. Who do you think you are?" Chuck Norris echoed.

"I'm not a fish . . . not a f . . . freshman anymore," I stuttered nervously, peering toward Reeser's car, the so-called Blaster. Would they perhaps notice my plight and come to my aid? Did the car seem to be oscillating like a boat on choppy waters?

"You think we give a shit, Ese?"

"Yeah, Ese."

"You need to stay in your place, Vato." Juan Diego had shoulder-length hair and a red bandanna hanging from his jean pocket. His most impressive tattoo was definitely the one of the Virgen de Guadalupe. She danced miraculously when he flexed his muscles.

"Yeah, your place," Chuck Norris repeated, pointedly placing his hand on a set of nunchucks jutting from his back pocket.

"Listen, vatos, I don't want any trouble." I detested the quiver in my voice. If Julia could hear me now, would she deem me worthy of being a paladin, or joining her group?

"Don't you try to talk like us or be like us, Ese. We know where you're from. You're not from the barrio. You went to private school before you came here."

"I grew up in Southmost," I blurted out. There had been a time at the nun's school when saying that earned me instant respect.

"You think we give a shit?"

"Yeah, you think?"

I stared sullenly at my tattered sneakers. My lunch simmered and soured in my stomach, morphing into a tightly raging ball of acid. I wondered what a paladin might do. What would Julia be impressed by, were she not distracted doing Satan-knew-what in the Blaster? I curled my hands into tight fists, my knuckles blanching white. "You know what I think?"

They jabbed their chins toward the sky, daring me.

"I think you two better leave me the fuck alone before I get pissed off. It's not right to bully people."

Chuck Norris pulled his weapon of choice out of his pants as Juan Diego recoiled his arm and readied to swing. I called upon everything my dad had taught me over the years, which—I now realized—amounted to a considerable cache of constant counsel. Waiting until the moment I saw Juan Diego's body begin shifting its weight toward me, I ducked and felt nothing but a whoosh of displaced air as his right cross narrowly missed my face. His momentum carried him forward, rendering it child's play for me to sweep his legs out from under him. Then I covered my head with my hands in anticipation of the nunchucks slamming down on my skull, but they never dropped. Whirling around as I rose back up, I was surprised to see Dante looming over us, his hand up in the air, grasping the nunchucks as my attackers—now the ones stuck in the corner—cowered against the wall.

"You two better split," Dante growled. "And I'll keep these."

The nunchucks slipped from Chuck Norris' hand as the fight drained from his eyes. Juan Diego slowly backed away. "No hay bronca, Dante," Juan Diego assured. "Go Cowboys, Ese."

"Yeah, go Cowboys, Ese," Dante replied coldly.

The two retreated without meeting my eyes again.

Dante patted me on the shoulder, handing me the nunchucks. "You can keep these as a memento. Or better yet, learn to use them in case you get in trouble and I'm not around."

As Dante strolled away, I stared at the pair of black sticks bound together by a short length of silver chain. Would a paladin use these? Would Julia approve?

————

"Nunchucks?" Reeser stifled a laugh when I posed my question in the art studio. "No way, dude. A paladin wields a holy sword, high-octane magic. Nunchucks are for thieves and low-level martial arts wannabes. Paladins fight evil head on, eye to eye."

Julia nodded, her eyes remaining fixed on her canvas.

"Maybe I'll paint them," I thought out loud, setting them on a stool in front of my blank canvas and reaching for my pencil.

"That could be interesting." Reeser leaned back in the desk he occupied, his feet draped over the seat in front of him, his eyes diligently tracing Julia's figure.

"Don't you have a class to be in?" Julia asked as she flowingly manipulated her paintbrush.

"I guess so," Reeser sighed, dragging his feet toward the door.

When he left, Julia's eyes finally detached from her artwork and slid in my direction. As she smiled, I dropped my pencil.

————

Cruising in the Blaster was like consuming an intoxicating potion imbued with superpowers. The vehicle possessed the power to leave the mundane and monotonous world of Brownsville behind in a cloud of dust and exhaust fumes, a blur of palm trees and little pink houses rendered meaningless beyond the dark gray filter of those tinted windows. The stereo system enveloped you, no, swarmed you in sound, the booming pile driver shaking your very soul from slumber. Shouting over the din of grinding metal axes, Reeser expounded about amps and wattage and the late great Randy Rhoads and how Black Sabbath was going to hell in a Hollywood handbasket now that Ozzy had gone solo. Had I heard about Ozzy biting heads off bats and pissing all over the Alamo? I nodded reverentially, pretending I knew what all he was talking about while actually wondering if my bones would ever stop vibrating. The other thing about the car, besides its smooth, supple black leather seats and all the chrome, was its air conditioner. It felt like a refrigerator in the Blaster, and this made it a most welcome refuge in the scalding South Texas heat.

My head stopped nodding in awed agreement with everything Reeser said when we drove up to what appeared to be a small Middle Eastern city. Behind towering wrought iron gates and a massive stucco wall rose countless turrets and shiny golden domes.

Reeser decreased the volume as he approached.

"Is this one of those new 'gated communities'?" I asked, gaping at the spectacular sight spread out before us like a brilliant city on a hill.

Reeser chuckled, lowering his window so he could punch the code into the security keypad. "No, man. This is where Julia lives."

I squinted and blinked at the bright sunlight bouncing off the minarets and basilica-like structures gleaming beneath the perfectly blue sky. Palm trees soared on either side of the driveway as we slowly prowled through the smoothly parting automatic gates.

"Like, in a country club?"

"Like in . . . this is her house, Dude."

"Shiiiiiit," I mouthed slowly, struggling to take in the magnitude of the place.

We drove up a long drive, swung around a massive fountain shooting jets of water about twenty feet into the air, and slowed to a halt beneath a vast, vaulted porte cochère. Next to that glorified carport sat a dazzling array of vehicular firepower that threatened to eclipse Reeser's Chevy Monte Carlo. There was a white Mercedes, a silver Porsche, the requisite red Ferrari, and a boxy black Land Rover SUV that appeared to be heavily armored.

As I stepped out of Reeser's frigid car into the intense heat, the arched, carved wood doors of the mansion swung open, and Julia welcomed us with open arms. She wore a black floor-length silk robe.

"Wow!" I said as she hugged me. Through her robe I momentarily felt her soft flesh press against me, causing me to swoon. "I like your get-up."

"I'm the wizard queen!" She bounded giddily to Reeser, throwing her arms around him and kissing him on the lips. "And these are my magic-user's robes.

"C'mon." She took us both by the hand, towing us into her palace.

D&D was surprisingly fun. Helmed by Julia's melodramatic cousin Aaron, who was a student at Southmost College, and accompanied by two other senior girls who were friends of Julia's, we embarked on an epic adventure that left us yearning for more. But what followed afterward managed to be even more astonishing and entertaining. Given the day's tremendous amount of what Julia and Reeser called "hacking and slashing"—which entailed rolling handfuls of many-sided dice, slaying monsters, and listening to Aaron graphically describe the spilling of their blood and guts all over stone dungeon floors—Julia proclaimed that we needed to be cleansed. Proposing we do this by going for a swim, she flung a variety of male swim trunks at Reeser and me, and the next thing I knew, we were floating in the largest swimming pool I'd ever laid eyes on. It made Mr. Aranda's once-idyllic pool seem like a bathtub. Long and rectangular, it was flanked on both sides by gargantuan white statues resembling Greek gods and goddesses. At the far end, Corinthian columns formed a portico, beyond which a large resaca sparkled in the late afternoon sun. Off to the side sat a covered bar area, from which

Reeser ferried ice-cold Coronas for everyone. Julia—barely contained in a black string bikini—held court on a giant pink floatie shaped like a donut covered in rainbow sprinkles.

Later that night, as Reeser gave me a ride to my Grandma Fina's house on the poor side of town where the houses were old and askew and still fashioned from horizontal slats of wood that had peeled and been repainted countless times since they were first erected in the 1940s, he went out of his way to take Coffee Port Road.

"What are we doing out here?" I asked as we headed toward the outskirts of town.

"You'll see," he answered cryptically. "Coffee Port has a couple of virtues that merit taking it, even if it doesn't lead to where you want to go."

As we drove, he surprised me by ejecting the Judas Priest cassette and speaking in a tranquil, sincere voice rather than shouting over the metallic fracas as he usually did. "I owe you a big thank you, man."

"For what?" I had no idea what he was talking about, but I started hoping he hadn't drunk one too many Coronas at Julia's house. As for me, I was certain I had definitely consumed one too many. Just one would have actually been one too many, given that I'd never had one before that day.

"For winning that big art contest last year. You wouldn't know it since Porter has such a bad rap, but some years back a fancy foundation started taking an interest in artists coming out of the barrio. They have helped some of the art show winners get ahead up north, recommending them to big-time art schools and providing scholarships even. If Julia had won yet again, she'd probably be going to New York for college this summer. It was her big plan. But instead, she's staying in Texas, which means we'll be able to keep seeing each other. And for that, I'll be thanking you the rest of my life, because I want to marry that girl first chance I get."

I gazed out the window at the shadowy, sparsely populated landscape blurring by in the dark of night at an alarming speed. I hadn't meant to derail Julia's dream of going to a great art school. Suddenly, I felt overwhelmed by guilt rather than the joy Reeser exuded at her falling short of her aspirations.

"But enough of that serious shit," Reeser declared as we finally turned onto the street he had insisted on taking despite it making no sense. "Coffee Port Road has only two lanes, one in each direction. And Coffee Port Road has no street lamps or stop signs or traffic lights. And Coffee Port Road is long and usually abandoned."

As he finished his love letter to Coffee Port Road, he abruptly swerved into the middle of the street, straddling the center stripe, and slammed his pedal to the metal with a loud thud. The car engine roared. The tires squealed as the car peeled out. My head whipped back, hitting the headrest. And then he punched the light switch, extinguishing the headlights and plunging us into absolute darkness as the car rocketed through the night.

———

I screamed so loud and so long that when Reeser dropped me off—dumbfounded—at my grandmother's house, I feared my ears would never stop ringing. Could you give yourself tinnitus? That night I couldn't sleep. I churned restlessly in my bed, alternating between dreams of Julia in her colossal swimming pool and nightmares of Reeser barreling down Coffee Port in the pitch black. What if someone else harbored the same insane idea, coming from the opposite direction? Paladins and demons seemed pretty tame compared to the adventures I was being drawn into by my newfound friends.

The following day was a Sunday, so my parents and Rubén paid their ritual visit to Grandma Fina's, braving the long line at the international bridge to spend time with us. After a hearty lunch, my father and I sat out on the back porch in the rocking chairs, as was tradition. I'd come to realize that he had some sort of preternatural sense for what was going on in my life, even though I'd now been living with my grandmother for the better part of two years.

"You look like you've got 'susto,'" he said.

"Susto?"

"Yes, you have to be careful who you spend time with at school, and also outside of school for that matter. You know how the dicho goes."

"What dicho?"

"Mejor solo que mal acompañado."

I mulled his message, that it was better to be alone than in bad company. "My friends are good people, Dad!" I replied defensively.

"Of course they are. But the inexperience of youth can lead to many mistakes, some of them ones that you can't take back, that you can't do over."

I nodded respectfully. He certainly knew about making mistakes. If he was so smart, why couldn't he seem to avoid them?

"Especially, be careful with the older kids and los gringos."

"Why? I thought it wasn't good to be racist toward people of other backgrounds."

"Racist, no! Dios, no. None of that. God created us all equal. What I mean is be careful because older kids may be doing things that you shouldn't be involved in at your age, and los gringos—well—they have some different customs."

"Like what?"

"Their parents didn't grow up here usually. They get transferred down here by the automobile manufacturers to manage the maquiladoras in Matamoros. And they have no idea what goes on down here. They give their kids the same privileges they would normally grant them up in Ohio and Indiana and Michigan. They buy them fast cars. They let them come home whenever they want. They let them sleep over at other people's houses. How do they know they're not sleeping with their girlfriends or boyfriends? The parents even go on vacations and leave the kids alone at home, trusting that nothing will go wrong. Don't they know their kids can cross the border, buy beer, and throw a big party?" He shook his head in disbelief at gringo naivete. "Life on the border is different from up in the Midwest, m'ijo. Those parents don't know what they're getting into down here. And if you run with their kids, you could end up in some bad trouble."

I nodded solemnly, wondering if he had a spy tailing me at Porter, watching Reeser like a hawk.

"Also, be careful with the muchachas. Mucho cuidado. Nunca les faltes el respeto. Respect is the key. Treat them as if their bodies and minds are sacred temples. You would not defile a temple, would you? Then respect women, m'ijo. Remember, there is a time and a place for everything, including lying down with a woman. That time is adulthood and that place is the marriage bed. Any other time and place can change your life—and hers—forever, and not in a good way."

"Who is 'her'?" I asked, knowing most of my friends would be shocked by his far-ranging intrusions into my private life, but at the same time finding myself completely accustomed to his wily, wisdom-dispensing ways.

"I don't know. You tell me? Who is she?"

I shook my head, determined to end this conversation before I regretted it further. As it was, his sage advice had already singled out my friends on multiple counts. I was surprised he hadn't mentioned them by name. "I'll be fine, Dad. I'm focused on my studies and my art classes. Besides, if I did things your way, I'd have no friends left. Please, just don't worry about me."

He furrowed his brow. "I'll always worry about you, Son. And, someday, if you're blessed, you'll worry about your own children. Ya veras. Whatever you do while you're young will come back to haunt you many times over when you get to be my age. What goes around comes around. And just remember, there's a time and a place . . ."

I wondered if he'd go for a trifecta of trite clichés, but he fell silent.

We rocked quietly until my mother called him back inside for their weekly commute back to their tiny cinder-block house deep inside of Matamoros' voracious concrete belly.

"How's business?" I asked as he opened the screen door.

"Slow. I'm still trying to get the tire recapping plant up and running again. I moved it to the ranch, but there are a lot of hidden costs. And that lime business really wiped me out."

I couldn't help myself even though I regretted the words the moment they left my mouth. "I guess that wasn't the right time and place either, huh?"

He hesitated and then turned back slowly, lowering his voice. At first, his eyes glowered with his trademark flash of anger, but then, as he assessed me, they softened uncharacteristically. He put his hand on my shoulder and said calmly, "Ramón, it wasn't necessarily a matter of time and place. See, the problem is the older you get, the more variables life throws at you."

———

Julia and I stood at our canvases, working late after class as the year-end art show approached. Hers was an elaborate drybrush painting of a beautiful Rio Grande Valley ranch scene. A Mexican American rancher and his wife fed chickens highly detailed corn kernels in a dusty corral fenced by rough wooden posts and barbed wire. Palm trees stood silhouetted against a glorious sunset rimming billowy clouds with purple, crimson, and gold. Verdant rows of crops arced toward the horizon. Mexican American Gothic. It was quite lovely really, a dazzling display of skill. I didn't even know how to paint in drybrush yet. But somehow, it felt "safe," a concept I had learned to avoid when it came to my art.

When I looked back at my painting for the contest, I saw a hyperrealistic portrait based on my indelible mental photograph of Juan Diego and Chuck Norris the day they had nearly beaten me to a pulp in the parking lot. It was rendered in various shades of blue for the jeans, the cornflower sky, the Virgen de Guadalupe tattoo; white for the wife-beater T-shirts and marshmallow clouds hovering overhead; gray for the concrete sidewalk and unyielding walls of the corner in which they had ended up trapped by Dante. The color scheme was punctuated by the vibrant red of Juan Diego's bandanna dangling from his pocket and the gleaming black and silver of Chuck Norris' nunchucks, hanging in surrender from his still-curled fist. The splashes of red and black were disruptive and dangerous. They foreshadowed bloodshed and pain. The true coup, however, was not the technical feat of achieving a nearly photorealistic effect but rather the look in their eyes. Everything about the image conveyed that these were two tough guys from the barrio, but in their eyes, one could glimpse their fear betraying them. Dante's tiny looming shadow lurked menacingly in their pupils' quivering miniature reflections.

My art teacher, Señora Martinez, had become enamored with the painting, staring at it for a very long period of time until she issued her final verdict, tears welling in her eyes as she spoke. "It breaks my heart, but it's stunning. You've painted a macho stereotype with a multitude of perfectly placed strokes and then you've flipped it on its head with just a couple dabs of your most delicate brush. There, in their eyes, you have planted the seeds of fear. And that makes them vulnerable. That helps any viewer—regardless of race or ethnicity or gender—connect with them because, m'ijo, if there's anything that binds us in common as humans, it is fear. We are all afraid of the day we will lose, the day we will hurt, the day we will inevitably face the ultimate challenge none of us can overcome. If we could see the fear in the eyes of those that would threaten us, what might we do? Might we rise up and fight back? Or might we give them a hug?"

Thrilled at her reaction, I ran my paint-splattered hands through my hair, smearing blue and white through it until I resembled a comic book character.

Julia, who'd been listening studiously while continuing her own finishing touches, had cheerily chimed in, "You're going to win again, Ramón!"

Now, as we toiled together in the studio, always the first to arrive and the last to leave, I couldn't help but be revisited by that wave of guilt that had swamped me when Reeser informed me about the consequences of Julia's loss the previous year.

"Reeser told me you've decided on an art college in Dallas?" I asked her as we both kept our eyes on our respective paintings.

"Yes," I could hear the disappointment in her voice. "But I'm on the waiting list for one in New York City. So who knows . . ."

I glanced at her painting and then back at mine. If she won the school contest, her work would be entered into the statewide event and she'd likely receive a slew of accolades. With that foundation Reeser had talked about watching the art show, it might be enough to nudge her from waiting list to admission. I'd been learning about the competitive processes and honors that drove the world of fine art education from Señora Martinez and Mr. Dean, both of whom expressed high hopes for my continued development. But I had time on my side, two more years. For Julia, time was running out.

———

When it came time to show our artwork at the contest, I hovered nervously by my easel, torn between my instinctive desire to win and the confounding urge to help Julia. Anxiously, I observed the gaggle of judges as they proceeded slowly up and down the aisles, scrutinizing the vast array of subpar artwork with feigned interest. A couple of their name tags bore the logo of an art foundation with a famous rich-person's last name: Guggenheim. I recognized it from one of the museums Mrs. Martinez often referred to when showing us famous paintings. The judges spent an inordinate amount of time poring over Julia's canvas, smiling and nodding their heads as they took notes. I watched their lips move from afar as they congratulated her.

As they turned the corner and headed down my row of students, a tight knot grew in my throat. Gazing across the sea of contestants, I stared longingly at Julia, realizing I didn't just yearn for her; I pined for her selflessly, like a devoted paladin would desire a sublime princess.

Stealthily, I switched my portrait of Juan Diego and Chuck Norris for a still life study of the latter's nunchucks. It was something I'd done in preparation for the larger piece, and its unfinished nature was evident. Having arrived at my easel with high expectations, the judges scowled at the work and peered at me quizzically. They were so disappointed that they didn't even place me among the finalists, which was a good thing because then nobody would have to see what I had ended up submitting. After the judges were gone, I put my portrait of Juan Diego and Chuck Norris back on the easel and watched Julia win the grand prize. I watched with pride as Julia strutted across the stage to gather her awards.

Her picture of the rancher and wife amid an archetypical Valley land-scape was lauded as an homage to our homeland and heritage.

———

When Julia was admitted to the art school in New York, her joy could not be contained. Massive festivities ensued at her palatial compound, some of them ending up with the Greek statues by the pool donning the partygoers' bathing suits.

Reeser, however, was devastated. He knew her good fortune spelled the end of their four-year romance. His middling grades had landed him at some third-tier state school in a rural part of north Texas. From there, it would have been easy to ride the Blaster to Big D and continue dating Julia until he could afford to put a mall-store diamond ring on her finger. But now his fate was sealed. On the outside, he forcibly main-tained a feeble smile and a supportive spirit, but inside he was seething, which led to the tragic conclusion of our D&D campaign. The last time we played, his fighter took out all of Reeser's frustrations on everybody in the group, picking a fight with each of us and slaying us one by one until he faced Julia's magic-user. She, however, turned out to be too powerful for him to defeat. And when he found himself at death's door, he defiantly declared: "I impale myself upon my magical broadsword."

Stunned, the group somberly dispersed. My dead paladin's ego bat-tered and bruised, I bummed a ride from Aaron the Dungeon Master in order to avoid refrigerating with Reeser in the Blaster.

A couple of nights later, though, Julia called and invited me to one of the end-of-year senior bashes, which were legendary for their excesses. Incapable of ever refusing her, I assented to her and Reeser picking me up, but only if she was already in the car.

Laughing, she asked, "You're not still pissed about the D&D game, are you?"

"No," I lied. "It's just a game."

"You're so cute." I could envision her smile, her lush lips hovering near the phone.

When they picked me up, it was dark already. The car smelled like an intoxicating blend of her high-end perfume, his cheap cologne, and marijuana. Reeser drove us to the northwestern edge of town, to an unfinished subdivision that had been abandoned when the developer ran out of cash. We meandered through what seemed like an endless number of barren cul-de-sacs. There were no streetlights, no houses, nothing but overgrown grass and weeds illuminated by the Blaster's headlights.

Finally, in one of the cul-de-sacs, we encountered a cluster of cars assembled around a fire raging in a large oil drum. In the flickering light, I could make out a significant cross section of the senior class which was soon to disintegrate, a few fortunate graduates absconding to college, the rest laboring in local supermarkets and flipping burgers at food chains.

Hovering near Julia, I did my best to steer clear of the rowdy guys gathered around the beer keg. Once in a while throughout the night, Reeser brought us a beer and offered us a toke, but we passed on both, instead nursing a warm Bartles & James wine cooler between the two of us.

At the end of the night, when everyone began to leave, Julia and I found Reeser passed out in the backseat of the Blaster. Failing to rouse him, Julia slid into the driver's seat and gestured for me to climb into the other side. She fired up the car so we could cool off in its prodigious air conditioner. As she leaned back, I watched her hair flow in the artificial breeze. Sensing my admiring gaze, she turned to me, her lips curving upward into a smile.

"Thanks for keeping me company tonight. Reeser's no fun these days. He's always wasted and depressed."

I nodded, still nervous in her crosshairs after all these months of hanging out together. I could feel my heart pounding in my chest as she leaned toward me across the console. Her left hand reached out and pulled the back of my neck gently toward her, our lips touching and then locking as one. We kissed for a long while, and before I knew what was happening, she had somehow maneuvered her lithe body onto my lap, straddling me, her black skirt riding up to her hips, her hair tumbling over my shoulders, my hands instinctively exploring her soft curves.

"I'm not wearing any underwear," she whispered, her breath hot and moist on my ear.

I wanted to ask her why, but found myself unable to speak, my tongue entangled with hers.

"I want to be your first," she said, her hand reaching for my zipper.

I could have died right then and there when I heard my father's voice ringing in my mind, droning on about respect and sacred temples and times and places. Then, his voice was joined by my dead paladin's imaginary one, proclaiming platitudes about honor and friendship and chivalric code. I wanted her more than anything I had ever wanted before, yet this holier-than-thou choir urged me to halt the proceedings, insisted on reminding me that Reeser was asleep in the back seat and that this was all terribly wrong.

"I can't." My hand parried hers.

"What? Why?"

"I don't know."

"You don't like me?"

"I love you," I confessed, startled as I heard the words slip from my mouth.

She released her tense grip on my hand, relaxing her shoulders and leaning back against the dash. After a long pause, she sighed, "You've been so sweet to me this year."

I just stared back at her, her hair all a mess, her mascara and lipstick smeared, her black blouse open, her bra rendered nearly pointless.

"If you want, we can take it slow. I'm here all summer. I don't go to New York until August," she added soothingly.

Overwhelmed by a swirl of feelings for her, ethical concerns, and downright fear of the unknown, I felt like weeping, tears welling in my eyes.

She leaned forward and wrapped her arms around me, holding me tight, our bodies oscillating gently.

Suddenly, a rustling in the back seat startled us. She wiggled into the driver's seat, pulling down her skirt and buttoning her blouse with blazing speed. I turned around to block Reeser's line of sight.

Sitting up groggily, he eyed me suspiciously. "How long was I out?"

"A while," I croaked, my voice brittle and cracking.

He reached over me and yanked clumsily at the handle, opening the passenger door, impatiently motioning for me to let him out. We both stepped onto the crunchy gravel of the abandoned cul-de-sac. Closing the door behind us, he edged up close to me. I could smell the sour stench of alcohol on his breath, the sweet scent of weed wafting from his Iron Maiden T-shirt and his rumpled dirty blond hair. His blood-shot blue eyes glared angrily into mine.

"I thought you were my friend," he snarled. "Find your own way home."

Brushing past me, he walked through a cloud of dragonflies and moths dancing chaotically in the headlight beams and got into the driv-er's seat as Julia shifted into the seat we had both occupied in a lustful frenzy moments earlier.

I banged my fist on the passenger window, shouting, "Julia, don't go. Don't let him drive."

But it was too late. He had shifted gears and the squealing tires were burning rubber, spitting gravel. She gazed mournfully at me through the smoky glass, her expression one of melancholy mingled with ap-prehension as the engine roared, the chassis fishtailed, and they sped ferociously away.

I ran desperately, chasing the receding taillights, futilely hoping to catch them, obstinately yearning to stop Reeser from doing what I knew in my churning gut he would do next. The cul-de-sacs in the unfinished neighborhood all flowed into one main street, and that one street led to Coffee Port Road.

———

Out on those desolate, windswept, pitch-black fields, sound traveled un-fettered and far. As I struggled to stay on the paved streets with only the starlight bleakly bathing the concrete in a dim blue glow, I was shaken to my core by what I could only describe as a sonic boom rippling across the long reeds of grass.

"No!" I shouted, terrified as I ran as fast as I could down the long subdivision avenue toward Coffee Port. Twice, I stumbled over the curb and fell into the grass. Twice, I rose, spitting dirt out of my mouth, pulling stickers off my bloodied arms as I continued my mad scramble. It must have taken about two miles to get out of the ghostly neighborhood that never was. On foot, moving as quickly as I could in the dark, it took about twenty minutes to find my way out of there. By the time I reached Coffee Port Road, I could see flashing multicolored lights about a mile away. Reeser had boasted that the '83 Chevy Montecarlo SS could zoom from 0 to 60 in 8.1 seconds, and that was without all the aftermarket customization that he'd put into the Blaster. By the time he'd thundered a mile down Coffee Port Road, he could have easily been doing 80 to 100 miles per hour.

As the math ran through my mind, I stopped running toward the crash. My blood-streaked arms dropped to my sides as I proceeded slowly, dreadfully, heavy with the burden of the knowledge that there could be no survivors. It seemed to happen every year around graduation. Usually on the two-lane highway between South Padre Island and Brownsville, kids coming back from parties on the beach, sometimes drunk, sometimes drag racing. Graduation gowns traded for funeral clothes, commencement ceremonies exchanged for wakes and rosaries and funerals. Futures buried in freshly turned soil.

First, I felt the tiny fragments of glass crushed beneath my shoes. Then, I smelled the gasoline fumes, spied pieces of rubber and metal flung far from the site of impact. A flash of blue light illuminated one of the Blaster's chrome hubcaps tossed into the weeds like litter by the side of the road. Up ahead, a cluster of black silhouettes circled two mangled and twisted hunks of steel melded into one steaming and bloodied maelstrom. Ambulances and police cruisers sat idly by as an enormous machine with mechanical jaws attempted to pry crumpled sheets of metal off the fused and distorted mass. Cringing, I expected to hear screams of agony, but the only sounds were the crunching and screeching of metal and the hissing and pumping of the hydraulically powered jaws of life. The paramedics stood along the side of the road respectfully. It was clear that there would be nothing left for them to do.

Before a sheriff's deputy noticed me and pulled me aside, I caught a glimpse of Julia's lustrous mane. It glittered—crowned by windshield glass—in the flashing blue and red lights. Her head lay slumped on what I assumed were the remnants of the dashboard. I couldn't see her face. She rested motionless. Tears streaming down my cheeks, I blurted to the officer that they were my friends. He nodded somberly and told me in a hushed tone that they were gone, that there was nothing anybody could do.

———

That night, like many nights that ended in loss or sorrow, confusion or despair, my father salvaged me from the scene in his rusty red pickup. He had to drive from Matamoros, but I couldn't picture the cops calling Grandma Fina and her having to wake up and drive to the middle of nowhere after midnight.

I thought he'd yell at me for being out so late or excoriate me for going against his advice and nearly getting myself killed. But he didn't say a word. As the police waved us past the accident, where they would surely struggle for hours to retrieve the bodies from both vehicles, I couldn't bear to look again. Instead, I followed my father's eyes. On the glossy surface of his black pupils, the police lights were mirrored as we glided by, and beyond that something else lurked, like a shadow, a flicker of weakness cowering in the depths of his soul. I'd never know for sure what he was thinking, but—if I had to guess—I'd say he was terrified that it could have been me in one of those cars; he was grateful that it hadn't been; and he was grief-stricken for the lives lost and the families now bereft of their children.

That night he took me home to Matamoros, to the tiny cinder-block hovel where they lived, and I slept wrapped in blankets on the cement floor in my parents' bedroom.

"¿Que pasó?" I heard my mom whisper when they thought I was asleep.

"Two of his friends died," he replied.

"Dios mio." The sheets rustled as she made the sign of the cross.

"Solo por la gracia de Dios . . ." he murmured. He left his thought unfinished, but it was clear he believed that only by the grace of God was I still alive.

———

I attended both funerals, extending my condolences to the parents and siblings. Reeser's parents appeared completely baffled as a small, sparsely attended ceremony unfolded silently around them at an impersonal funeral home. There would be no burial because Reeser would be laid to rest up north in their family plot. My dad had been correct in assuming that his parents had been shipped down to the Valley to manage a maquiladora, only to now find themselves shipping their son's body back to be buried among kin in Ohio.

The border specializes in cruel trade, I realized, wondering how quickly Reeser's parents would pick up their things and follow their son back where they came from. Hopefully, they would do so before their two younger children reached driving age.

Julia's funeral was sharply contrasting. So many people attended the rosary that my parents and I were forced to sit in an overflow room. The next day at the funeral, throngs clad in black swarmed the Buena Vista cemetery. We had to park on a side road and traverse the entirety of the graveyard to reach her family's ornate mausoleum, which looked like it had been designed by the same audacious architect to blame for their grandiose house. There was much crying and hand wringing. Her mother wailed inconsolably. In the sweltering heat, we stood in line to pay our respects and give our pésame to her parents. Mariachis played mournful songs as her shiny black coffin laden with red roses was lowered into the ground. Afterward, as we walked away with our heads hung low, a man in a distinctive pin-striped suit intercepted us. He wore sunglasses and his hair was slicked back.

"Excuse me, Señor López?" he asked my father.

"¿Sí?"

"Julia's father wishes to speak with your son before you leave."

My father nodded gravely, motioning for my mother and I to join him in following the man back to the family's tent. Weaving our way through the crowd, we eventually reached the shaded Astroturf where Julia's father stood surrounded by what looked more like bodyguards than mourners.

Spotting us, the tall, broad-shouldered man cut off his conversation and waved us over. Standing in front of him, in his custom-tailored black suit and shiny shoes, I felt that we must look like a ragtag band of hobos, our clothes outdated and ill-fitting, our shoes scuffed, our eyes unshielded by designer sunglasses like the ones he and his entourage wore. Yet I also knew none of that mattered at a moment like this. Because despite all this man's wealth and power, Julia was in the ground. And we were alive, whether we deserved it—or carried it off with dignity—or not. It wasn't fair. And it wasn't right. But—like most things on the border—this was how it was.

"López," he acknowledged my dad, nodding.

"Señor Guerrero," my father answered, shaking his head sadly. "Una vez más, sentimos mucho su pérdida."

My mom nodded, staring glumly at the artificial grass.

"This is your son?" He looked down at me.

"Sí. This is Ramón."

"Ramón." Mr. Guerrero removed his sunglasses, revealing light gray eyes that sparkled against his dark skin. "You were a good friend to m'ija. She spoke a great deal about you."

I struggled to keep my voice steady as I thought of her talking about me to her father. What had she said? How had she really felt about me?

"You're a bit younger than her . . . than she was . . ." he continued, also battling his emotions to produce the right words.

"Yes, sir. Two years younger. I'll be a junior next year."

"Si Dios quiere," my mom murmured, nodding in deference to the Almighty and His unpredictable and inscrutable will upon which all of our fates invariably turned.

"Sí," Mr. Guerrero supported her statement. "Well, Ramón, Julia told me that you lost the art contest on purpose this year so that she could win it and get into that art school in New York."

I stared back at him in disbelief. I'd had no idea that Julia had figured out my scheme. "I . . . She . . . Sir, Julia was a great artist. And she was an even greater friend."

"Well, m'ijo, you made her very happy. That day she came home with the awards, she lit up the house with her smile. And then when they let her into that school in New York after all that waiting, she was over la luna! I'd never seen her more excited, more full of life. She was eager to meet her future. That's how I will remember her. So I wanted to say gracias to you for being such a friend."

"I wish I could have done more."

"We all do, m'ijo," he replied. "And if you ever need something, no matter how big or how small, you come see me. ¿Me entiendes?"

I nodded.

"Pues, ándale, que nos quemamos en este infierno," he concluded, gesturing for his bodyguards to escort him toward the waiting black limo.

On the drive over to Grandma Fina's house, my mother asked, "So is that the Señor Guerrero that is well known for his 'business'?"

"Yes," my dad replied, morosely viewing the road ahead.

I knew they were referring to the drug trade, but it would be disrespectful to cast aspersions at a time like this.

My mom pursed her lips, staring out the window at the passing palm trees.

"How did he know you, Dad?"

"We grew up together, ran in the same circles as kids, like you and his daughter I suppose."

Somehow, I pictured that whatever those two men had done together as teenagers was far from what Julia and I had shared while painting in the art studio or playing D&D or stealing glances here and there.

"¿Le vas a decir algo? ¿Al niño?" My mom asked, still looking out the window. What did she want him to tell me that I didn't already know?

He sighed, obligation weighing down his words. "I know Julia's father told you that if you ever need anything, you can call him, but with people like this, you must keep your distance."

"But he's Julia's dad," I protested.

"You never want to be indebted to someone in his . . . profession. If approached, be respectful, but go your own way. Let's just leave it at that. Trust me. I know what I'm talking about."

I frowned as we approached Grandma Fina's house. If he knew so much, why wasn't he as rich and successful as Julia's dad? Was he just jealous or did he really want to protect me? It was pointless to continue the conversation. There simply was no arguing or debating anything with him.

As they dropped me off at my grandmother's house, he addressed me through the truck window. "I'm very sorry about your friend. She was a beautiful young woman."

"Yes, she was."

He gazed at me wistfully. "Keep yourself alive, son. With a little luck, someday you'll meet someone like her again."

I fought back the tears as they drove away.

———

Graduation was a somber affair that year. In memory of Julia and Reeser, the school band didn't even play Pomp & Circumstance. The seniors all filed in silently, the rustling of their robes filling the tense auditorium. The valedictorian spoke sorrowfully about Julia's squandered promise and Reeser's unforgettable style. Afterward, as a long and vacuous summer stretched out before me, I gathered my meager savings and rode my bike to Curiel's flower shop. I recalled the scent of Julia's signature perfume, one she told me exuded the fragrance of her favorite flowers. I asked Old Man Curiel to fashion a small garland of gardenias, with a metal stand to hold it up. Then I pedaled out beneath the blistering sun to lay the white wreath at the spot where she perished, where her racing heart marked its last beat.

Laying my bike on the ground, I closed my eyes and inhaled the invigorating aroma of the pristine blooms before propping the garland up amid a clump of dry grass and withered weeds. On the scorching pavement, through ripples of rising heat, I could still make out shards of glass, chunks of rubber and slivers of shiny metal scattered like ashes, the remains of that night where our paths diverged on Coffee Port Road.

DEL RÍO

When Abuela Carmela died, it was like she took part of my mother with her. Sure, my mom still carried Rubén up in arms as if he were a newborn despite the fact he was nearing nine years old, but while she managed to keep her spine straight, her eyes now seemed vacant, the bones and skin around them hollowed out.

"I'm an orphan," she murmured to me, staring absently into her mother's coffin in the Matamoros funeral home.

I gawked at Abuelita Carmela, her alabaster skin, her pink lips, her perfectly coiffed auburn curls. She looked like a doll, like a fictionalized replica of the woman I'd known in life, the one always on her knees in her garden, pulling weeds, pruning rosebushes, harvesting peaches and pomegranates and guayabas and avocados. I would miss her, even though I had never spent as much time with her as I had with Grandma Fina. In some ways it was less like losing a relative and more like the Earth itself dying. It also made me worry, for the first time, about Grandma Fina's longevity. How could I even consider life without her? She provided the roof over my head, my foothold in this country I so believed in. She was my constant unsung heroine.

I'd never thought about orphans as adults, but then I realized that if nature took its course, we all were destined to become orphans at some point or another. Regardless of age, it seemed like a milestone for which nobody could be prepared. Parents seemed like an impenetrable, lifelong line of defense between oneself and death. And, once that mighty, previously invulnerable generational shield was gone, what—if anything—stood between one's self and one's obliteration?

With Abuela Carmela gone, my mother and Rubén began to commute on a more regular basis from their cement prison in Matamoros to Grandma Fina's house in Brownsville. One day after school, I found them in Grandma Fina's neglected backyard, staring at the old fire pit.

As if to spite both my father and me, a lime tree had sprouted from the ashes of the award-winning painting I'd torched there. A waxy emerald shrub now filled the crumbling brick grill. Its roots twisted through the cracks in the decrepit structure, wrapping themselves around the base and burrowing into the ground.

My grandmother's gaze shifted from the vibrant plant to my mother's ashen face.

Rubén crawled over the unkempt grass, oblivious to the ant piles that surrounded him.

My mother stared blankly through the tree's leafy branches.

Removing her glasses, Grandma Fina asked, "Marisol, didn't your mother love gardening?"

My mother nodded slowly, Grandma Fina's words taking a long time to reach her.

"We should fix up this garden in honor of Carmela," my grandmother declared. "That way, when you're here, you can remember her with joy. Would you help me, Marisol?"

My mom nodded again, wiping a tear from a corner of her eye and absent-mindedly scooping Rubén up just as he was about to plow into an anthill towering in his path.

Day after day, I came home to find them devotedly digging and planting and watering.

Grandma Fina appeared obsessed with perfecting the garden at the same vigorous pace with which the lime tree was flourishing.

"Lime trees usually take three to four years to bear fruit, but this one is going to do so much sooner. I must have the garden ready by then," she huffed as she gardened in her flowery housecoat, pink curlers dotting her gray hair, oversized sunglasses sliding down her aquiline nose.

Nobody asked why she felt compelled to meet this deadline, but her energy was contagious.

I'd never seen my mom on her knees in the soil, but there she was like a schoolgirl making mud pies.

"What was Carmela's favorite flower?" Grandma Fina asked.

"Tulipanes," my mom answered.

"Then we will plant those along the fence," Grandma Fina said, placing her hands on her hips as she surveyed her modest parcel of land.

The next day, my mother was the first to get her hands dirty, kneeling next to my grandmother as they planted a row of hibiscus along the back fence line. Grandma Fina glanced frequently over her shoulder at the lime tree. It was rising rapidly from the fire pit, which had now disappeared beneath a canopy of low-hanging branches thick with dark green foliage. She seemed paranoid, like the tree was trying to beat her in some sort of race. Toward what, I had no idea, but sitting idly as they toiled ushered a wave of guilt over me. Slipping on a pair of canvas gloves Grandma Fina had purchased, I began tilling the ground to install the new grass.

A few weeks into the project, Cousin David rolled out the sod. Even Rubén wanted in on the action, sitting at the edge of the brick patio with a small red pail and yellow spade meant for building sandcastles at the beach. He dug awkwardly along the perimeter, slowly filling his bucket with dirt.

"Good job, Rubén," our dad said during one of his Sunday visits, spreading fertilizer over the grass and then using a shovel to quickly transform Rubén's feeble effort into a bona fide planting trench. "We'll plant rosales around the patio in the holes you're digging. This way your grandma and mom can always have roses." With his mighty girth and trunk-like arms, my father made the labor look easy. By the end of that day, an entire hedge of rosebushes flanked the patio.

At first, I feared this was a final admission of defeat from my father, a vocalized realization that we would never cease depending on Grandma Fina's home. The place seemed to possess some unfathomable gravity destined to draw back her progeny. But as the garden took shape, and we began to enjoy the cooling evening breeze that whispered through its shimmering leaves, I found myself lulled into a surreal state of comfort. The Gulf winds now carried the scent of jasmine from vines that laced through the chain-link fence hanging heavy with white star blossoms. The lime tree towered, casting a soothing shade over the patio, where my father arranged a string of wrought iron rocking chairs.

When our work was finished, the whole family sat on the patio. We rocked quietly as the sun set, sleepy smiles gracing our faces. The cicadas hummed. The palm trees became black cutouts against the deep blue sky.

"Even the bees are happy," Rubén noted as a straggler bumbled casually past him on his way back to the hive. He had finally begun speaking, often surprising us with his insights.

Despite the disruption, I felt oddly unperturbed by Rubén's presence as he settled back in one of the rockers, closed his eyes, and let the breeze caress his curls. Watching the bee vanish into the leafy shadows, I realized my brother was correct. As we'd brought the garden back to life, the bees had been drawn to it, yet they had not bothered us one bit. They seemed as content as we did.

"My mamá is with us," my mom sighed. After a long pause, she added, "We finished just in time. Tomorrow would have been her eightieth birthday."

At last, I understood why Grandma Fina had been in such a hurry.

The two women smiled with satisfaction.

"What will we do now?" my mom wondered aloud, a flicker of life creeping back into her voice.

I could tell from the moonlit glint in Grandma Fina's eyes, she had an answer in store, but she pursed her lips demurely, allowing us to relish the rare moment of peace.

———

The next day, the baking began.

Converting the kitchen into their war room, my mother and Grandma Fina commiserated about the inconsistency of men, reminisced about their departed parents, and—well—they baked. They not only baked; they also cooked, made sandwiches, and whatever else people might need for family parties, receptions, reunions, funerals, and other assorted festivities. And after they were finished on Fridays, my mother insisted on taking me back to their house in Matamoros for the weekend. Ever since Julia and Reeser's catastrophic accident, my parents believed I would be safer with them than at parties with my classmates.

The López women's catering endeavor may have been sparked by my father's failed lime venture, but it blossomed into so much more. It wasn't long before my cousin David and I had been recruited to make deliveries on our bikes.

The López men observed this bustling commerce with skeptical eyes, usually from beneath the shade of the avocado tree in the front yard. They watched like envious, sidelined buzzards as customers came and went, picking up orders at the kitchen's screen door. They gathered like a dark cloud, brooding, resenting the obvious success of their mother and sister-in-law and wife. Why were customers not knocking down their doors? Why weren't their phones ringing off the hook? They blamed it on the economy and on the fact that everybody still had to eat, whereas recapped tires or used cars could wait for better days.

The unprecedented success of the López women's catering venture spurred my father to toil harder and longer than ever, if that was humanly possible. He had finally succeeded in getting his tire recapping plant up and running in México. Trade was booming. Tractor-trailer trucks lined the roads leading to the bridges that spanned the Rio Grande. And he was determined to provide the tires that would propel those eighteen-wheelers across the border and the nations. Uncle Nick joined him as a sales agent, and soon the shade beneath the avocado tree found itself lacking in human inhabitants.

Everyone, it seemed, was busy. And, at the same time, I could not imagine that anyone could feel—or be—busier than me.

While at home, I ran deliveries for the catering service. On weekends, I helped my dad at the tire plant in Matamoros. And at school, I had begun my junior year. During the first week of classes, Señora Martinez and Mr. Dean sat me down in the art studio for what they called a "come to Jesus" conversation. I had never heard the phrase before and feared they were going to attempt to convert me to some form of Protestantism, which was my mother's greatest fear. But quite to the contrary, their focus was not religious but academic.

"After what happened to poor Julia," Señora Martinez said, "it occurred to me to nominate you for this special program, Ramón."

Mr. Dean nodded in agreement.

"What special program?" The only special program I had ever heard of was special ed, and that was reserved for students like my brother, Rubén, not for me.

"It's an amazing opportunity," Mr. Dean explained.

"I had spoken to Julia about it when she became a junior, but her parents wouldn't hear about it," Señora Martinez lamented. "If she'd applied and gotten in, maybe she'd still be . . ."

I stared mournfully at her as she bit her lip and looked away.

"Basically, it's a program for art students who qualify to finish their senior year of high school in New York City, Ramón," Mr. Dean continued.

"My parents couldn't afford that," I immediately interjected. "They can barely keep the lights turned on at their house in Matamoros."

"There's a scholarship," Mr. Dean said. "It's paid for by a prestigious foundation in New York. The idea is to give artists from diverse cultures the opportunity to learn from the best, to have a chance to make something of themselves with their artistic talent."

"Yes," Señora Martinez added. "And—if all goes well while you're there, you can then get into one of the top art colleges in the city."

"Like Julia?"

"Yes, like Julia," Señora Martinez nodded ruefully. "A place like the Pratt Institute or the Cooper Union could change your whole life, Ramón."

I stared at them both as if they were ambassadors from a different species. Why did they care? Why were they trying so hard?

"My dad wants me to study business," I told them.

"Do you want to study business?" Mr. Dean asked.

I thought about it for a while, turning and scanning the easels scattered about the room, the art lining the walls, the ceramics and pottery perched on the shelves. What did I want?

"When I was a little kid, I thought that was what I wanted to be, an entrepreneur. But as time has passed, I'm not so sure. I've seen a lot of businessmen, including my own dad, struggle, fail, and worse, even die doing their jobs."

"You're a natural-born artist," Señora Martinez said. I wasn't sure if she was trying to convince herself or me.

I knew she was undeniably biased, so my eyes naturally sought out Mr. Dean's for his opinion. "What do you think, Mr. Dean?"

"Remember that test I had you take at the counseling office one day?" he asked.

"Yes." There had been a long series of inkblots and questions that made no sense to me, and then I'd forgotten all about it.

"Your responses in that test indicated that you will always be torn between two sides of your personality: your creative side and your pragmatic side."

"What does that mean?"

"It means," he said, "that it is quite likely you will need to search for a balance in your life that enables you to harness the energies of both sides in order to succeed and feel fulfilled."

"Fulfilled?" He was touching on a subject I'd never even considered, much less heard about from my parents. Success, on the other hand, had always seemed like a clear concept to me, a very American idea. Money, cars, clothes, Rolex watches, fancy houses, and foreign travel had all long stood as symbols to me of what success looked like. "What's the difference between success and fulfillment?"

Mr. Dean smiled warmly. "We might have to make a series of appointments to explore that question, but it's a good one."

Señora Martinez, however, couldn't hold herself back. "In America, people tend to think of success as financial, something sort of outside of yourself, embodied by the things you own or the attention and respect you receive publicly. Whereas, fulfillment is something more personal and internal. If you spend your time and your life doing things that make you feel good inside, make you feel happy or better about yourself and your life when you do them, then you feel fulfilled. One feeds your wallet and your ego while the other nourishes your soul."

Watching my face contort as I struggled to grasp the difference, Mr. Dean chuckled. "Let's make those appointments to discuss it further. In the meantime, discuss this application for the arts program with your parents."

Señora Martinez handed me a heavy, colorful folder stuffed with brochures and forms. "Remember, it's your future. Not anybody else's."

———

"New York?!" The way my father exclaimed the words made it so I couldn't discern if they represented a question, an indignant proclamation, or all of the above.

My mother looked anxiously at him as we sat in Grandma Fina's kitchen. The pocket folder Señora Martinez had given me a few weeks earlier had spewed its contents across the table, my parents gawking at the overwhelming array of information and photos of happy young artists living large in the big city as if it were one of my brother Rubén's disastrous dinner messes in desperate need of cleaning up.

"I didn't even know you wanted to be an artist!" my father continued, rubbing his temples as if my aspirations had caused him a massive migraine.

"I thought you were interested in business, Ramón," my mother added, trying to steer the conversation in a constructive direction.

I shrugged. "The teachers say it's a great opportunity."

My father shook his head. "Those meddling gringos will take our son away from us if we let them. They don't care about family the same way we do. You don't belong in New York for your senior year or college. You belong close to your flesh and blood. What can we do for you up there, so far away? What if you needed something? No, no. You have to beware of those gringo ways."

He pushed his chair back, and it was like he'd mentally scooped all the program materials back into their two-dimensional Pandora's box and emphatically closed it shut.

I yearned to tell him it wasn't a gringo who had brought the program to my attention. The source had been Señora Martinez, someone who knew what it was like to have talent, yet toil in the shadows because of a mediocre education and lack of opportunities beyond the border. But it was clear my father would have nothing further to do with this conversation at that particular moment.

As he exited through the screen door onto the front porch, my mother looked back at me quietly. I stared despondently at the forms, surveyed the smiling faces of the students pictured in the glossy brochures.

My mother knew a thing or two about dreams deferred. I doubted that she had ever imagined her life would turn out as it had. She had been a smart student, placing at the top of her high school class, but she had not been allowed to go to college simply because that notion was not conceivable to her parents. She was meant to take care of them when they grew old, to be a stolid wife and devoted mother. What good could be achieved by filling her mind with knowledge and ideas that she could never act upon?

She leafed through the papers gingerly, as if they might crumble in her fingers if she pressed too hard. My father stood outside the screen door, but within earshot. So she kept mum, discretely sliding a particular paper toward me, her pointer finger lingering over a block of bold red print in its corner.

Focusing in, I read the deadline for the application. It was still a couple of months away. She was telling me—without speaking—that there was still time. Glancing at my father, who had his back to us as he stared out over the front lawn, she tapped her chest with the same finger and gestured with her hand that she would talk to him.

I was surprised and impressed by her willingness to champion my cause. She still came across as meek and submissive in group settings, but perhaps the growing success of her catering business was fueling a newfound—if quiet—confidence deep within herself.

―――

The Del Río brothers made other bullies, like Juan Diego and Chuck Norris, look like amateur circus clowns. There were three of them: El Gordo, El Flaco, and El Güero. Their names were apt descriptions of their physical appearance. El Gordo was a behemoth, more muscle than fat really, but the point was that he was heavy and large, like a human wall with a thickly bearded double chin. El Flaco was tall and thin, his face narrow, his chin pointy, his hair long and stringy. And El Güero was somewhere in between the other two in terms of size, but what stood about him were his blue eyes, light skin, and blond hair. How they could all be seniors while not being triplets was somewhat of a mystery, as was the question whether they could truly be 100 percent brothers at the genetic level given their disparate looks. It was rumored that El Gordo had been held back at least two or three times along the way, and El Flaco had been flunked at least once, which could explain how they might all end up in the same grade. But what they lacked in book smarts, they certainly overcompensated for in the street savvy department, where their claim to fame was running the primary drug operation not just at Porter but also at several other public and private schools.

"Organized crime," Dante told me over lunch in the cafeteria one day as our eyes followed the Del Río brothers' march to their reserved table against the far wall, from where they could sit and watch all of the entrances and exits. He spoke the term as if he were privy to some proprietary knowledge. "That's what the Del Río brothers are. I hear they sit around watching Scarface over and over. They want to be just like Tony Montana."

"Tony Montana ends up dead," I retorted.

"Just stay away from them," Dante chewed on his Americanized school enchilada, yellow cheese oozing from the corner of his mouth. "If they came after you, even I couldn't protect you."

I looked at Dante's bulging biceps and then glanced at the Del Río brothers. There were three of them, which would definitely make it tough on Dante, but they weren't massively fit athletes like him. "You look like you could take them."

"These guys don't mess around with nunchucks and switchblades."

Word around school was that they actually kept guns concealed in their black monster truck.

Dante lowered his voice to a whisper, "Rumor is they have slaves."

"What? How?"

"I don't know. It's best not to talk about it. Don't even look at them. Don't even think about them," Dante said as he finished wiping his plate clean. "Just stay out of their way."

I really wished I could have done that. In fact, I literally did stay out of their way, but soon enough they found their way to me.

———

Those weekends in Matamoros were not exactly my idea of relaxation. On Saturdays, my dad would drag me with him to the tire recapping plant, where I helped Pedro load worn tire casings into the giant steel molds where they would be given a new lease on life. The smell of baking rubber seared my nostrils, and the soot clung to our sweaty limbs and faces, stinging my eyes. I complained, but my dad told me that the work would make me strong.

"Look, m'ijo. This is better than lifting weights," he grunted as he showed me how to tighten the wheels that secured the mold lids in place. "C'mon. Show me how it's done."

Straining as I put his teachings into practice, I asked him if he'd pay me, and he replied that he was paying me "in kind," that it was like a free gym membership.

Then on Sundays, my mom dragged us all to the cathedral to attend mass in Spanish. I usually lurked near the wall at the back of the church, occasionally taking short strolls outside in the plaza to break up the monotony of the priest's chants and recitations.

It was on one of those Sundays that I wished I'd sat—and stayed—in the front pew with my parents, Rubén, and the other groups who brought disabled family members. While fleeing sanctification beneath the meager shade of the plaza's dusty trees, I felt my stomach turn upon a hauntingly familiar sight. Coming toward me diagonally across the square were three distinctly recognizable human forms: one huge, one skinny, and one crowned by shiny golden hair.

I pretended not to notice them, adjusting my trajectory to loop back toward the cathedral, but before I could reach the beggars panhandling in the shade of the arched entrance, I heard one of them call my name. Freezing in place, I turned slowly to see their shadows creeping toward me as they climbed the steps up from the street.

"¿Que honda, güey?" El Güero asked in a cheery singsong voice. He acted as if we were lifelong friends. He was disarming, charismatic even. I could immediately see why people said he had many girlfriends as a result of his looks and charm, not to mention the wads of cash all three of them invariably carried in their wallets.

The other two brothers nodded and crossed their arms, standing slightly behind him on either side.

"Nada," I tried to respond nonchalantly.

"You like church?" El Gordo huffed.

I shrugged, squinting in the bright sunlight.

"It's boring right?" El Flaco grinned, a gold tooth flashing brightly. "That's why you're out here skipping the sermon."

"Let's take a walk." El Güero gave me little choice, swinging a friendly arm around my shoulders and guiding me back down the steps toward the plaza. "We've got much more interesting things to talk about."

As we crossed the street, El Flaco added, "Yeah, who needs to hear all the things they've done wrong and all the ways they're guilty of being sinners?"

"Not me," El Gordo breathed heavily, lumbering behind the rest of us. "I already know everything I do is wrong, but I do it anyway."

They all laughed in unison. Then they fell silent together. And when we reached the old wrought iron gazebo at the center of the plaza—where the mariachis would play after mass ended, they delivered a sermon of their own to me.

————

"They want you to what?" Dante smacked his forehead with his giant hand, knitting his thick eyebrows together as he looked up from his math homework during our tutoring session in the library.

In hushed tones, I patiently recounted the Del Río brothers' instructions to me in the plaza.

"I heard you the first time," Dante replied.

"Oh, so it was a rhetorical question?"

"I don't know what that means, but I know what they want you to do. And there's no way you can do it. You can't get involved."

"They said if I did it just this once, they'd leave me alone."

"They won't. That's how they draw people in. They act all nice, like they're your best friends and they're not bad, just misunderstood. They just need a favor from you. Then, next thing you know, you're their slave."

"C'mon. It can't be that bad."

"Talk to Manny Hinojosa if you can find him. He's usually hiding."

"Who's Manny?"

"Exactly. You haven't seen him because he's either busy moving drugs for them or he's hiding so they don't make him do other things he doesn't want to do."

"Why did this have to happen to me?" I lamented my fate.

"Because you're going back and forth to Matamoros every weekend and they figured it out. They spotted you. They need mules, man."

"Mules?"

"Yeah, mules to carry their merchandise for them. The border agents know them, so they can't get anything through the checkpoint from México. They get inspected every time they cross the bridge. So they have to find fresh meat, people who aren't suspected by the authorities, inocentes like you to do their dirty work for them."

The term "inocentes" made me uncomfortable. I didn't want to be a naive idiot, a patsy, just another victim in the making.

"If you let them, they'll use you until you're burned and then they'll get rid of you."

"Aw, c'mon. They haven't actually gotten rid of anyone, have they?"

"Just talk to Manny, if you . . ."

"Yeah, yeah. If I can find him."

———

Manny did not turn out to be an easy person to locate, much less lure into a conversation. The first time I caught a glimpse of him, he wore a hoodie in hundred-degree heat. His eyes were hollowed out, deep shadows ringing their sunken sockets. Like a frightened raccoon, he scurried away when I called his name, disappearing into a crowd near the senior lockers.

During the weekend pilgrimages to Matamoros, I began to sit in the front pew, sandwiched between Rubén and my dad. My mom was thrilled by my sudden interest in mass, but my father scrutinized me suspiciously.

As the weeks passed, I hoped that the Del Río brothers had forgotten all about me and our pleasant chat in the shade of the gazebo. But eventually the terrifying trio approached me in the parking lot before school.

"Where've you been, López?" Güero feigned chumminess.

"You're not avoiding us, are you? We haven't seen you outside the church or in the plaza," El Gordo added.

"No, I've just been busy."

"On the weekends? Weekends are for chilling, vato," El Flaco said. "Even God took it easy on Sunday."

I hesitated before replying, "I've been busy helping my mom. You know, my brother's handicapped. She needs my help." I hated myself when I heard the words coming out of my mouth. I never helped my mom. I never helped Rubén. But here I was using them in a vain effort to garner sympathy and protect my own skin.

The Del Río brothers seemed caught off guard, as if they rehearsed and choreographed these encounters beforehand and I'd derailed their routine by improvising my lines.

When the bell rang, I didn't wait for their response, flying into class as if I actually wanted to learn something. Later that day, when Señora Martinez asked me if I'd worked on my application to the New York art program, I lied and told her I was almost done.

"Has your father approved? Will he sign it?" she asked, concern lacing her voice.

"My mom will sign it," I guessed.

That night, while my cousin David strummed his guitar in the bed next to mine at Grandma Fina's, I hunched over the application forms, urgently scribbling my responses to the questions.

When I finished, I lay awake for a long time. I couldn't sleep all night. My stomach felt sick, but it dawned on me—as the light outside the window morphed from black to blue—that it was not due to anything I'd eaten. The cause of my nausea was the realization that up until I now, I had always been motivated by a deep desire to reach for my dreams, to accomplish something big, to go places, but suddenly—after meeting the Del Río brothers—all I yearned for was to flee.

———

I finally ran into Manny when I wasn't even hunting for him. He was dispensing illicit pharmaceuticals at Amigoland Mall on Black Friday. I happened to be there with my mom and Rubén. The line to get to Manny competed with the one for a portrait with Santa, but I cut straight to the front and cornered him.

"Is it true what they say?" I whispered into his ear. "That they've got you literally enslaved? How? And what do I do?"

His eyes glinted with terror as he gawked back at me. He seemed unable to produce a word, opening and closing his mouth without a sound, like a guppy in a fishbowl. Was he scared speechless or had he simply forgotten how to communicate outside of his sales and collection efforts?

"Talk to me. They're after me," I implored.

"I have two sisters," he finally mustered. "They say they'll do horrible things to them if I don't follow their orders."

"What do I do, Manny?"

"Just stay away from them, man."

"They say it's a one-time favor," I replied.

"That's what they always say, but once they have you, they won't let go. Now get away from me, before one of them sees us talking."

I let the queue resume its flow and put distance between us. All around me, shoppers milled in a frenzy, a mixture of English and Spanish bubbling energetically from the crowd. Everyone seemed buoyed by holiday cheer, except Manny, and me.

———

As Christmas neared, I told my mother all I wanted as a present was for her to sign the forms, lending her consent to my application. She said she'd think about it and discuss it further with my father.

I'd overheard them talking about it, and I knew he would not be easily convinced. The phrase "over my dead body" might have been thrown about. But, perhaps not too coincidentally, the Saturday the Del Río brothers showed up at my parents' doorstep to ask for me, she took matters into her own hands.

They knocked in the early evening. My dad and I had just returned from the tire shop and he was in the shower. Acting as if it were not at all out of the ordinary, she told me some friends were there to see me.

I was covered in grease and grime from working at the recapping plant when I met them at the door.

"I guess you weren't kidding about being a hard worker," El Güero greeted me.

"What do you guys want?"

"We need you to do that favor for us," El Gordo cut to it.

El Flaco shoved a nondescript backpack into my hands.

"We'll get it from you at school on Monday," Güero concluded.

The three nodded in sync and walked away briskly.

I quickly skulked to the room I shared with Rubén and shoved the backpack under his bed, hiding it behind a wall of stuffed animals. Then I sat on the bed and let my head slump down into my hands, my elbows propped up on my knees.

Rubén sat in the corner of the room listening to an Olivia Newton John song on his record player. When he saw me, he looked up from the spinning vinyl disc and drawled in his distinctively wavering voice, "You sad, Ramón."

I wasn't sure if it was a question or an observation. Rubén seemed to be strangely wise in that way.

After dinner, when my father went to bed, my mother signed the forms.

Once everybody was asleep, I finally dared peek into the backpack. It was bursting with a variety of plastic Ziploc bags crammed full of pills of varied colors, dried and shriveled leaves of what resembled grass clippings, and a shrink-wrapped white brick. Hastily zipping it back up, I held no doubt the contents of the bag were worth more than the entire inventory at my dad's tire retread facility.

———

Monday, I ran straight to Señora Martinez's art studio and handed her my application forms. From there, I took a seldom-used service hallway to reach the nurse's office and declare myself ill. Grandma Fina escorted me home in her beige VW Beetle, where I pretended to be sick for the next several days.

Cousin David, who now attended a small Christian school his mother's family had begun paying for, was the first—aside from the Del Río brothers, no doubt—to suspect my ruse.

"What's going on?" he asked me, plucking the strings on his acoustic guitar as he sat across from me on the edge of his bed. "This isn't like you. You like going to school, something I've never understood by the way. Are you finally joining the rest of us in our absolute disgust with the daily nightmare of it?"

"Have you heard of the Del Río brothers?"

"Of course I have. Everyone has. They're like gangsters." He kept strumming, finding a steady rhythm.

As he played, I confessed my quandary. He never skipped a beat. When I finished, he stopped playing and put his guitar down. It was then I realized he not only had a musical gift, he also had perfect timing. He'd been playing so that Grandma Fina wouldn't overhear our conversation. He motioned with a head movement for us to go out into the backyard.

Out by the barbecue pit, he paused. "So where's the bag?"

"Behind an army of stuffed animals under Rubén's bed."

"That's not good."

"I don't want to bring it across. It's a no-win situation. If I bring it, I'm breaking the law and I'm trapped in their game. If I don't bring it, they're probably going to kill me. And if I bring it and get caught, I'll be sent to Juvi, and they'll probably have God-knows-what done to me in there."

"But if you leave it there, what if they go mess with your parents and Rubén?"

I hadn't thought of that. It was hard to imagine anyone "messing" with my dad. His glare alone could scare off an intruder.

"Christmas vacation starts this weekend," I said. "I'll just stay home sick until then, and hopefully that will buy me more time."

"More time for what? Now that you have that stuff, they're going to be after you."

"They were already after me."

Cousin David shook his head and put his hand on my shoulder as if he were offering his condolences. "Just remember, brother. You're not alone."

With that, he picked up a plank of wood from a pile by the chain-link fence and set it across two cinder blocks. He struck a serene pose and proceeded to split the board into two with his right hand.

I knew he'd been taking karate classes but had never seen him in action. I stood speechless as he stepped back from the broken board and gazed at me mournfully.

"I don't want to drag you into this," I said.

"If you need me, I'm here," he answered.

———

Christmas came and went, and I was beginning to hope that, through some form of divine intervention, perhaps the Del Río brothers had perished in a shoot-out or been caught by the cops and thrown in jail. I was praying for myself at Christmas Eve mass in the Matamoros cathedral when I saw them standing against the wall to the right side of the front pew. They stared straight at me.

Afterward in the plaza, mariachis played in the bandstand. Families and couples packed the square beneath the colorful Christmas lights strung between the trees. Street vendors sold corn on the cob and churros and hot chocolate. And as we strolled through the plaza, I sensed the brothers around me.

"Where have you been, López?" El Güero hissed, the time for his nice-guy routine apparently expired.

"Sick," I answered.

"You don't look sick no more," El Gordo responded.

Worried my father would spot the Del Río brothers, I slowed down so more people could fill the gap between my family and me.

"When school's back in session, you bring the stuff across," El Güero commanded.

"Or else." El Flaco made a fist and pounded it into the palm of his other hand.

"And not just you, but your retard little brother," El Gordo threatened.

A sudden wave of rage rushed through me. I had no qualms lamenting my brother to myself and my parents, but it angered me to hear somebody else disparage him. "You do something to my brother and you'll burn in Hell, the three of you."

El Güero stopped in his tracks and smiled. "Vato, we're already gonna burn in Hell."

The other two flashed sinister grins as they allowed the crowd to fill the space between us.

When I caught up to my parents, they were gathered around the Nacimiento, a life-sized Nativity scene with real humans playing the parts of the Holy Family in a makeshift manger made from plywood. In the center, a small pile of hay in a rickety cradle waited for Baby Jesus to arrive. The throng chanted a Spanish hymn about the Savior. And I couldn't help but pray that He would take mercy on me and help me find a way out of my situation.

———

The part of me that sat in mass all those Sundays, and the part of me that listened to my dad's own sermons night after night sitting on the porch in the rusting metal rocking chairs, and the part of me that briefly portrayed a holier-than-thou paladin in Julia's D&D campaign, all those parts harmoniously rang in my ears with disapproval and disappointment the day before school began, when I stuffed the bag full of drugs into my duffel for the ride back from Matamoros to Grandma Fina's house.

There was a long line at the bridge, as there always was after the holidays. Everyone was busy returning or exchanging gifts, and shopping for bargains at the post-Christmas sales so they could provide yet another round of gifts to their children on el Día de los Reyes Magos.

I stared sullenly out the back window, listening to my parents bicker about Rubén's endless physical therapy and speech therapy and doctor's appointments and medical bills, and leaks in the roof and whether they would ever be able to afford moving back to Brownsville. Rubén played with his two favorite stuffed animals, a cute dog he called Kawa and a strange creature—whose species I never did figure out—named Ramona Rosa. He babbled unintelligibly, clumsily moving the stuffed toys as they conversed. I wondered what he thought they were saying. I rankled at the word Güero had used to describe him. I'd heard my parents argue about the formal version of the diagnosis too. One neurologist had told them that he was mentally retarded and would never amount to anything more than "a vegetable" and that they would be doing their whole family a favor if they put him in an institution. My father refused to accept the doctor's assessment, and they both categorically rejected his recommendation. Instead, they took him to more appointments and clinics and curanderas and shamans on both sides of the border, leaving every peso and dollar they could get their hands on in somebody else's pocket in search of hope.

As the traffic inched along, I gazed down at the river, past the plaque with the vertical line that divided México from the United States. On the northern riverbank, tall reeds of grass grew nearly ten feet tall. I watched as a young man waded through the murky river water and crawled naked onto the muddy banks, slipping and sliding into the cover provided by the lush vegetation. Moving in parallel, I strained my eyes to keep him in sight, wondering if maybe—just maybe—I could witness him sneak over the levee to safety without being caught. For a moment, I lost sight of him deep in the thick reeds. Then, I realized it was because he was down on the ground getting dressed. For a moment, as if he sensed he was being watched, he looked over his shoulder up toward the shiny cars on the bridge, squinting, the distance between us stretching and tensing like a rubber band pulled beyond its breaking point. And then, he scrambled up the verdant slope toward the dirt road at its crest, dashing east along the levee, away from the barbed wire and the guards and the inspections and the arrests and deportations, running from the indignity and the inhumanity at breakneck speed. I watched him go until he disappeared around a bend. I knew the direction in which he was headed. Just a few years earlier, I had ridden my Evil Knievel bike on that same dirt path over the levee in Southmost. How different were we? I thought of him as our car finally reached the checkpoint. I pushed aside the knowledge of what my duffel carried inside, stashed in the trunk with Rubén's wheelchair. And when the customs inspector asked us, I replied in chorus with my parents, "American citizen." He nodded and waved us through, a green light flashing before our eyes.

———

At school, I told the Del Río brothers to come to my grandmother's house that night, to meet me in the alleyway so I could give them their bag. They weren't thrilled, but they had little choice at that point.

When dusk fell, Cousin David and I stood on the back porch, waiting. Once the alleyway was plunged into darkness, we heard the rumble of the Del Río's lowrider approaching, its headlights cutting through the chain-link fence, casting a crisscross pattern across Grandma Fina's brittle grass.

We descended the steps and crossed the yard, exiting to the alleyway through the rusted gate. David wore his white karate gi, cinched by his wide black belt.

Standing in the beams, we squinted into the light, moths and dragonflies chaotically filling the illuminated space between us and the Del Río clan with their frenzied dance.

The doors to the low-slung muscle car swung open. The engine still running, the brothers stepped out and walked slowly toward us.

"Who's this, López?" El Güero asked.

"This is my cousin, David."

"Why's he dressed in his pajamas?" El Flaco asked as his brothers snickered.

David stared back at them impassively.

"Where's our bag?" El Gordo demanded, switching into a serious tone.

"About that," I replied. "Before I give it to you, I want your word that I will be left alone after this. I will not become the next Manny Hinojosa."

The brothers looked at each other, then back at me.

"That's not how this works," El Güero explained. "We make the demands, not you."

I could feel my heart rate accelerating, my breathing becoming agitated. Glancing at David, I could tell he was completely unfazed, completely ready.

I swallowed hard. "Then I won't give you the bag."

It was obvious the Del Río brothers were not accustomed to any pushback. Güero hesitated as his brothers exchanged glances.

"If you don't give us the bag, we'll go into your abuela's house and take it," El Gordo stated plainly. "And we'll make you sorrier than you can imagine. Think about it. You could still enjoy a few more years of that old lady cooking for you before she croaks."

"You're not going into that house," David said calmly. "Now promise you'll leave Ramón alone, and he'll get you the bag."

"Have it your way." Güero shook his head, stepping toward the gate into the backyard.

In one lithe movement, David was between Güero and the gate. Güero raised his fist to strike, but before he could even move it forward, David had him face down on the caliche, his arm pulled behind his back, his eyes steadily on the other two.

I was quickly overpowered by El Gordo and El Flaco, forcing David to relinquish his hold on Güero to come to my assistance. And, thus, the melee broke out in earnest. No more words were spoken. All I could hear over the car engine were the sounds of our feet sliding and crunching on the gravely caliche, the muffled pounding of fists landing blows, pained grunts and anguished exhalations. Soon, David dealt Güero a knockout lunge punch to the chin, sending him sliding toward the front of their car, where he lay inert. In that moment, we took the advantage as David delivered a flurry of round kicks to El Gordo, backing him up like a giant bobblehead against the cinder-block wall opposite our grandmother's fence. Meanwhile, El Flaco and I wrestled somewhat evenly, stumbling to the ground. In the headlights, I saw a flash of steel emerge from El Gordo's pocket, heard a sudden yelp from David. A red bloom appeared on his white karate shirt. He quickly disarmed El Gordo, the blade spinning overhead and clattering in the shadows. It had fallen somewhere near the fence, ringing against one of its metal posts, but I couldn't see it anymore. As I looked for it, while trying to force El Flaco into a stranglehold beneath my superior weight, I noticed that Güero no longer lay motionless. Doubled over and moving slowly, he circled toward the driver's seat, reaching in for something. In the dim interior car light, I saw him raise a gun and back out, turning toward us from behind the door. David had El Gordo against the wall, slamming his fists into his mammoth body. El Gordo's eyes fluttered shut as he began to wobble. Güero took aim at my cousin.

I struggled to rise and throw my body toward David, but El Flaco had me tangled up. "David! Gun!" I yelled.

And at that instant, I heard a loud thud instead of a gunshot. Güero's head had been slammed into the side of the car's roof. His body crumpled to the ground. The gun spun on the caliche at the foot of the car's headlamps. From behind the open driver door, a powerful shadow moved swiftly toward us, picking up the gun and using its butt to finally knock El Flaco unconscious. I felt his body go limp in my grasp, recognizing the black Mexican botines that stood before me.

My dad pointed the gun at El Gordo, motioning for David to stand aside. Clutching at his wounded rib cage, David complied.

"Get your brothers in the car. And get out of here," my dad growled. "Ándale. Muévete."

El Gordo blinked unsteadily but followed my father's orders. First, he dragged El Flaco and loaded him into the back seat. Then, he helped a groggy Güero into the front passenger seat, closing the door. Standing in front of the car, he looked at me and then at my dad. "What about our bag?"

"Tomorrow morning I'm turning your bag into the sheriff. And if you ever come near my son or my nephew or anyone in my family again, I will tell him who the bag belonged to, but only after I hunt each one of you down and kill you."

The way my father spoke the words was not menacing or melodramatic, just a matter of fact.

El Gordo eyed the weapon in my father's hand. I knew he was wondering if he should ask about his gun, but it was clear my father had convinced him that this was not the time to try and negotiate. Slowly, he shuffled to the driver side and got into the vehicle. We stood to the side and watched him drive away.

My father tucked the gun behind his back, hidden under his guayabera. He then looked at David. The whole right side of David's shirt was sopping wet with blood. "Let's take a look at you. You may have to go to the hospital," he said.

We helped my cousin inside, where Grandma Fina washed his wound and poured alcohol over it. David winced and let out a gasp. As I watched her, I got the feeling that this wasn't her first rodeo. After all, she'd raised five boys in the '50s, all prone to violent confrontations. I'd once heard her say that the school principal had called her and asked her why her sons were so violent. Her response had been, "Mis hijos no son violentos, solamente no son dejados," which roughly translated as: "My sons aren't violent; they're just not pushovers."

When she'd gotten a good look at the cut, she determined that he would need stitches.

"¿Al hospital?" my father asked.

"Nick can do it," she said, picking up the phone. My uncle was now living a couple houses down the street. He had been a medic in the Korean War. And he kept a load of supplies on hand.

A couple minutes later, he was there, looming over my cousin. As he worked, David couldn't contain his pain any longer, moaning in agony.

Stepping out onto the front porch with my father, I braced myself for his reprobation.

"You're grounded for the rest of junior year," he stated plainly.

I nodded.

"The moment those boys came after you, you should have told me."

I nodded again.

"You can't mess around or take chances with these things," his voice roiled with dark emotion. "Times are changing down here. This is not the border I grew up in. Sure, we had rumbles and knife fights over things like girls and honor and then got sent off to war with our street smarts and the illusion we could survive anything life threw our way. But these days, it's drugs and guns and people killing for pleasure. La raza se ha vuelto loca. You're lucky you're alive, son. And you're even luckier you didn't get your primo killed." He shook his head and spit disgustedly from the porch railing onto the darkened lawn.

I stared out into the inky night, toward the park and the resaca I couldn't see beyond the black ribbon of street. I felt a hollow pit within myself, a dark depth of disenchantment in my own poor decision-making. *How could I have been so stupid?*

"Where's the bag those guys gave you?"

"In my room."

"And you brought it across the river when we brought you back to school?"

"Yes."

"And before that you hid it in Rubén's room?"

"Yes." How did he always know?

He shook his head again, signaling the colossal burden of his disappointment and loss of trust in me.

"Bring it to me."

I retrieved the bag, relieved to see that David's torso was being wrapped in gauze and the worst seemed to have passed. I handed the bag to my father and he deposited it—and the gun—in his truck.

"What will you do with it?" I asked as he stepped back up on the porch.

"What I said I would do," he replied sternly. "Haven't you learned by now? I always do what I say."

He was right. I should have learned by then.

———

There were no parties and no visits to friends' houses. My life consisted of going to school and coming home and doing chores at Grandma Fina's house until she said the work was done, which involved helping her and my mom with their endless cooking and baking, plus helping with the laundry, which she washed in a machine in the carport but then line dried in the backyard. My tasks included carrying the baskets of clothes out to the washer, helping her load and unload, ferrying the wet clothes to the backyard, and handing each piece to her so she could stretch it out and fasten it with wooden clothespins to the wires that spanned the yard. The nights ended with the washing and drying of dishes, which was all done by hand as she did not have space for a dishwasher in her cramped kitchen.

At school, I kept to myself as much as I could, hiding from the world in Señora Martinez's art studio, immersing myself in my painting.

I found myself lost in a triptych of a young man fleeing his past yet running toward an uncertain future. The first canvas involved the river. It was wet and brown and muddy, dirty and filthy and repulsive. I started and stopped and destroyed my work, and started over many times, struggling to get the ripples in the water just right, the balance of transparency and murkiness through which one could discern the man's feet and kneeling legs still submerged in the shallows as he dragged his naked body onto the soggy bank like a prehistoric creature striving to rise from the muck and the grime toward light, toward safety. I pushed myself to an obsessive level, straining to convey the determination and the anguish with which the man dug his nails and fingers into the chalky supersaturated clay, slipping and sliding, desperately clinging to whatever hold he could purchase.

The second piece was wider, greener, lush vertical reeds filling the canvas from side to side, bottom to top, like a photorealistic Rousseau jungle. And there, nearly lost in the foliage, angled brushstrokes brought a dark silhouette from the shadows. The young man was pulling on his pants over his glistening legs. His wet black hair clung to his forehead and cheeks. His eyes met the viewer's in surprise. Was it fear or shame or obstinate hope that dodged about the edges of his irises, shimmered in the slick void of his pupils? I wasn't sure. I was trying to figure it out as I went along.

The third piece remained in sketch form for what seemed like an eternity as I toiled on the details of the other two. The canvas was divided by sweeping graphite lines fashioning broad horizontal planes, where I envisioned the dark but shimmering river below, the emerald levee between, the blue sky above. On the crest of the levee, the young man ran for his life. What would he find around the bend, I wondered. Would it be the freedom he sought and left everything behind for, including shreds of his dignity? Or would it be something far different from what he had expected, from whatever motivated his courageous journey?

———

"Congratulations, Mr. and Mrs. López," Señora Martinez said. "Ramón has been accepted into the art program in New York. It is a most prestigious accomplishment."

My mom nodded, smiling tightly as she wrung her hands in her lap. My father frowned and knit his eyebrows together in consternation, as he often did.

"So he's not in trouble?" my father asked.

"Oh, no. Ramón is a model student. Of course he's not in trouble. He's a star!"

"A star?" My dad looked at me, sitting nervously at my mother's side, as far from his potential recriminations as I could possibly position myself. "This star's been grounded for the last three months. I didn't even grant my permission for his application. My wife must have signed it behind my back." He glared at her. Surely, their arguing would shake dust from the cinder blocks tonight. I felt sorry for Rubén, perpetually stuck there with them, spinning vinyl to drown out their sorrows.

"Yes," Señora Martinez acknowledged. "He told me that it's been a difficult time, that he has been working hard to earn back your family's trust."

"Looks like he won't be alone in that regard," my father fumed.

My mom sniffed, as if she might start crying.

My parents were accustomed to sitting together at Rubén's doctor appointments, where they generally received all sorts of bad news. This must be an alien experience for them, I realized.

"What do you want from us, Señora Martinez?" my father demanded to know. "I cannot afford to send Ramón to New York. That's why we have a college here in Brownsville, so our children don't have to leave us, so they can get an education we can afford."

I had warned my art teacher that this would be a difficult climb. Mr. Dean had asked if he could help, but I had determined that—alone— Señora Martinez had the best chance of anyone to get through to my father. Largely because she was Mexican, but also because she was a woman. I figured—given his macho pride—my father might go into combat mode if he felt remotely threatened by a gringo male encouraging him to ship his son to the Northeast.

"Señor López, este es un honor para su familia," she said, adeptly switching into Spanish—as I had hoped she would—to connect on a cultural level. "This program is paid for by a scholarship. It pays for the tuition and the housing for his senior year of high school. And it gives him a great opportunity to go straight into a top art college after graduation. It's a chance of a lifetime."

"Congratulations, Ramón." My mom patted me on the knee. "You have made our family proud."

We all looked at my dad. His broad shoulders and thick arms made his chair look too small, like it might collapse beneath the weight of his stout body.

Clearing his throat, he replied, "I'll be honest, Señora. I don't want my son to go."

We shifted uncomfortably in our seats as he paused. He always had a way of building suspense when he spoke, making you wonder what he might say next, hanging on his every lingering word.

"I'm glad he has a hobby like art, but business is his future," he affirmed.

Señora Martinez pivoted gracefully, rising from her desk and motioning for my parents to follow her so they could view some of my recent artwork.

I watched them as they stood before my triptych of the young man crossing the river.

They were speechless as she made various proclamations about the merits of my work. "Ramón has a keen vision for our culture, Señor and Señora López. He can help others understand our world, where we come from, who we are and who we're trying to become. And, to your point, art—like everything else—*is* a business. If Ramón gets the training that is available to him in New York through this program, he could become successful. This triptych just won him the school art contest for the second time. Imagine what he could do with the right education and opportunities?"

My mother leaned forward, her nose nearly touching the center panel, where the subject lurked naked in the vegetation. My father studied the paintings from further back, scratching at his chin as his eyes absorbed the scenes. I wondered if they'd ever heard the term "triptych" before, if they knew what it meant.

"A son belongs with his family," he professed. "But . . ."

Yes? But! Out with it, I thought.

"But . . ." he scoured his mind for the right words to express what he was thinking. "I have been thinking about this for a long time now, ever since the terrible accident that happened last year."

Señora Martinez quickly made the sign of the cross. "Poor Julia." It was as if Reeser had never existed.

"Then, there were the problems this year," my dad labored on, un-accustomed to explaining—or justifying—the inner workings of his cryptic mind to others.

"Yes, we've been worried for Ramón's safety," my mother added.

I thanked her silently for helping build his momentum.

"Yes, his safety." My father nodded, glancing in my direction. "So, even though he belongs here, and even though I am not convinced by this whole art thing . . ." he waved his hands dismissively at the canvases in front of them and those scattered throughout the room, "I would rather he not get himself killed before he can make something of his life."

Jumping at the chance, I shot out of my chair and joined them, "It's not just my life, Dad. It's my dreams."

"Well, my dream was to keep my family together," he said, "but without you, all our dreams will be for naught, so the most important thing is for you to stay alive. And, unfortunately, this has become a dangerous place and time for you."

"So, you give your permission?" Señora Martinez folded her hands beseechingly.

Feeling the pressure of our combined gazes, my father finally relented, "I will not stand in his way."

———

Sometime that summer, not long before I was due to leave for New York, my father finally lifted my punishment. To celebrate my impending departure, David and I walked across the Gateway Bridge to eat tacos and have drinks at the bars across the border. Afterward, as we worked our way back toward the tollbooth to return to Brownsville, we ran into someone familiar at the median between the lanes of busy traffic. As the cars rushed by, I recognized Manny Hinojosa. It had been months since I'd seen him. Beads of perspiration dotted his forehead and he had a wild look in his eyes, that of a hunted animal.

"Ramón," he panted. "Do you have some cash you could give me? I need to get out of town fast. I need money for a bus ticket south."

"Why? What's going on?" I asked, as David's eyes opened wide and he tried to steer my line of vision down to Manny's stomach.

"I don't have much time. I have to get to the Central de Autobuses. The Del Río brothers are after me, Ramón. I've gotta run."

I finally saw what David was gesticulating about. Blood oozed around a hole in Manny's shirt, despite the fact he had a hand over it.

I reached into my wallet and gave him everything I had. "Good luck, Manny."

"You too."

We watched him weave through the passing cars as he scrambled desperately toward a dark neighborhood street and vanished into the trees.

The next day, a local student was found dead from a gunshot wound, slumped on a bench—ticket in hand—waiting for a bus out of Matamoros.

———

After I said my goodbyes to my mom, Grandma Fina, Rubén, and David, my dad drove me down Boca Chica Boulevard to the airport. His truck crawled so slowly I thought we'd never reach it in time for me to catch my flight.

Along the way, he stayed quiet for the most part, opening his mouth only a pair of times to counsel me. He said, "Remember, son, when you get there: just because the buildings are taller, that doesn't mean the people inside are any happier or more important."

I nodded, still having a hard time believing that he was letting me go.

As the diminutive, beige cinder-block airport slid into view, he added, "Don't forget where you came from."

He carried my bag as we walked beneath the palm trees toward the entrance. Once inside the small terminal, he moved so hesitantly toward the single gate that when we got there, the waiting area was vacant and the airline agents were getting ready to shut the door to the tarmac.

"Hurry!" the uniformed woman called urgently. "You'll miss your flight."

He handed me the bag and gave me a tight hug. I always felt so small and weak—yet loved and protected—within his powerful arms. Somehow, he rendered me both vulnerable and safe at the same time. And then, I was free of his grasp and being towed by the insistent flight attendant toward the gate. Hot air blasted in through the open doorway. I turned and waved at my dad. He stood there, staring grimly at me in his khaki pants and white guayabera, his Stetson in his hand, his thick mustache quivering slightly over his impassive lips. He waved, silently mouthing the word, "Adios."

———

I'd never flown anywhere in my life and here I was dashing across a steaming tarmac toward a flight of steps to a jet powered by screaming engines. Moments later, I was belted into my seat as the airport terminal glided by. Through the oval double-paned window, I gawked at a cluster of people waving at the plane from a fenced area outside the gate. At the back of the enthusiastic throng, I spied my father standing stoically beneath his hat. His hands behind his back, he glumly watched the plane roll away. The knot in my throat and the tears stinging my eyes surprised me as he too receded from view. Was this a hint of what my poor mother had felt when she lamented becoming an orphan? Could I survive alone, without her and my father and my Grandma Fina?

My heart momentarily plummeted through my churning stomach as the lurching metal beast defied gravity. And then, I marveled at how small everything below became, how quickly the airport shrank into a tiny dot and the fields around it unfurled into a green patchwork quilt. A winding sliver of silver gleamed beneath the sun as it carved through the earth on its obstinate, meandering route to the vast and sparkling Gulf of México.

As the airplane turned northeast, the Rio Grande and the towns huddled on its treacherous banks, and my family and friends—as well as those who might do me harm—were all left behind in its invisible wake. Ascending through the feathery clouds, I closed my eyes, took a deep breath, and dreamed of all that lay ahead.

OUR LADY OF LEVEE STREET

I longed for home. Grandma Fina's constant presence in the kitchen, her fresh handmade tortillas, the warm scent of toasted corn wafting through the house in the cross breeze from the front screen door to the back patio, her picadillo con papas and key lime meringue pies. My father's incessant advice. My mother's silent support. Even Rubén's amusing antics, which had once aggravated me, now seemed perfectly harmless and endearing.

Although I talked to them every Sunday, there were more subtle dimensions of home that were not only absent from my daily life but had been replaced by much harsher substitutes in New York. I missed the sonorous yet soothing song of the cicadas. I longed for the melancholy cries of the mourning doves at dusk. In the middle of the night, as I tossed in my cold cinder-block dorm room chasing sleep, I wished away the ambulance and fire truck sirens that pierced the night, yearning to be lulled by the soulful hymn of trains burrowing through darkness over rusty railroad bridges.

My time at the High School of Art & Design moved more swiftly than any of those modes of transportation. I learned more in that year than I had in the previous dozen. Soon, I was admitted with a scholarship to the Cooper Union. Over the phone, my parents did not understand what that meant. They had never heard of Cooper Union or its history as an art college.

"Son," my father said. "If it's what you want, then we will support you. I can keep wiring you a little bit here and a little bit there to help you get by . . . but . . ." His voice turned glum as he confessed they simply could not afford the trip to New York for my high school graduation. It was not what I had expected, to march across the graduation stage completely alone, my family thousands of miles away and unable to witness my success, but—despite the sensation of solitude—my enthusiasm soared to such heights that none of that could bring me down. My whole upbringing on the border, I had been led to believe in this so-called American Dream. At times it even seemed like a fable too good to be true, but I had clung to it and clawed toward it and now here it was. I felt like I was living it. Its energy pulsated around me in flashing lights, chaotic traffic, masses of people churning through broad streets, hunger defining and driving their every purposeful step. After a lifetime languishing on the inert edge of the world, I was finally making progress, even as I often found myself confused.

At the Cooper Union, the professors talked ad nauseum about advancing the artist's role in "cultural production." Spanish may have been my first language, but I was now far more fluent in English. Yet, I'd never heard most of the buzzwords and phrases swirling about me. Much less had I imagined the lofty concepts. I yearned to ask someone, anyone, what "cultural production" even was. But I was afraid. I was almost as frightened as I was excited by everything I was going through. Half the time I didn't think I was worthy of belonging, but yet here I was. I rarely knew whether I should ask a question to enrich my knowledge or stay silent to avoid exposing the depths of my ignorance.

When I arrived, I thought I knew what art was. I thought I was a painter. Little did I know, as it turned out. Quickly, I was schooled in the physical aspects of working with wood, metal, plaster, and plastics. I studied "color." I didn't know one would have to do that. The course was a deep dive into everything one could ever imagine about color, from its physical nature to the principles of light, from its role in art history to its cultural significance. I learned about two-dimensional design, exploring the visual and intellectual aspects of form. I took a course in freehand drawing designed to emphasize perceptual and inventive skills. Then there was Advanced Painting, where I focused on water media—acrylic, transparent watercolor, and gouache—working on canvas and paper. I even studied lithography, making images on lithographic stones and commercial aluminum plates.

Toward the end of the first year, my painting professor presented my ode to New York, inspired by a ferry cruise through the harbor. The glossy acrylic on canvas brought to life my vision of the Statue of Liberty as an apparition of the Virgen de Guadalupe. Lady Liberty's hard angles were softened and flowing, her robes curved and undulating. In place of the rigid and muted tome in her hands, she clasped a bushel of vibrant roses. In lieu of the cold, septic patina, her cloak radiated emerald green. In her other hand, she still held aloft her brilliant torch, guiding and welcoming the world's lost souls—like me—toward safety.

The reactions in the classroom ranged widely. While most of my fellow students sat in stunned silence, one of the young men in the room spoke up indignantly. "I don't get it," he said. "What is the artist trying to say? That Mexicans are taking over our country? That their Virgin is better than our Lady Liberty?"

Audible gasps followed as the air was sucked out of the room.

The professor, an elderly woman always clad in flowing black robes, diffused the tension expertly, responding, "Sometimes art can be seen as a positive vision by some and an attack by others. Do we have diverging interpretations, perhaps?" She scanned the room hopefully, her eyes landing on a pile of wavy blond hair in the back row, a hand half-raised. "Back there, do you have a different perspective?"

"Yes," the defiant blond answered. "I think it's beautiful, a vision of how America's beacon is universally appealing to people from around the world, regardless of where they come from. People driven by their dreams can see themselves in America. To me, that's what this painting says. It says, Liberty is for everyone, even if they speak Spanish and come from Latin America."

"Bravo." The professor smiled as the bell rang and the class dispersed.

Afterward, as I lingered to collect my artwork, the professor approached me, patting me gently on the shoulder as I wrapped the piece.

"It is a lovely piece, Ramón," she assured me. "And a fascinating cultural reinterpretation of an iconic form."

Unsure if she was taking pity on me, I shrugged my shoulders, hanging my head.

"Do not be deterred," she urged. "There will always be doubters and naysayers, those that not only question your work, but also lash out and rebuke you for simply being yourself. You should always listen to their concerns and question your approach, but never let them stop you from expressing your vision or fulfilling your calling."

Surprised by her fervor, I gazed into her blue eyes, wondering what sorrow filled them with such aqueous portent, empathy deep as the waters threatening to drown Lady Liberty. I thanked her, forcing a smile before I lugged my beleaguered Virgen back to my cramped studio space.

The next day I received a note in my mailbox informing me that the professor had selected my painting for the school's annual art exhibit, which was a significant fundraising event attended by alumni, paparazzi, and New York's art intelligentsia.

At the exhibit, I recognized one of my work's admirers from a show staged by the performance art class. Her name was Clara. She was a blond model masquerading as an art student, as far as anyone could tell. Her "performance" had entailed a tribal dance and song in a fabricated language, which was primal and ironic in that it seemed inspired by the cultures of African or Native American civilizations yet was enacted by the whitest of white girls I'd ever seen. Still, somehow, she had the moxie and the cool factor to pull it off without being flunked, ridiculed, or accused of cultural appropriation.

"I like the Virgen," she asserted, assessing the painting with the detached assurance of one raised amid art and artists and art openings and members-preview nights at the Met and the Whitney and MOMA. She glanced at me dismissively and then did a double take. Perhaps the lower reflection level of my skin sent her a message.

"Is she yours?"

I nodded.

"She's lovely. I defended her—and you—in class."

My eyes widened. "That was you, in the back row?"

When she smiled it seemed like the wattage from the spotlights doubled. A moment later she delicately placed a glass of white wine in my hand. "Try this. It's Chardonnay," she instructed.

Two hours later, we slung across the backseat of a shiny black sedan that was always available wherever she went, no matter the time, a darkly tinted window shielding our impatient indiscretions from the chauffer's rear-mirror gaze.

———

"Her name is Clara," I told them over the phone.

"Es Mexicana," my father proclaimed over the tinny speaker.

I winced as I realized I'd inadvertently pronounced her name in Spanish. Should I let it go? Would they ever meet her or know the difference?

"What part of México is she from?" my mother chimed in from the background, probably ensuring that Rubén didn't tumble out of his kitchen table booster seat. Just as I had graduated from high school, he too had been liberated from his growth-defying highchair. But he required constant supervision due to his lack of equilibrium.

"New York," I answered. "She's from New York."

"I didn't know there were Mexicanas in New York," my father answered, confusion lacing his voice.

"You'd be surprised," I answered, thinking of all the housekeepers and nannies and waitresses I saw every day on the subway.

But Clara was not one to be spied underground or toiling in the shadows. Clara flew in her own stratosphere. Thanks to her, my painting of the Virgen sold for a record price, a record for a student show at the Union to be precise. She recommended it to someone she knew.

"I don't want your family spending money on my paintings," I protested.

"Oh, trust me. They wouldn't. It's a family acquaintance. Big difference. My family never risks their own money. They risk other people's money. That's the way wealth works, according to Daddy."

I nodded as if I understood. It sounded like one of the entrepreneurial concepts my father used to marvel at, back before his business dreams had been crushed by the overwhelming reality of his ineptitude and bad luck.

High on the proceeds from my first major art sale, I was eager to celebrate with her when she invited me to a Fourth of July picnic at her family's estate somewhere outside of the city. She hadn't been too specific, just told me to meet her at her apartment on Central Park West. I'd been there a few times, lost in long nights of partying followed by sex until the sun rose over the park and poured in through the windows, illuminating her naked form wrapped around mine. Black leather sofa. Drained bottles of champagne strewn across hardwood floors.

The morning her car took us out to the Hamptons, I wore a pair of sunglasses I borrowed from her. I wasn't about to ask why she had expensive men's sunglasses on the console table in her foyer, which incidentally was the size of my dorm room. Maybe they were her brother's. Did she have a brother?

We stared vacantly into oblivion—phasing in and out of sleep—as the chauffeur ferried us east and then north, over bridges and highways and causeways.

At a waterfront house the size of a luxurious resort, the party swarmed with rich white people dressed in crisp linens, Wall Street financiers, and their spouses. The only dark-skinned faces, aside from mine, were those of the waiters who circulated through the crowd carrying trays laden with canapés and crowned by champagne flutes.

As Clara air-kissed countless family acquaintances, I made a feeble attempt at mingling, but after being asked for the third or fourth time to refill a drink or ferry away a dirty plate, I skulked down a long, abandoned hallway to what appeared to be the bedroom wing of the rambling beachside mansion. I decided to take refuge in what I assumed was Clara's room. It was decorated in pristine white furnishings, white electric guitars hanging on the wall alongside photos of her cavorting backstage with assorted rock stars.

After surveying the pictures of her and her similarly model-like friends at some fancy prep school, my eyes landed thirstily on her white princess phone. Rich people didn't scrutinize their long-distance phone bill the same way the rest of us did. It wouldn't even matter to them if I called home, would it?

I felt like a thief and a scoundrel as I punched the buttons and pressed the phone against my ear. Sitting on the edge of the cloud that was her bed, I heard Grandma Fina pick up.

"Grandma Fina?"

"¡M'ijo!" she exclaimed.

I was immediately transported to her stuffy kitchen, the screen door overlooking the hardscrabble yard, Lincoln Street, and the resaca and park beyond. An aching knot grew tight in my throat.

"How are you?" I asked, choking back the sudden threat of tears.

"Bien, m'ijo, bien. And you? Is everything okay?"

"Sí."

"Are you looking for your mamá and papá?"

"Are they there?"

"No. They don't come until mañana, Sunday."

I shrugged sullenly, hoping that—as a Mexican abuela—she possessed the preternatural ability to interpret my body language from two thousand miles away.

"We miss you, m'ijo. It's been so long since you came home. You should make a pilgrimage. Even people who aren't from here are doing it."

"What do you mean?"

"Haven't you heard?" Grandma Fina asked.

"Heard what?"

"About the apparition."

"No. What apparition?"

Grandma Fina gasped as if a miracle was taking place before her very eyes in her kitchen on Lincoln Street. "La Virgen has manifested herself here."

"In Brownsville?"

"Sí. On Levee Street," she declared emphatically.

"On Levee Street?"

"Sí. On a tree trunk behind Texas Commerce Bank."

I'll believe it when I see it, I thought, but I had too much respect for my grandmother to voice my reaction. After all, she'd practically raised me. "Wow," was all I could muster in response. I'd been gone a long time, longer than I'd even realized up until that moment. Suddenly, even the concept of home didn't make sense. I had anticipated feeling alien in New York, but to grow estranged from the place I'd been born and raised was deeply disconcerting. I had never expected anything to change down there. I had not imagined that life would go on without me, that people would grow old, that the city would grow larger, and that supernatural powers would make their mark on the landscaping.

"You should come home, m'ijo," Grandma Fina wisely concluded. "It's been two years."

She had never told me what to do. My eyes narrowed as I focused on a photo of Clara with David Bowie pinned to the mirror over her white vanity lined with crystal perfume bottles.

"I should," I heard myself mumbling in a hypnotic daze. "I should go."

After I put the phone back in its cradle, I sat on Clara's bed until she made an apparition of her own. She said there were people I needed to meet, reps from the record label that was courting her. Maybe they'd like my artwork and commission me to do some album covers. I nodded and followed her like a zombie in a B-movie trudging after the brains of the operation. Outside, the Fourth of July fireworks exploded over the water.

Countless drinks and quickly forgotten conversations later, we dozed intermittently in the black sedan, gliding back toward the Upper West Side. The back of the car was filled with the swirling haze of a fine Guatemalan blend of sinsemilla that Clara fired up and sucked on expertly.

"So, who were you talking to in my room?" she asked sleepily.

"My grandmother," I replied, bleary-eyed. "I hope you don't mind."

She smiled lazily. "That's cool. What's she like?"

"She's a badass."

"Like the Virgen?

"Even better."

"Why?"

"She's for real."

"You should go visit her."

I nodded, peering out the tinted window in the inky night dotted by the lights of thousands of apartments suspended in concrete, steel, and glass towers as we shot across the Harlem River into Manhattan. I missed home more than I'd realized. Somehow it had taken a trip to the Hamptons to slap me out of my daze and put life in perspective. "She says there's some sort of divine apparition going on down there."

"You should bring me with you."

"Yeah?" I asked, taking the joint from her and inhaling.

"Why not?"

Through the smoke, I squinted at her, a golden-haired goddess that would seem more at home on the cover of Rolling Stone or Vogue than anywhere near the Rio Grande. Smiling mischievously, I replied, "You're quite the apparition yourself. I think you should come with me."

"Yeah?" she asked, taking the toke back.

"Why not?" I exhaled.

———

"It's so hot!" Clara proclaimed. "Is this place closer to the sun?"

"I told you."

"The asphalt is melting under my feet," she noted. A syrupy strand of black goo dangled from one of her white Gucci shoes.

"You shouldn't have worn those heels. Who flies like that? I've never seen anybody travel with such uncomfortable footwear."

"I'm not 'anybody,'" she clipped. "I'm me."

"Touché."

Melting in the airport parking lot, we sought refuge in the slim shadow of a soaring palm tree. Clara wore skintight jeans, a black tank-top, and white sunglasses, her golden hair floating in the balmy Gulf breeze.

"So this is the Brownsville–South Padre International Airport," she mused with the pomp of someone checking a monumental milestone off her bucket list.

"The 'International' part is a bit of a stretch," I conceded. "But the border is pretty near."

I heard my dad's pickup truck before I could see it, the brakes squealing as he approached, the truck bed rattling under the weight of whatever tire casings he happened to be hauling.

"Son!" he bellowed, descending from the cab and wrapping his arms heartily around me, his bushy mustache prickling my sun-starved cheek.

I hugged him tightly, longer than I ever had, fearing the moment I'd have to let go, like someone lost at sea who'd just found a sturdy rock to cling to during a tempest.

When I finally loosened my grip, he stood back and turned his gaze to my travel companion.

"You don't look Mexican, not that there's any one way that Mexicans look, but I can tell you're not from around these parts." He smiled broadly, gallantly removing his Stetson hat.

She slowly removed her sunglasses as her lips curved into a dazzling smile. "I'm Clara."

"Yes, you are," he replied, nodding in approval.

As we drove to Grandma Fina's house, my dad gave Clara the royal tour of Brownsville, taking the scenic routes to impress our important delegate from the great city in the North. He took Boca Chica Boulevard so she could catch a fleeting glimpse of our many storied and recognizable fast-food restaurants. Then he rambled down Palm Boulevard so Clara could view our tropical landscaping and historic mansions. This was followed by a circuitous route through downtown so he could point out Market Square and the Cathedral of the Immaculate Conception.

Finally, we traversed International Boulevard and headed down Lincoln Street to Grandma Fina's humble home, the summer-scorched yard in full desiccation mode. I was chagrinned to see a long picnic table set out beneath the large tree in the front yard. A slew of family members loitered in the shade of its broad canopy, waiting for our arrival.

Grandma Fina was flanked by Cousin David who sported long hair and a mustache of his own, my mom in a flowery dress, Rubén clinging precariously to his walker, Little Bobby—whose nickname was now ironic—hulking in a taut muscle T-shirt, and Uncles Nick and David chain-smoking in the background. It was a veritable family reunion. My innards twisted. We were far from the Hamptons. What would Clara think? There were no art collectors or record-label executives here. No investors or venture capitalists. No real estate developers or Ivy League graduates. Just my familia. Just the López clan.

As I stepped down from my dad's rattletrap pickup truck, the brown grass crumbled beneath my shoes. Just as I feared I'd made a terrible mistake bringing her along, the family's eyes collectively shifted from me to Clara. As jaws dropped, eyes widened, and audible gasps arose from the audience, I realized I had nothing to worry about. As misguided and objectifying as it was, there was no doubt in my mind that in their limited view I was returning home as a bona fide conquistador, and I was delivering to their dusty and dilapidated doorstep a sparkling and unprecedented symbol of none other than the unreachable, unrivaled, inimitable American Dream.

———

There were many macho slaps on the back and bear hugs exchanged. Everyone from Cousin David to Uncle Nick seemed fully confident that I was in the process of putting the López clan on the map. I wasn't sure how a family got on a map since it wasn't a geographic location, but I understood the point and let go of the incongruous metaphor.

At the picnic table, Clara deftly eluded the clamoring López men by cornering my mother into conversation.

"So what do you do?" Clara probed.

"Nothing really," my mother modestly demurred.

"What do you mean nothing? You have to do something. There are a lot of hours in the day," Clara insisted.

I ripped a napkin into shreds beneath the table, worried whether Clara's brash northeastern style would rub my parents the wrong way.

"Well, I do take care of Rubén," my mom conceded.

Unabashed, Clara asked, "And Rubén has what?"

I cringed, grabbing an ice-cold Corona that Cousin David placed in my hand and taking a long swig.

My mother balked a bit, but politely pushed on, "The list is long. There's cerebral palsy . . ." She lowered her voice to a whisper. "Some doctors say mental retardation, but Ramón's father won't accept that."

"Uncle Joe punched the last doctor who told them that," David interjected as he eavesdropped gleefully.

"And there's the Dandy Walker's Syndrome. That's why he can't walk on his own," my mother explained.

"He's made a lot of progress though," I noted, hoping to steer the conversation in a positive direction. "He's grown a lot too."

"Yes, yes, he's doing well. When he was a baby, a neurologist told us he would be in a vegetative state and that we should put him in an institution, but we refused. And now, he's in school. He's talking. He's learning to read. And he's getting around with his walker."

Clara processed that for a bit. "So you're a full-time caregiver."

My mom nodded.

"And what else?"

I winced.

"Well, I clean house. I make beds. I wash dishes. I do laundry."

"And what else?"

"Well, there's the baking. I do that to help pay the bills because . . ." She lowered her voice even further than the previous time. "Ramón's dad's business is sometimes not too steady, you know."

"Uncle Joe's an entrepreneur," Cousin David added unapologetically. Heads bobbed up and down along the picnic bench as my dad either pretended to not hear any of the conversation or was thoroughly lost in his thoughts about his prodigal son and his gringa girlfriend.

Not one to get thrown off track, Clara continued. She was like a dogged investigative journalist dissecting a fascinating foreign leader. "Baking? Like what, cookies?"

"Sure. Cookies, pies, sandwiches, taco trays. Also, cakes for the birthdays and the weddings and the quinceañeras."

"So people pay you to cook?"

I half-expected Clara to take out pen and paper and start jotting notes.

"Tía Marisol invented the Sandwichón," Cousin David boasted.

"What a lovely name! Marisol . . ." Clara smiled gloriously, reaching for my mom's hand. "You're an amazing woman."

My mom blushed, unaccustomed to attention and accolades. "No, no. I'm just doing the best that I can, with God's help. And with Grandma Fina's help too. Without her, I don't know where I'd be after losing my own mother."

"Well I think you're incredible," Clara proclaimed. "You're a special needs caregiver, a homemaker, a wife, and a businesswoman with a blossoming catering company. Most importantly, you're a mother, and a good one at that, from everything Ramón has told me. I'm so glad I got to meet you."

I was worried Clara's words might come across as condescending, but her delivery was so genuine and her charisma so overpowering that suddenly it seemed everyone at the table was seeing my mother for who she truly was for the very first time.

"What's a 'sandwichón?'" I turned to Cousin David in utter confusion.

Finally, my dad—quietly hunched over his food all this time—cleared his throat. All eyes turned to him. The López men were notoriously mercurial. Would his macho side lash out at all this praise being heaped on his typically under-the-radar wife? Or would he manage to get through the moment without embarrassing us all in front of our honored guest from New York?

I watched my mom's face turn to stone as she stared down at her uneaten barbecue plate. Rubén even held his spoonful of ketchup tenuously aloft, waiting to put it into his mouth.

Slowly, my father rose from his seat at the far end of the table, resolutely knit his eyebrows together, and glowered at us all. "Esta mujer, this woman . . ." he motioned with his beer bottle in my mother's direction, ". . . is a saint. My sons and I have been blessed by her. ¡Salud!" He raised the beer in my mother's honor.

"¡Salud!" the family chanted happily.

My mom and I sighed in relief, our eyes meeting as we smiled gratefully. Meanwhile, Clara shifted her interest to Rubén. It was the first time I ever heard him engage in a conversation with somebody, beyond his typical requests for more food, CDs, and batteries. The López men brandished their guitars, belting boleros beneath the giant avocado tree, accompanied by the cicada rhythm section. Awash in forgotten comfort, I wrapped my arm around Clara, closed my eyes, and basked in the moment.

———

The next day, Clara and I observed as my mother and Grandma Fina labored lovingly over their signature culinary creation. El Sandwichón turned out to be an absurdly long, multilayered sandwich assembled on a massive tray. It was custom ordered for large parties and then cut into slices and distributed like cake. Apparently, it was taking the city's social scene by storm, overshadowed only by the apparition of the Virgin Mary's likeness on a gnarled and ancient cottonwood tree. After several servings of my mother's decadent delicacy, I borrowed Grandma Fina's beige Beetle and took Clara downtown to witness the divine spectacle.

As we drove past used clothing stores and shuttered movie theaters, it became painfully obvious that Brownsville had hit hard times. Maneuvering past Elizabeth Street, downtown's main drag, I made a beeline for the towering Texas Commerce Bank sign. There on Levee Street, a crowd gathered around an enormous tree in front of a boarded-up wooden shack. Before I could find a parking spot along the car-lined street, Clara hopped out of the car, her fancy camera strapped around her neck.

"I'll catch up to you," I mumbled to myself as I parked a couple of blocks away.

As I approached the reverential throng, I spied Clara near the tree trunk. Her hair glinted in the sunlight like a royal crown as she towered over her subjects. The prayerful susurrations of the faithful were occasionally punctuated by the clicking sound of a camera shutter.

"She's a real beauty," a familiar voice whispered into my ear.

I turned to see my old friend Dante, smiling at me.

"Who, La Virgen?" I asked.

"No, your girlfriend."

As was the custom in Brownsville, just as in México, we embraced tightly, patted each other three times on the back, and gruffly shook hands to shake off the display of affection.

"She could make this place famous," Dante continued.

"Who, my girlfriend?"

"No, dummy, La Virgen." He smiled mischievously.

I chuckled. "It's good to see you."

"You too, Bro."

"How'd you know that was my girlfriend?"

"C'mon. I may have needed your tutoring, but I'm no idiot."

"Understood."

"I always knew you'd do great things." Dante said. "Looks like you're a hit up in New York."

"Well, I'm trying."

"No, man. You're doing."

"What about you? You playing ball in college somewhere?"

"No, man. Just working. Trabajando."

I nodded, "No hay otra." This was the ritual response to the traditional answer to my question. Work was pretty much all anyone around here did. After the school years came the work years. And those lasted a very long time, basically until you died.

"Are you disappointed in me?" Dante asked, his eyes betraying hints of fear and shame.

"No way. I'm sure you're doing what you need to do."

"I'm working at the Pronto Mart on Paredes Line Road."

I hesitated uncomfortably. How had this guy—who had not long ago lorded over the football field and ruled the corridors of Porter High—ended up working at a run-down convenience store? It wasn't even a Circle K or 7-Eleven.

We both stared somberly at the tree, unsure of what to say next. Fortunately, the crowd parted like the Red Sea as Clara emerged, still snapping photos as she came toward us.

"You guys have to get in there and see that," Clara urged, lowering the camera after one last close-up. "It is frickin' unbelievable."

"It's a miracle," Dante explained, his voice devoid of sarcasm.

"This is my old friend Dante," I introduced them. "Dante, this is my girlfriend, Clara."

"Oh my God, *the* Dante?" Clara oozed. Already having acclimated to the cultural customs, she threw her arms around his broad shoulders and planted a kiss on his rosy cheek. "You've got the face of a cherub. I've heard so much about you. You're this guy's hometown hero." Turning to me, she asked, "How many times did he save your life?"

"Countless," I answered.

Dante lowered his head sheepishly. "He's always liked to make things look better than they are."

"That's what an artist does, isn't it?" Clara smiled.

Together, the three of us approached the tree, threading our way through the crowd of worshippers. As Clara snapped away and Dante—entranced by the apparition on the trunk—reached out to trace its delicate lines, I marveled at how lucky they seemed. For Clara, this was either the equivalent of a carnival sideshow or a fleeting flirtation with cultural anthropology, a subject to scrutinize and memorialize, potentially even exploit for some artistic purpose. For Dante, and the others assembled about us incanting prayers in Spanish, this event was a miracle, and its witnessing was an act of passionate faith. Why could I muster up no emotions beyond confusion and discomfort? I had been raised Catholic, taught to believe, even been instructed by nuns for years, but still I was filled with doubt. For Clara, it was fine to observe this phenomenon as a detached outsider. Nobody expected her to believe. But I couldn't help but feel that my skepticism rendered me deficient in some capacity, either as a Mexican American, a local, or at the very least as a member of the devout López clan. What was wrong with me? Had I simply become too American? My eyes sank into the grooves which formed the outline of La Virgen's head within the mysterious bark. My troubled gaze followed their shape, tilting in the classic, sympathetic pose of most artistic representations of the Virgin Mary. There was no denying the likeness, but had this simply been a random act of nature, an odd occurrence bound to happen on one tree eventually due only to the sheer numbers of trees in the world and the countless patterns that could emerge on their surfaces? Or was this truly an act of God? Was there even a difference? Was La Virgen truly here to help the myriad needy and poor and sick of the Rio Grande Valley, as many local parishioners and pilgrims from afar contended? I yearned to touch the trunk, to caress the slightly smoother plane that formed La Virgen's soft cheek, but something held me back, some invisible force. I felt unworthy, lacking in faith. I feared the multitude would see right through me and begin casting stones.

My reverie was shattered by a boy staring in our direction. Innocently, he asked his mother, "Can I take a picture with her?"

When the mother nodded and motioned for him to stand next to the tree and pose, the boy giddily bounded toward Clara, who instinctively took his hand. A round of suppressed chuckles rippled through the crowd as the mother shook her head, sighed, and took the picture of her son and the golden-haired apparition. Our Lady of Levee Street lurked out of focus in the background.

We took a few more pictures, bid adios to Dante, and strolled hand in hand to the car.

"You rescued me from an uncomfortable exchange with Dante earlier," I confessed. "I don't even remember telling you about him and his high school heroics."

As she ducked into the car, she winked at me naughtily. Clearly, I didn't remember because I'd never told her. She'd somehow made it all up and yet been spot on. Smooth and silky. That's how she rolled.

———

After a few days of stuffing ourselves with Grandma Fina's cooking, lounging on the beach, and partying with Cousin David and Little Bobby, the time neared for our return to New York. Clara urged me to take her to Sunrise Mall, where she flashed her Black Card to procure a trove of parting gifts for the family. I was worried that somehow her generosity would backfire and be perceived as patronizing charity, but she selected each present with such meticulous insight that each recipient's face lit up like a little kid's on Christmas morning. Grandma Fina received an apron worthy of Betty Crocker. My mom got a book about the rise of female entrepreneurs. Cousin David got a hand-tooled belt with a gleaming silver buckle that was sure to enhance his Cowboy Rocker look. He vowed to wear it onstage. Rubén salivated over a Sony Discman with a massive packet of batteries. And for my dad, Clara chose a bolo tie. He struggled to contain his smile as he put it on beneath his Stetson, looking every bit the vaquero Tejano.

Out on the back porch, sitting in the rusted rocking chairs after Clara's gift-giving ceremony, my dad pensively stroked his mustache, squinting into the lush backyard with a wistful air, as if he were contemplating the Rocky Mountains or Lake Titicaca. The intricately etched silver slide clip on his new bolo tie glinted in the golden light of the setting sun. I waited for him to dispense his judgment. After an exasperatingly long wait, he began.

"Your friend has a good heart," he spoke slowly.

I could hear Clara and Rubén laughing indoors as she taught him how to operate his bright yellow musical gadget. I nodded respectfully and waited for the inevitable conditions and disclaimers to follow.

"But . . ."

The chairs rocked creakily as we swayed.

" . . . you have to be very careful," he said.

I wasn't sure if he meant "careful" as in avoiding an unwanted pregnancy or "careful" as in wary of not hurting her feelings, or "careful" as in not getting in over my head and ending up devastated myself. Maybe he meant all of the above?

"Careful, how?"

After several oscillations he proceeded. "A woman like that will have certain . . . requirements."

I shifted uncomfortably in the hard metal seat as he weighed his next words.

"It is clear she comes from money, but she also has been taught how to use it, and—more importantly—how to treat people that don't have it."

I nodded.

"She's good people. Right now she's young and you're an exciting and interesting friend. But as time passes, and she matures, she will need to be with her own kind."

It pained me to hear his words. Was he being racist? And, if so, was he prejudiced against her or me? Did he perhaps mean she could not possibly choose to stay with me because of the color of my skin, my heritage, the very background that he had raised me to be proud of and to cherish?

"Don't get me wrong," he added quickly, as if he could read my troubled mind. "I don't mean that she belongs with other gringos. I mean she'll need to be with someone who can maintain her in the lifestyle in which she has grown up, someone who can be her equal."

A current of anger shot through me. "And you don't think that could be me?"

"I didn't say that. I just think you should move slowly. Don't get ahead of yourself. Make yourself into someone that's strong enough to swim against those currents before you wade too deep into the waters. Think of her like the ocean out at Boca Chica Beach, where the river flows into the sea. The waters are warm and inviting. On the surface they are still. But underneath, like I taught you when you were little, the currents can pull you out, drag you down, drown you if you're not careful."

I wasn't sure whether I should feel grateful for his advice or be insulted by his lack of faith in my prospects. On the other hand, young artists weren't exactly known for raking in the big bucks. Did he have a point?

"The last thing you want to do is become a mantenido," he concluded, his voice laced with disdain.

A "mantenido" was a kept man, the antithesis of an independent macho like my dad. It was somewhat ironic since, at various times, he and his brothers had all depended on Grandma Fina's open-door policy and their own wives' resourcefulness for shelter and survival. He wasn't simply being racist and classist; he was topping that off with some old-fashioned sexism to boot.

"You'll see, Dad," my voice trembled. "I'm going places. I'm working hard. I've got my dreams. And I'll make you—and Clara—proud." My throat tightened with pent-up emotion, forcing me to stop there. I wasn't sure if I was trying to convince him or myself.

I could not bear to hear any more of my father's unsolicited wisdom, to be made to feel even less worthy of Clara and more doubtful about my future prospects. Standing abruptly, I headed inside, the screen door swinging shut behind me more loudly than I'd expected. Startled by the clapping sound, I turned and caught him looking at me through the metal mesh. I couldn't discern whether his expression was one of disappointment or yearning for the innocent child I'd once been, the son still full of undefined promise.

———

On the flight back to New York, Clara could not stop talking about Brownsville. She rhapsodized about the place like it was up there with such exotic destinations as Istanbul, Cairo, Kyoto, or Hong Kong.

Exasperated, I finally asserted, "It's Brownsville," struggling to hide my bitterness. "Get over it."

"Didn't you have a great time?" Concern filled her face, softening its angles.

"Yes, yes, but I'm ready to return to school and work." Something about being back in Brownsville unnerved me. Moments like those spent beneath the shade of the holy tree made me feel like a stranger in my own home. If I didn't belong there, where in the world would I ever fit in? Every day magnified my insecurities and increased my fear that the gravity of my birthplace would deepen exponentially with each passing second, eventually preventing me from ever escaping its grasp again. It was an instinctive dread nearly impossible to explain to someone like Clara, whose home was a metropolis where everything happened and dreams were built into reality as opposed to a small town where nothing ever changed and dreams were born to die.

"I can't wait to develop the photos of the tree." She closed her eyes, no doubt envisioning the images she'd captured. "You should use them to make a series of paintings."

"I don't need you to tell me what to paint," I snapped, surprising even myself with how curt I sounded.

Immediately, I could tell my angry words stung like an unwarranted slap across her graceful cheeks.

I yearned to apologize, but I couldn't bring myself to do it. I wallowed in my confused macho bitterness. Who did she think she was, anyway?

She sulked silently for the rest of the flight. Even though we were inches apart from each other in the first-class seats she'd paid for, I might as well have been back in coach by the stinky bathrooms.

When we landed in New York, instead of inviting me to her apartment to frolic in her king-sized bed, she parted awkwardly outside the baggage claim. Her chauffeur whisked her away in the shiny black sedan as I rode the bus to the subway station, took the train to campus and my tiny cinder-block cell.

Holed up in my dorm room as it snowed outside, I sat on the floor and wept. What was wrong with me? How could I carry so much bitterness about where I came from that I would let it imperil where I was going? Despite my negative ruminations on the airplane, and my resentment toward Clara for falling in love with Brownsville and my family, the truth was I already missed them both. Wiping the tears from my eyes, I reached for my tools.

Through the long night, I painted the puzzling place I already missed even though I'd woken up there that very morning. I envisioned and replicated the silhouettes and outlines I yearned to see again, the familiar comforts of the place I'd been born to love and grown to hate.

Swirls and slashes of vibrant acrylic poured like blood from my veins onto canvas after canvas. I didn't care if anyone ever saw them as long as I knew they existed. I placed them on my dorm room walls like windows into a distant world far from here, far from the cold and the bleak and the brutal, scintillating memories of heat and sweat, love and labor.

Channeling a handful of my favorite artists—Henri Rousseau, Wilfredo Lam, Frida Kahlo—I sensed the echoes of my past and the roar of my present harmonize and resonate in my voice. Unspoken but seen. Unheard but felt.

Palm trees jutting defiantly into the turquoise sky. The river carved deep like a wound, snaking east toward the Gulf of México, a blur of red, white, and blue streaking along the northern bank. Me on my daredevil bicycle before I knew better. The river yet again, shimmering beneath the blasting sun. A hazy figure emerging from the verdant reeds on the levee across the treacherous waters. A hint of a Stetson crowning his head. Was it my father? I could not tell but I suspected he was there, still watching me, still worrying, still wondering what I might become in this faraway land. Shiny wet gobs of green. The lush lime tree towering in Grandma Fina's tropical garden, laden with glistening green gems reincarnated from my dad's desiccated dream. Hibiscus flowers opening like ripe red fruit. A lone bee, rendered in a flash of saffron and onyx stripes and graceful gossamer wings, not lost in the jungle but rather seeding it.

Slick with paint and perspiration, I collapsed on my rickety bed. Resting atop my frayed childhood sarape, I dreamed not of the big city and its spoils, but of home and its fertile soil. And at last, for a fleeting night, I slept warmly beneath a blanket of memory.

———

A few days later, she called me, acting like nothing had ever happened. We met at her workspace in Soho. It was a full floor-through in an old cast-iron building inhabited by a handful of other performers, artists, and dancers. She'd set up a recording booth in one corner, where she and her band lay down demo tracks. In another area, she'd erected a makeshift dark room for developing film. I marveled at all the space she had access to, from her parents' Upper East Side townhouse with five floors of museum-quality art and antique furnishings to the compound in the Hamptons, from her Upper West Side penthouse with views of Central Park to this vast wood-floored, stamped-ceiling artist's loft in the neighborhood where luminaries like Warhol and Basquiat had lived and worked. She semi-apologetically explained it was good to have a space to go to work. I couldn't help but agree, especially when it was a space like this.

Standing by the soaring arched windows overlooking Grand Street, she asked me to wait while she brought something out. A few moments later, she emerged from the darkroom's black velvet curtains carrying an easel and a bolt of gray fabric.

"What's this?" I asked.

"My way of apologizing." She unfurled the drop cloth onto the floor beneath the windows, setting the stand atop it.

"Apologizing for what?" I was flummoxed.

"I shouldn't have told you what to paint. I didn't mean to boss you around. I was just in a creative brainstorming mood." She nervously swept her blond hair behind her ears, jamming her hands into the back pockets of her jeans. In the light filtering through the windows, her indigo eyes glowed like twin gems, sparkling in their search for needless forgiveness.

"I'm the one that should be sorry." I shook my head. "And I am. I shouldn't have snapped at you. Going home just affects me in strange and confusing ways. It's like living in two worlds at once. It's hard to find a balance."

"Thanks for taking me with you. At least now I can understand where you're coming from. Seriously though, I won't tell you what to paint, but if you want to work here alongside me, you're welcome. The light's good, right?"

"You look stunning in it."

She smiled and pulled me toward her, our lips meeting as our silhouettes became one. "I think we both just get edgy when it's been too long. And there was nowhere to do it at Grandma Fina's house."

She led me by the hand to the mattress flung on the floor in the back of the apartment. I followed as my heart pounded in anticipation.

———

Outside, the sky was dark, but the streetlights diffused an eerie orange glow into the loft. The fire escape attached to the exterior of the building cast intricate shadow works across the glossy floor. My eyes traced Clara's nude form across the rumpled sheets, mapping every square inch of her smooth pale skin, her lustrous hair. I yearned to paint her and only her, to capture her poetic majesty, her overflowing heart, her casual courage, and her brazen imagination. But despite my initial reaction on the airplane, I knew she was right. I needed to paint that tree—La Virgen's likeness carved cryptically into it by the inscrutable genetic code of nature herself. I yearned to channel the image of Our Lady of Levee Street onto canvas the same inexplicable way La Virgen de Guadalupe had miraculously been emblazoned onto the innards of Juan Diego's leather tilma in the misty mountains of the Valley of México. I wanted to be a conduit for something greater than myself and my earthly desires. I longed to believe in something not because others did so, or because I was told by my elders that it was the right thing to do, but because— with every fiber of my being—I simply knew it to be true, to be real, to pulsate with power that resonated in each and every one of my cells.

My eyes drifted expectantly to the easel, standing empty and aloof by the windows, a skeleton waiting to be draped with flesh. Tomorrow, I would study the photos hanging in the dark room, stretch a canvas, and commence my labor of love. Clara would pen a song about blind faith and those sorry souls desperate enough to cling to it, no doubt strumming guitar chords that conjured up daydreams of angels playing on harps before the disruptive boom of a heavy rock drumbeat and the dissonant thunder of an electric rhythm guitar tore the bark off the tree.

The future looked wide open as my hungry eyes grazed over the curved landscape of Clara's skin outlined in the haunting auburn light. But I worried that like any apparition, either it might not be real or it simply wouldn't last long. At that moment I realized I could not wait until tomorrow to capture my vision or else it might slip away. The miraculously grooved image of the Virgen on the tree flashed through my mind, beckoning me, compelling me. I had to begin now. Stealthily, I rose. I peered at the photos in the shadows. I stretched the canvas in the bathroom to not wake Clara. My breath shallow with anticipation, as my brush hovered over the blank surface, I balked for an instant, my eyes fluttering shut, the image I envisioned disrupted by nagging doubt. What if I wasn't good enough? What if my promise would prove to be as mercurial as Uncle Bobby's had been? What if nothing was real unless you believed in it with the blind faith of a pilgrim? In that moment, I was unsure whether to pray or to paint, but I chose to dip my brush into a color so dark that in the inky light its true hue eluded me.

NO TIME TO SAY GOODBYE

Our Lady of Levee Street propelled me to new heights. I chose to render the apparition as a duotone of sorts. To play off the dichotomous supernatural and natural aspects of a divine manifestation on an actual product of nature, the tree trunk, I painted the series of canvases in black and white with touches of deep, dark green. It was as if black-and-white pictures had been converted into photorealistic paintings and then flourishes had been colored in, leaves and moss and grass, nature's flesh on supernature's skeleton. I felt this color choice was a nod not only to nature but also to La Virgen de Guadalupe, whose resplendent cloak shimmered like an emerald. But perhaps the most enthralling paintings of the series were the ones in which Our Lady of Levee Street was not in sharp focus on center stage, but rather blurred in the background. Modeled faithfully after the photos Clara had taken at the site, in these images the adoring pilgrims were rendered crisply. And in the most dazzling one of all, Clara herself was standing next to a young boy holding her hand, both smiling for the audience.

The paintings were somewhat of a sensation within the art department at the Union. When I graduated, there was an exhibit at which my professors waxed philosophically about the potential of my work to transcend the issues of culture and race and render those borders and barriers moot as we confronted as humans—regardless of our earthly differences—the immutable boundary between the physical and the ethereal, the natural and the supernatural, the living and the after-living. It was an intoxicating environment in that campus art gallery. As champagne flutes were circulated to nourish the heady mood, Clara strolled up in a slinky gold dress with a silver-haired man in a white suit and purple tie on her arm.

"This," she said, "is Montgomery Franklin."

I opened my mouth to speak but unapologetically paused in my tracks. My eyebrows rose in awe. He was a New York City art scene icon. He owned his own gallery in Soho and had represented some of the greats of the pop art scene, including Andy Warhol, Roy Lichtenstein, and Lee Krasner. Clara recounted how they'd met at one of her daddy's investment bank's parties at Studio 54, as I nodded and swigged my Louis Roederer, swiping a replacement off a passing tray.

Cards were exchanged and talk ensued about representation and a show and international buyers, and how he was there to help artists build their long-term oeuvres. I was thrilled, of course, swooning in the high-society swirl, but as Montgomery Franklin waxed poetic about bodies of work, all I could do was consume Clara's glittering presence.

———

As senior year had drawn to a close, my mother had regretfully informed me that—yet again—they could not afford to fly up for my graduation. She sounded even smaller than usual through the tinny telephone speaker. They'd never been beyond the border, she explained by way of apology. Clearly, the first López to graduate from college would not be enough to merit the sacrifice. My initial reaction, as usual, was anger. Couldn't my parents have seen this day coming years ago and planned for its eventuality? Why was the concept of savings more difficult for them to grasp than a fish swimming in the Laguna Madre? But as she rambled on about all of their financial woes due to Rubén's ever-expanding needs and appetites, the resentment faded and I was left unsure whether I was disappointed or relieved. On one hand, I felt alone and unappreciated, adrift in New York's vast urban chaos without a familial anchor. On the other hand, it was hard to imagine my parents in the city. On the border, my dad strutted like a king, his white guayabera a regal tunic, his Stetson hat a defiant crown, but on the streets of Manhattan, he would be seen as a caricature of himself. And my mom, she was barely beginning to emerge from her shy shell. In Brownsville, she was a budding businesswoman as Clara had pointed out, but in New York, she would be shocked back into her turtle shell, a timid provincial woman unable to process the magnitude of her surroundings. It was better, I assured myself, that I handle this phase of my life on my own.

When my mom handed my dad the phone, he spoke gruffly. "Congratulations, son. You will be our first college graduate. That papelito, that little piece of paper you'll have in your hands is something nobody can ever take away from you."

"Thanks, Dad."

"So when are you coming home?"

"I don't know," I stalled, as I always did. It had become somewhat of a shtick. He would ask and I would evade, delay, and prevaricate. Then, he would relent and I would thank God for him letting me off the hook and not pressing any further.

"If you have the summer free, I could use your help," he pushed.

"Oh?"

"Yes, I'm thinking of moving us back to Brownsville and bringing the plant too."

"Really? Why now?" They'd been living on the southern side of the Rio Grande for eight years.

"Well, son," he sighed. "It turns out maybe you were right."

"What?" I couldn't believe what I was hearing.

"Moving to México might not have been the best idea after all."

My dad had never admitted being wrong, ever. "Why do you say that?"

"The Maña is trying to extort all the local businesses, demanding what they call 'protection fees.' It's basically so they don't simply take your business or your money straight out of your hands."

The Maña was a sort of Mexican mafia that dealt in all sorts of organized crime, including kidnappings but also basically holding small
businesses hostage while draining their profits. "So why are you also
thinking of moving the family and not just the business?" I asked.

"Well, Ramoncito," he answered, a sharp pain evident in his voice,
"the Maña is not the only one pressuring me. So is the Brownsville Independent School District."

"The BISD?" I asked, the overlords of my alma mater Porter High
School? How dare they?

"Yes, they told us that if we don't move back to Brownsville, your
brother, Rubén, will not be able to continue attending the school and
receiving the special ed he needs. And he's making great progress, he
really is. He's reading. He's writing. He's coming out of it, Ramón. Soon,
he'll be walking, I just know it."

"He does walk, with his walker," I clarified.

"Yes, but I mean on his own, without help."

I grimaced, knowing that he would not be aware of my disapproval,
but wallowing in it anyway.

"I guess it makes sense," I mustered.

"What does?

"The BISD wanting you to live in the district. After all, property
taxes fund their schools. If you don't live in the city, you don't pay taxes.
If you stay in México, you're benefiting from the public schools and their
services without paying for them."

My dad hesitated for a long time on the other end of the long-distance
phone line. I could picture him stroking his mustache and staring at
Rubén spooning his ketchup tableside.

Finally he spoke. "You deserve to be the first López to graduate
from college. The nuns told me that you were the smartest kid they'd
ever seen."

"What? What are you talking about?" How had he never mentioned this before?

"The first year you were there at the nuns' school, you took some
sort of national test . . ."

"One of those achievement tests?"

"Yes, that's it. Anyway, after that they called me for a meeting, and the Mother Superior, that Sister Marie Antoinette that shut down your chile business, she told me that you had scored off the charts, higher than anyone in the history of not only the school, but the whole town. She said you were destined for something special, something only our Lord could decide."

"Obviously she didn't think it was selling chile."

He laughed, and then I thanked him for telling me all that, and we said goodbye.

Afterward, I realized I couldn't recall if I'd ever heard him laugh before.

———

Surviving without a regular nine-to-five job after college is tough, to say the least. Nobody had prepared me for that cruel reality. Sure, there was an Office of Career Services at the Union, but none of the jobs were titled "Emerging Latino Artist" or "Brilliant from Brownsville." Luckily, I had Montgomery Franklin's crisp, sleek business card with print so small and fine that it almost disappeared into the endless white space around it.

I met with Montgomery at his gallery on Spring Street, on the ground floor of one of those cast-iron buildings with the bubbled glass inserts on the metal steps leading up to the door. In fact, it was a short stroll from Clara's studio.

Montgomery's assistant, a comely Japanese woman dressed in a striking black kimono, placed a glass of Chardonnay in my hand as he gave me a tour of the space. He rambled about the many greats he'd represented and how all it would take was one respected collector to fall in love with my work for my future to be cemented. There were contracts signed, all standard of course. And then, as champagne was poured, he disbursed his creative direction, which he assured me was a critical part of his role.

"Listen, Ramón." He sat behind his vast white marble desk, fidgeting with his purple tie. "I love your style . . . but . . . there's just one thing."

"Yes?" I leaned in, setting my bubbly down in anticipation.

"Your portfolio is very, how can I put it delicately . . ." He squinted up at the lofty ceiling as if he might find the answer there. "It's very . . . ethnic."

"I'm Mexican American."

"Yes, yes, of course." He waved his hand as if to dispel smoke being blown in his face. "But do you think wealthy art collectors really want to hang pictures of poor people and Mexican idols and barrio gang members on the walls of their penthouse apartments and townhomes?"

I stared back at him nonplussed. "So, what are you saying?"

"I'm saying, if you want your first show to sell, you have to give them what they want, something they can understand. And if, in the process, it makes them feel a little better about themselves—and where all their riches come from—to support an ethnic artist, then more power to us."

I scrunched up my eyebrows the same way my father always did, disapprovingly. "I see. And what do they want?"

Opening my portfolio, he leafed through photos of my work to date. Eventually, he arrived at some of the pieces from my series on Our Lady of Levee Street, stopping at the one of Clara holding the young boy's hand in front of the sacred tree.

I stared at the image of the painting. It was lifelike, were it not for the color scheme, which rendered it surreal. If it weren't mine, I would still be in awe of it, I thought. But was it really the best piece? Or was it simply what this market could relate to, as Montgomery characterized the matter?

"This is what they want," he pontificated. "Beauty."

I nodded, unsure whether I understood or was simply pretending.

———

As Clara lay down tracks with her band at the back of the studio, I painted up front by the arched windows. Often, I would sneak into the recording area and watch her sing her heart out in the isolation booth, take mental notes or actual photos with her camera, and run to the easel to capture images of her in the midst of her ascent. Her voice rang along the metal pipes clinging to the whitewashed, stamped ceiling. Guitar riffs and drumbeats thundered beneath my feet through the hardwood floors as my paint flowed onto the canvases.

When the frenetic burst of creativity concluded, my art show opened to a designer-clad crowd, courtesy of Montgomery Franklin's Rolodex and Clara's family connections and club memberships. I stood frozen, like a javelina in headlights. Black jeans. Black turtleneck. Blank mind. The only painting sold went to Clara's mom and dad, despite her declaration that they never risked their own funds. At dinner in a lofty aerie with floor-to-ceiling glass walls, glumly sipping a four-digit bottle of burgundy while staring glumly at the glittering skyline, I listened dutifully to Clara and her well-intentioned parents make excuses for my abysmal commercial failure. There would be other opportunities, they said. An artist's road was long and arduous, they said. All I had to do was hang in there and keep painting, they said. All I could think of was how much more feasible that would be if I had parents like them bankrolling me as I "developed."

The next day, Montgomery decreed I'd lost my focus. "You drifted away from what made your work unique. If people want to look at pictures of a pretty girl, they can buy a limited edition print of one of Warhol's Marilyns."

"Someday Clara will be as big as her," I retorted in a surly tone.

"Perhaps, but she's not there yet. And you may never be," he concluded bitterly. "I'm afraid we'll have to part ways. But I wish you the best of luck. I can store your unsold paintings," he added. "But I'll have to charge you the standard monthly fee."

I wanted to blame him, this glitzy gallerist, for sending me down the wrong path. But was it his fault or mine? Had I misconstrued his abstract counsel? People like Clara could afford missteps and mistakes. The same could not be said for people like me. What if this was my one chance? No other agents would be lining up for a boy from the border. No cush job at daddy's investment bank waited for me as a safety net. No trust fund sat between me and sleeping on the streets.

I stared at my paintings still hanging on the walls. Not one of them, except the one Clara's parents had so mercifully purchased, had a red sticker by it. They all starred Clara herself, singing, writhing behind the microphone stand, her golden hair undulating Medusa-like as the band jammed behind her. He'd told me to give them what they wanted. Instead, I'd given them what I wanted.

——

When Clara and her band signed their record deal with Arista, there was a blowout party at Studio 54. The best DJs officiated, and Kristal flowed from the open bar. Models from the Ford Agency danced on tables, and Russian oligarchs gathered at the foot of the stage. At the end of the evening, Clara and the boys stormed the stage and played an intense three-song set, the soon-to-be released singles from their album. She wore a gold miniskirt, and her legs seemed as endless as they were flawless from the dingy floor below the footlights. The first hit single had to do with blind faith. I drank hard as I squinted like a nocturnal creature in the dazzling glare of the crowd-scanning laser beams and pulsating strobe lights. Javelina. Deer. Lost dogs. They all met the same fate where I came from.

——

"You should go do this job interview," she urged as we sat at the kitchen table in her penthouse, sipping our morning coffees. "Daddy has it all lined up for you. One of the partners is his yachting buddy."

Yachting buddy? People had those? I had heard of golfing buddies and bowling buddies, but I suspected this was a whole other league.

"Okay," I answered somberly.

"Art takes time, Ramón." She made excuses for my failure. "Nobody makes it right away and everybody needs a day job."

"And you?"

"Well that's just different."

"Different why?"

She hastily drained her coffee and bolted out of her chair, dashing to the elevator. "I've gotta run, but please call them. You can't just sit around and mope while I go on tour."

She was right, I considered, as the elevator doors closed shut behind her tight jeans and silkily flowing white gauze shirt that was probably worth more than my entire bank account had ever seen deposited over the last four years. But then again, the record label that had signed her band was owned by one of her father's venture capital firms, and her apartment and her studio and her clothes were all paid for by some trust fund set up in her name back when I was still sitting on the floor of a temporary classroom at a public grade school in Brownsville.

———

Before heading to the interview at Young & Rubicam, I called my dad at the new phone number he'd given me for the tire shop in Brownsville.

"Son! You made my day!" he exclaimed.

"Thanks, Dad." I smiled.

"How are you?" he asked.

"I'm okay," I lied, thinking of all my unsold paintings and the storage fees I could not afford, and the job I was about to interview for that I didn't really want. "How are *you*?"

"Like always, I'm working hard and making progress, Son," he exalted. He sounded on top of his game, brimming with exuberant energy. "I've got the plant moved back. I just need to reconnect the electricity and order the rubber from Akron and we'll be rocking and rolling." I could picture him standing in that dilapidated shack by the railroad tracks, the faded "Joe's Tire Shop" still dangling outside all these years later, waiting for him to return home.

"And how about the family? When do you all move to the new house?"

"Soon, Son. There's a little place near Grandma Fina's I've got an eye on. It would be great for all of us."

"That's wonderful." I hesitated.

"You can always come home, son. You have to know that."

"I know."

He could sense the solemnity in my tone, the desolation, I was sure of it.

"Remember, Ramón, never give up," he urged. "No matter what challenges you run up against, stay true to yourself, follow your course, never give up."

I suppressed a despondent sigh. "But I thought you didn't want me doing this whole art thing in the first place?"

He took his time, mulling my words. "Son, you have taken a path I would have never imagined or picked out for you. It may not have been the path I would have wanted for you. It seems like a hard way to make a living, painting pictures. But this is your life. These are your choices. You make them. And you should never cower in the face of adversity. Fight. And never give up. Remember how the dicho goes: Cuando la rama cruje, el águila no teme, porque a sus alas se atiene." *When the branch sways, the eagle does not fear, for to its wings it clings.*

I quietly admired his fortitude and perseverance. My instinct was always to cut and run. I had often thought he would have been better off if he did give up, if he hadn't kept trusting in his brothers to run his businesses into the ground or hadn't kept trying to import his perishable produce from México on rickety trucks without the proper permits. But what did I know? Had I ever raised a family? Had I ever paid a light bill? Had I ever taken a disabled child to countless doctors in search of a miracle?

"Thanks, Dad," I said.

"Just be yourself, Son. Be who you are. And don't give up on your dreams to settle for something less, something that serves another master. That's not what you went up to New York for, is it?"

"No, it isn't." I shook my head.

———

Pierre Bernard was a long-haired Eurotrash snob if ever I'd seen one. Unfortunately, he was not only Clara's dad's boating pal, he was also the

Executive Creative Director at one of the hottest ad agencies on Madison Avenue. Pierre brandished his vaguely French accent like it was a flashy souvenir acquired at a trinket shop in the Latin Quarter. He led me through countless hallways and seas of cubicles crammed with artists and copywriters hunched over campaigns in development for an endless name-dropping slew of high-wattage brands. Illustrators sat at drafting tables crowned by massive carrousels filled with an impressive spectrum of colored markers, and boxy beige Macintosh II computers dotted the landscape.

After a tour of several floors in the Midtown building, he showed me into a conference room with an inspiring view of the Chrysler and Empire State buildings gleaming in the midday sun.

As he reviewed my art portfolio, he blinked nervously, asking to see my spec creative advertising campaigns. I told him I didn't have any because I'd studied art, not marketing.

"I see," he huffed. "Well, we have been talking about gambling on a multicultural division. Do you think you could help us sell Coke to Mexicans? Or McDonald's to the Blacks?"

"I'm not sure that's a good idea," I answered naively. "We already drink and eat enough unhealthy stuff. Do we really need it to be sold to us in ways we can't resist?"

"I like your style." He snapped his fingers and jumped toward the whiteboard at the end of the long white table. "Irresistible!" He scrawled the word in red marker. "That's what you'll make our brands and products to Hispanic and Black consumers. Impossible to resist! When spoken to in their own languages and within their own cultures, they will not be able to stop themselves from buying our clients' fast food and soft drinks, their chips and their cookies and desserts, their cereals and their beers and their cigarettes."

"Irresistible. It's the same spelling in English as it is in Spanish," I noted, repeating the word with a Castilian accent, rolling the "r's" for dramatic effect.

"Exactly," he proclaimed. "You just named our new division. When can you start? You'd have to first learn the ropes in our graphic arts department, but you could also work simultaneously on this new concept. Entry-level pay is not that great, but—given your special connections—and your unique potential, I think we could make you a handsome offer. It would certainly beat being a starving artist while running with the likes of Clara."

I hesitated, peering at him suspiciously, wondering if Clara's father had orchestrated all of this down to the salary so that I could keep up with his daughter's social circle and lifestyle. I wondered how many of the brands the ad agency handled were owned by companies in which her father held shares and board positions. "I need to think this over. I am not sure this is exactly what I had in mind."

"Take your time," he delicately placed the red marker on the ledge beneath the board and flashed a saccharine smile at me, his pristine white teeth glowing brightly against the deep orange hue of his artificially tanned face.

————

On the way back to Clara's studio, I pondered the possibilities. Accepting the job would go against everything I'd ever been taught by my father and everything I'd worked toward in my art education, yet at the same time it would help me fulfill my lifelong dreams of financial success, begin to satiate my desire to belong to America's high society. The steady paycheck would enable me to move out of the tiny apartment I was sharing in Hell's Kitchen with a handful of other impoverished artists. I'd be able to pay my way at meals with Clara and not feel like a "mantenido," as my father had termed the ignominious fate of one who married a wealthy woman while remaining unable to provide his fair share. And I could even afford my art storage and supplies as I picked up the pieces of my disintegrating career as a painter. Heck, I could potentially even put my art dreams on hold and spend some time climbing the ladder at Y&R, building that "Irresistible" multicultural division, making a fortune, and blending in with Clara's sophisticated social set. Wasn't that the epitome of the American Dream? Small-town boy makes good in the big city? Wasn't this what I'd come here for, what I had always wanted since I was a young kid selling chile to buy my Evel Knievel bike?

In the elevator up to her floor, I barely recognized myself in the mirrored doors. Who was this fool in a gifted Armani suit? It looked good and it fit perfectly, thanks to Clara's tailor, but something about my reflection just didn't feel right.

I found Clara lounging lazily on a blue velvet sofa in her studio.

"I got an offer," I said, standing awkwardly in front of her, watching her tune a white Fender.

"When do you start?" she asked, not even glancing up from the fretboard.

I felt my father speaking through me as I answered, "I'm going to pass. I have other options."

"Okay," she answered nonchalantly.

Apparently, what tormented me and kept me up at night barely made a dent in her psyche. She was about to go on tour and she had bigger things on her mind, like promotional photo shoots, media interviews, and merchandising agreements, and apparently, tuning guitars. Her group had just been selected as the opening act for some hotshot grunge band from Seattle, and her single was charting on Billboard.

The next time I saw her dad, I was waiting tables at a Mexican restaurant called La Frontera. As my borderline luck would have it, his entourage included Pierre Bernard. In vain, I tried to enlist another server to switch sections with me, but he had his hands full with a large party, so I gritted my teeth and approached the table.

The men didn't bother to look up at me, instead focusing on their menus and placing their orders without meeting my eyes. In shock, I shuffled back to the kitchen to convey their order. Had my black-and-white uniform rendered me invisible to them? Or had they recognized me, playing dumb to spare us all the embarrassment of seeing me in this servile position? I made it through the whole meal without being acknowledged, and when the men left, I found a hefty tip on the table.

After the lunch rush, as the staff ate family style at a long table in the back of the restaurant, I recounted my panicked brush with potential humiliation.

Juan, the head cook, a burly dark-skinned man from Veracruz and the elder of the team, spoke slowly as he chewed on a taco al pastor. "Why be embarrassed? Hard work is not shameful. If you were stealing or dealing drugs, now that would be cause for humiliation. But working here, you should be proud."

I was new to this line of work, and it was not what I had expected after graduating from college, but suddenly I was truly ashamed, not of working there but of having exposed my fear to the rest of the staff, who no doubt had way fewer options than I did at their disposal. "You're right, Juan. My father always said that he who wets his brow with sweat is embarrassed before no one."

"El que de sudor la frente se moja, ante nadie se sonroja," Juan recited the dicho as my colleagues nodded in agreement.

"I'm sorry, I did not mean that I find this work shameful. It's just that these gringos are very rich and I worried they would look down on me," I explained.

"You should have strolled right up to them, said hello, and offered to pay for their lunch with pride!" Juan proclaimed from the head of the table. "I am proud to be from México, and I am proud to cook our delicious cuisine for these rich New Yorkers!"

The group around the table clapped, all of them from various parts of the interior of México, ranging from Yucatán to Oaxaca, from Sinaloa to México City.

"Besides, you had nothing to worry about," one of the line cooks added. "Most gringos don't see us as individuals. Most of them don't recognize or remember our names. We are just here to serve. We are interchangeable. We are invisible to them."

———

Clara broke up with me over the phone. It was somewhat unexpected, but at the same time strangely unsurprising. I was more taken aback by the way she did it than by the fact that she was ready to move on from me. If I were her, I would have dumped me too. I had spiraled into a sad state since declining the advertising job. I was working double shifts at La Frontera to make rent and never had time to see her or to paint at the easel she kept at her studio for me.

"Is it something I've done?" I asked, struggling to steady my voice as I gripped the receiver, pressing it hard against my ear. Had her father mentioned seeing me at the restaurant? I had told her about my job, but I had not revealed the run-in with her dad and Pierre. Was she ashamed of me and my situation? Was she disappointed in my dimming prospects? Or was I simply not interesting anymore?

"No, it's nothing you've done," she claimed. "We're just moving in different directions."

Was that ever the truth. How could I deny it? "I'm just going through a bit of a rough patch, but things will get better."

"It's not you," she insisted. "It's just. Look, I'm about to leave on tour and I'll be gone for months. I just don't think a long-distance relationship at this stage of our lives is going to work for either of us."

Any kind of relationship with her would work for me, I thought. But I could certainly understand that it might not for her. Struggling to contain my tears and keep my voice from cracking, I wished her well and tried to end the conversation as quickly as I could.

"Do you want to come pick up your stuff? I mean, we're still friends, right?" she asked.

"Of course we're friends," I answered. "If you don't mind, keep the easel and the canvases. I don't have room for them."

And that was that. It was over. Nearly three years of my life were down the drain and I had nothing to show for them. I was subsisting in a tiny room barely large enough to contain the mattress on which I slept. When I rolled out of bed, I had to squeeze through the door to access the cramped kitchen and sitting room I shared with my roommates. Our view through the dingy windows was the fire escape and the brick wall across the alleyway. We couldn't even grow a houseplant on the windowsill. We had tried time and again, but the scarcity of sun had killed our dreams.

When I talked to my parents, dragging the telephone's serpentine cord into my room and shutting the door behind me, I had a difficult time concealing the depths of my dejection. Yet I continued to paint a rosy picture for them of my charmed life in New York. Fortunately, my mother was constantly distracted by Rubén's incessant requests and my father seemed absorbed in his latest machinations.

"I've got the electricity connected at the plant and all the molds are tested and ready to go," he informed me in a buoyant mood. "All I need is that rubber, but they want cash. My credit is shot, so I'm trying to gather the funds by selling off old tires here and there. It's a little bit stressful, but it's all going to work out, I'm sure of it." His practiced positivity came across a bit frayed as he strained to convince both himself and me of his latest gambit's impending success.

Instinctively, I changed the subject. "And the family? How's the move going?"

"We just moved into that little house down the street from your Grandma Fina," he replied. "Your mom's been busy settling in. And Rubén now gets picked up by a school bus every morning. I'd never seen a bus so short. He's growing up, that Rubén. He'll surprise everyone, you wait and see." My dad, ever the optimist. "When are you coming home?"

I didn't want to let him—or any of them—down. Coming home in defeat would surely disappoint them. And then, what would become of me? At least for now, my legend remained intact even if I knew I was living a lie. "I don't know, Dad. I'm pretty busy up here."

"So things are going well?"

"Yeah," I forced unconvincingly, my voice wavering and my uncooperative lips drawing the word out longer than they should have, almost turning the answer into a question of its own.

"You can always come home, Son," he assured me, his voice taking on a serious tone.

"I know."

"Has there been a setback?"

"Well, you know, it's up and down. New York's a tough place."

"And the girl? Clara?"

I was afraid to talk about her, dreading that I might break down crying, which was the ultimate taboo in the López clan's macho culture. "She's okay."

"Remember, son, a las mujeres, ni todo el amor ni todo el dinero." It was one of his classic macho dichos. It meant that to women, a man should give neither all of his love nor all of his money.

Suddenly, my sorrow channeled into anger, and my father was the unfortunate and unwitting bystander. "Dad, that's sexist!" I fumed.

"Sexy?" He seemed puzzled.

"No, not sexy. Sexist." Did he even know the meaning of the word?

"Oh, sexist? I don't have anything against women. I'm just giving you advice so you can protect yourself."

"Dad, I've been taking your advice or—in some cases—not taking it, my whole life, and no matter which decision I make, it doesn't seem to work out so well. Do you think maybe something's wrong with your advice?"

My dad took a deep breath before he replied, his tone of voice even and cool. "If no matter what you do, you feel that the outcome is bad, maybe it's not my advice that's the problem. Maybe it's the positions you keep putting yourself in. Have you thought about that?"

He was right. And it made me even angrier. "You ought to know," I concluded.

Undeterred by my defiance, he urged, "Just come home, Ramón. It's not giving up. It's just coming home and getting your feet back on the ground and staking out a new direction, your next move. You're a López. You've always got a next move."

"We'll see," I answered, but it was the last thing I wished to do. After all, things were already so bad, I figured they could only get better from here on out.

———

A couple of weeks later, I was startled to find one of my roommates loitering outside our apartment building when I returned home from the restaurant. He was a tall, scrawny sculptor from the Midwest named

Noah. Next to him on the sidewalk loomed a row of bulging black trash bags. It was dark already and I hadn't noticed them at first.

"What's going on?" I asked.

"We've been booted," Noah explained flatly.

"But why? We were current with our rent."

"Apparently, the guy we were subletting from didn't pay the rent to the owner and we weren't even authorized to be in the apartment." He glanced at his watch and then down at the bags. "I waited for you, but I've got to run, man. This bag has your stuff. The rest is mine."

"And our money?"

"That dude hasn't returned any of our calls. I think he's skipped town," Noah guessed. "We're screwed. I'm gonna go crash at my art studio until I can figure something out. I'd invite you, but it's pretty small and grim and cold."

"Sure. No worries." I nodded, shaking his hand and picking up my belongings. "Good luck."

"See you around." Noah forced a tight smile, grabbed his bags, and rustled away.

I was basically penniless and now homeless. It wasn't winter yet, but the temperature was plunging. Whatever tatters remained of my pride had to give way to sheer necessity at this point. I took the train to the Upper West Side and found myself knocking at Clara's door, my black trash bag at my feet. After a long while, Clara cracked the door open, peering at me suspiciously.

"Ramón. What are you doing here? It's kind of late," she whispered.

"I have nowhere to go. I got evicted from my place. I'm sorry to bother you, but I wondered if I could just stay on your couch until I figure something out."

She balked at my request, glancing furtively over her shoulder. She wore a black silk robe, her hair cascading over it carelessly. "I don't think that's a good idea, Ramón. We don't want to end up in a dysfunctional relationship."

It dawned on me that she was not alone. She hadn't even waited for her tour to start before she moved on from me.

"Oh," I replied awkwardly. "I see. Okay. I get it. Thanks." Slowly, I picked up my bag and dragged it to the elevator.

"I'm sorry," she called out. "I tried to help you." Her voice was laced with pity.

Waiting for the elevator, I stared glumly back at her, garbage bag in hand. That's when it hit me like an express train. She hadn't cared if I turned down that ad agency job, not because she thought I was destined for something greater but because she had already planned to break up with me. She had not been trying to mold me into a suitable partner or potential spouse that could afford to move gracefully in her circles. No, she had simply felt sorry for me. The whole notion had been a way of assuaging her own guilt as she left me in her dust.

As she retreated into her apartment, tears crystallized over my eyes, rendering the cool gray hallway like a fragmented Picasso painting from his cubist era. When the elevator finally arrived, I didn't simply board it. I fled.

———

That night I slept on a bench in Central Park. Garbage bag pillow. Jacket and sweatshirt quilt. Calling it "sleep" would be an exaggeration, however. Between the harsh discomfort of the hard wooden surface, the paranoia that someone would steal what little I had left, and the nagging doubts regarding how I'd ended up in these dire straits, there was little rest to be found beneath the falling leaves of the park. My ruminations ran the gamut from Clara to my father, from my quick fall from grace in the art scene to how I could possibly reverse my current direction in life. Had I lost Clara because of my own bad decisions? Or, truth be told, had I never had a chance at being anything more than an exotic flirtation for her? Was my father correct in wondering whether I was putting myself in positions where there was little choice but a bad one? Should I have sold out to the ad agency in an effort to hang on to my material and personal aspirations? And what could I do now to salvage my fate? There were no easy answers, I realized. But I concluded that going home to Browns-ville would not solve any of my problems. It would simply kick the can down the road for a few weeks or months or—worse even—years. And by then, perhaps all my options of today might be moot and I'd discover myself trapped in a dead-end scenario with no hope of escape. My dad had always said to never give up, so how could I? But was that good advice in every situation? I imagined how he would react if he could see me now, shivering on a bench like a junkie. When I finally dozed off, I dreamed of him staring sadly at me, great pity filling his dark and troubled eyes. And when I awoke, I felt he'd been there in the park watching over me as much as ruing my predicament.

At work, I was so stiff and sore I could barely move. Detecting my state of distress, along with the bulging trash bag I'd brought to the restaurant, Juan pulled me aside between shifts in the kitchen.

"¿Camarada, qué pasa?" he asked. "Something's not right."

He was only about ten years older than me, but he was already married and had young children, so he seemed like enough of a father figure that I suddenly found myself confiding in him, pouring out my sad saga.

"Tonight, after we close up shop, you come home with me to Jackson Heights, okay?" He patted me on the shoulder. "It may be a bit cozy but, hell, I grew up with six brothers and three sisters in a two-room hut in Tampico."

I toiled hard all day, striving to generate some extra tip money. José and I both knew it might take weeks for me to save up enough cash to put down a deposit on a new apartment, not to mention find roommates with whom to split the costs. It was very generous of him to open up his home to me, without even asking his wife. I'd never met her, but I sincerely hoped she would not be disgruntled by my sudden presence.

As we shut down the restaurant, propping the chairs upside down on the tabletops so we could mop the floors, the phone rang. Juan scrambled to pick it up. I wondered if it might be his wife telling him that by no means could he bring a stranger home to spend the night with her and the children. Eavesdropping from around the corner, I immediately discerned that the caller was not his wife. Juan spoke in halting English and then emerged from the hallway with a troubled expression on his round, deeply creased face.

"It's for you," he said. "I think you better take it."

I walked to the small cubbyhole at the end of the corridor, where the phone was located. "Hello?" I asked, growing concerned.

"Ramón?" It was Clara. Her voice sounded strangely fearful.

"Yes?" Had she changed her mind? Did she want me back? She had nothing to fear if that was the case.

"I'm sorry to bother you at work, but your mom called me. She's looking for you, and I guess you hadn't told her about being evicted or where you work . . ."

Or about us breaking up, for that matter, I heard her thoughts. "No. I didn't want to worry her. Is something wrong?"

"You need to call her," her voice wavered. "Call her at your grandmother's house. I'm so sorry," she said hurriedly, her voice cracking before she hung up.

The way the phone was set up, the only way it could be used long-distance was by making a collect call, so I dialed the operator and went through the motions. When I finally got through to Grandma Fina's, I heard Cousin David's voice on the other end of the line.

"Primo," he said softly. I knew immediately that my fears would be confirmed. Something terrible must have happened. Usually, he would have been boisterous and overjoyed to catch up with me. And, besides, what was he doing in Brownsville? He was supposed to be in Austin singing and playing guitar in an up-and-coming rock band.

"Primo," I acknowledged. "What's wrong? I heard my mom has been trying to reach me."

"Yes," he replied in a hushed tone. "Since last night. Hang on a second."

I could hear him whispering to someone in the background. Whoever it was, they sounded like they were crying.

"Listen, Ramón," Cousin David resumed. "Your mom doesn't want to come to the phone right now. The thing is: something's happened to Tío Joe."

"My dad?" My heart skipped a beat. I had thought maybe something was wrong with Grandma Fina given her age, but my dad was relatively young and always bursting with boundless energy and entrepreneurial zeal. "Was there an accident?" Had he been crushed beneath one of the giant tire molds at the tire plant? Had they not been set up properly after the move back from México? Had there been a fire? It was always so infernally hot in there.

"He had a heart attack, Primo. It was a real bad one. The doctors say he might not make it, but you know your dad, he's fighting as hard as he can. He's in the hospital. Your mom wants you to fly down to see him . . . just in case."

I stood motionless at the phone hanging on the wall, unable to speak.

"Primo?" Cousin David asked. "Primo? Are you still there?"

I turned slowly. Juan stood at the end of the hall staring at me glumly, a bucket in one hand and the mop in the other. I wouldn't be imposing on his wife and family after all.

"Yes, David. Okay, tell her I'll get down there tomorrow."

"Do you need us to wire you money for the airplane ticket? Your mom said I should ask."

"That might not be a bad idea," I replied, my hand shaking as we ironed out the details and I placed the receiver back in its cradle.

When I told Juan, he gave me a tight hug and insisted I spend the night at his apartment before heading to the airport in the morning. There, he gave me a faded duffel bag to transfer my belongings into for the trip. I ate his wife's pozole and played video games with his two boys until the three of us fell asleep on the couch. In the morning, I thanked them all for their kindness, picked up my wire at the corner store, and boarded the subway to La Guardia. My time in New York was turning out differently than I had ever imagined. But none of that seemed to matter now. Not Clara. Not my career. No. All I could think about was what I might find in Brownsville when I landed. And as the plane took off, for the first time in many years, I closed my eyes and I prayed.

BETTER PLACES

I always imagined that upon saying goodbye forever to someone vital in my life, the occasion would be momentous and memorable, rife with emotion and closure. What I didn't realize was that—more often than not—none of us know at that very crucial moment that it will turn out to be the last time we see our loved one, the last time we hear their voice or feel their warm embrace. I hadn't been given a chance to say a proper goodbye to Julia and Reeser, or to my Abuelita Carmela. And this is how it now threatened to be with my father.

When I landed in Brownsville, Cousin David was waiting at the gate. He looked like a bona fide rocker in black jeans, a black Fender shirt, and black steel-toe boots. His wavy hair had grown to his shoulders. And although he was thin, he was also tall and broad-shouldered. He might have resembled a menacing modern-day Angel of Death had he not brandished a warm and sympathetic smile as he greeted me with open arms.

"Primo," he murmured.

"How's my dad doing?" I asked as he led me to his car outside.

He simply shook his head as we walked beneath the whispering palms. Even though autumn was here, Brownsville still simmered in scorching heat. I recalled Clara's heels sinking into the supple asphalt when she'd visited.

We cruised quietly in his black GTO, the growl of its formidable engine filling the silence as we drove straight to the old Mercy Hospital on Jefferson Street. There, I went through the motions of an unanticipated and unscheduled family reunion of the worst kind. Uncle Nick, Uncle David, and Cousin Bobby lined the hallway, their backs against the wall. Cousin David left me at the hospital room door. Inside the hushed, cold room I found my mom, Rubén, and Grandma Fina, huddled somberly around my dad, who lay unconscious and intubated on the hospital bed. My mom and Grandma Fina flanked the bed on opposite sides. Rubén sat at the foot of the bed in the only guest chair, his metal walker to his side. After exchanging sober hugs with them, I hovered over my dad's inert form. I'd never seen him at rest, immobilized, not struggling against every obstacle in his world. It was an eerily alien sight to witness. Always, he had been in motion. Up before dawn, cooking breakfast and whistling or singing as the rest of us stirred in our beds, dashing off to work, coming home late covered in the grime from the tire shop. He never took a day off. He never took a vacation. He never lounged by a pool or a beach. He never rested until he was left with no other choice.

"What happened?" I whispered.

"He had a heart attack," my mom answered, staring despondently at him.

"When? Where?"

"He was at the tire plant, working. Someone stopped by, a customer, and he found the keys in the door. The door was open. He went inside and your father was on the floor. The man called 911." My mom recounted the events for what was probably the hundredth time. She sounded more like an emotionless recording than like a mother telling her son that his dad was at death's door.

"So is he going to be okay?" I asked hopefully.

My question was met with silence, except for the rhythmic mechanical breathing of the machines pumping air into his lungs and the steady beeps issuing forth from the heart monitor.

"Mamá?" I prodded.

She looked down at the floor, her knuckles as white as the tiles beneath her feet as she clutched a rosary between her fingers.

"Grandma?" I sought.

She glanced first at Rubén and then back at me. Slowly, she exited the room, something in her gaze silently instructing me to follow.

Out in the hallway, a few feet from the rest of the family, she spoke to me calmly in a hushed tone. "Ramón, the doctors say your father is probably not going to make it."

"What? Why?"

"We don't know how much time passed between his heart attack and when the ambulance got to him, but it might have been a couple of hours. During that time, his heart could not pump enough blood to his brain."

I stared at her in disbelief. "But he's too young."

She nodded in agreement, her eyes wobbling like melting Jello beneath the hospital's unforgiving fluorescent lights.

Grandma Fina, my mom, and I listened—in their due order—to the cardiologist and the neurologist and the doctor in charge of the ICU. Rubén and my father in the background, the cardiologist diligently explained to us that several factors, including multiple arterial blockages, had caused my father's cardiac arrest. When caught quickly, these events could often be resolved through multiple bypass surgery. But when too much time passed between the heart attack and the attempt to intervene, the brain was deprived of essential oxygen. That was when the neurologist stepped in and showed us a bunch of black-and-white images that he said were scans of my dad's brain. None of it made any sense to us, but he explained that what he was seeing in the picture was a brain that was dead. Without oxygen, the brain cells had died. Like when the electricity got cut off, the lights inside my father's mind had been extinguished.

But how could this happen now? He had just gotten his recapping plant up and running again. They had just moved back to Brownsville. They were starting over. And to make matters worse, our last conversation had been horrible. I had questioned him, doubted him, rebuffed him, offended him. He had to wake up. I desperately needed to tell him how sorry I was, for disrespecting him, for disobeying him, for disappointing him. How could we never, ever, speak to each other again? We hadn't even had time to say goodbye.

When the doctors left the room, an administrator shuffled in with a stack of forms. She explained that since my father had no advanced directives or living will, that we—his next of kin—must provide consent to remove life support.

The train was moving so fast and I had not even agreed to step aboard. "What's happening?" I asked.

My mom looked at me with the deepest degree of sadness and compassion I'd ever found in her large brown watery eyes. "We have to give them permission."

"Permission for what?"

"To let him rest," Grandma Fina said.

"I don't know if I can do that."

They looked at each other oddly. And then it dawned on me. It wasn't up to me, was it?

"It's best if we all can come to the same understanding," Grandma Fina said slowly. "None of us want this. But the Lord has called my son home, Ramón. I wish he would take me instead. I would trade my life for his right now, to spare you and Rubén and your mother this pain. But we have to understand. He is already gone. His soul, his mind, his consciousness are already in a better place."

I hated talk of better places. I'd spent my whole life looking for them and I was yet to find them. And, somehow, I had trouble believing that in death any of us would get so lucky as to discover what we couldn't in life.

Standing around his hospital bed again, it was torture to look at him. This man who had dominated whatever room he inhabited—with his macho presence, his bold attitude, his piercing eyes—was now an ashen shell wrapped in wires and tubes. This man who rejoiced in donning his Stetson hat and his pristine guayaberas when he wasn't covered in the grime and soot of his physical labor was now clad in a faded hospital gown. This man who thrived in the heat of his recapping plant or in the liberating breeze of the tiny scrap of ranchland in México that still belonged to our family was now confined to a sterile room surrounded by machines maintaining his body alive.

As the family filled the room, I struggled to breathe. All I could think of was him, his unfulfilled dreams, his tireless spirit, his ambition to get ahead and make a better life for his family, all of it coming to an abrupt end. "He tried so hard," my voice splintered as I fought back the sobs.

I felt a hand on my shoulder and turned to look at my Uncle David's face looming over me. "No, Ramón, your father didn't try. That's just who he was."

All our eyes shifted to my father, lying defeated on the hospital bed.

———

"How will we explain to Rubén?" I asked.

"I will tell him. All Rubén needs to know is that your dad will be in Heaven," my mother answered.

I nodded. Suddenly, religion made sense.

———

In the dark of night, I was left alone in the hospital room. My mother and Grandma Fina had taken Rubén home. When they rolled away the machines, the room fell silent except for my father's gentle snoring. And then, it was like all those times we sat in the rocking chairs on Grandma Fina's back porch, where he would dispense advice as he dozed off. I half-expected him to part with a priceless pearl of wisdom, but instead the snoring grew softer and further apart. I talked to him, whispered to him.

"I'm sorry, Dad. I love you, Dad. I wish I would have been a better son." And I waited.

———

I had always chased something so elusive and somewhat undefined while taking for granted all that I'd been born with, all that I had around me.

Now a big part of that birthright was gone. When the nurses confirmed he had passed, they allowed me some time in the room. I sat precariously on the edge of the hospital bed, wondering where he was now, if anywhere. Did any echo of his consciousness and indefatigable spirit remain? Or was he simply—and completely—gone forever? Could he see me from some vantage point floating overhead? Did he yearn to console me and stay with me? Did he stand nearby but unseen beyond some invisible and impenetrable wall that divided us, those breathing in this world and those journeying in the next?

I kissed his cooling forehead and whispered goodbye, my tears baptizing his new birth. Outside by the parking lot, on a patch of damp grass, I crumpled to my knees beneath the stars as the cicadas drowned out my bereaved cries.

———

In our tradition, there was a wake and a rosary the night before the funeral. As I stood before the open casket, I realized it was the only time I'd ever seen my father lie completely still. He'd always been up with the sun, working while the rest of us still slept. He wore a black Western suit with snap buttons, a crisp white shirt, and the bolo tie Clara had given him. I'd never seen him dressed so fancily. I yearned for another glimpse of him in one of his soot-streaked guayaberas frayed from years of wear, his brow damp with sweat, his black hair tangled and slick with tire grease.

Retreating from his repose, the family stood stoically in the front pew as well-wishers filed by to pay their respects to the dead and share their condolences with the living.

Like a ghost of myself, I shook the hands of his old friends and customers. Some of them I knew from my childhood days at the plant. Others I failed to recognize, nodding robotically as they voiced their regrets. A dark-skinned woman with piercing gray eyes, accompanied by her wispy teenage daughter, wept as she clasped my cheeks between her calloused hands. Her tears flowed down deep cuts in her cheeks grooved by years in the sun. She looked vaguely familiar, but I could not recall who she was. As she and her daughter shuffled morosely by, I was surprised to see Dante, soaring like a mountain in front of me.

Skipping the perfunctory handshake, he wrapped his thick arms tightly around me. "I'm sorry about your dad," he said. And I knew he was. He patted me firmly on the back. "I'm here for you," he said. And I knew he would be.

At the funeral the next day, a trio sang at my father's gravesite as his casket was lowered into the ground. Accompanied by Cousin David on guitar, they played his favorite songs, classic tunes of love and loss like "Sin Tí" and "La Barca de Oro."

Rubén collapsed into tears, his whole body shaking in grief. My mom and Grandma Fina sat on either side of him, wrapping their arms around him, blanketing him with their love.

Little Bobby, now a burly behemoth who repaired air conditioners for a living, sauntered toward me in an ill-fitting black suit. He put his arms around me and said, "You were lucky to have him as your dad."

I knew he meant it. None of us, including him, had heard hide or hair of Uncle Bobby since he'd vanished years ago with my dad's tire money.

I stared up at the overcast sky and wondered what in the world would happen next.

———

"The funeral wiped us out. And your father had no life insurance," my mom lamented.

Reality is oblivious to grief, I realized in the sparse living room of the house they'd recently rented a few doors down from Grandma Fina.

My mom and I sat on a ripped couch we'd ferried around since our stint in Southmost. The fabric had once been sky blue, if I recalled correctly. It was now so faded, it was hard to tell whether the image was remembered or imagined. The only decorations in the barren room hung on the wall: one of my still life paintings of limes and a picture of the Virgen de Guadalupe. An exhausted Rubén slept in his room down the hall.

"What will you do?" I asked.

"Keep working. What else is there? I have to keep a roof over our heads."

"Is the catering business enough?"

"I don't know. I've never had to do this alone."

"Dad always struggled."

"But he never gave up."

"He always came through," I agreed.

She looked at me for a long time before speaking. "When will you go back to New York?"

"I don't know. I haven't even thought about it."

She nodded. "Well, you can stay here as long as you want. But, please know, I understand you have your own life to live."

"Did you know he was sick?" I wondered aloud.

"No. He never said anything about feeling bad."

I thought about all the times he had asked me when I might come home for a visit. Over time—especially more recently—his inquiries had transformed into increasingly urgent suggestions. I had ignored them all, oblivious to the possibility he might have feared we'd never see each other again.

"Do you think he knew?" I asked.

"The doctors said he should have had warning signs. But he never went to the doctor. He never complained about any pain. You know how he was . . ."

"Puro macho," we mourned in unison, morosely shaking our heads.

———

I needed to put gas in my dad's rusty pickup, so I swung by the Pronto on Paredes Line Road. The pump sported a sign that instructed customers to pay inside first. All I had were a few crumpled dollar bills and some assorted coins, which I spread across the counter in front of Dante. He didn't bother to count them as he told me to fill her up.

"You don't have to do that," I assured him.

"I want to."

"It's very generous of you."

"It's not my gasoline. But thank you."

I smiled.

"You want a beer?" he asked.

"I don't have money for that either."

"Just come by later and I'll give you one of mine. We close at midnight."

At midnight, I returned to the Pronto. I shadowed Dante as he turned off the lights and pulled a couple cold ones from the beer cave. Beneath the roof that sheltered the gasoline pumps, we sat on the tailgate of my dad's pickup and clinked beer bottles before drinking.

"To your dad," Dante offered somberly.

I nodded, and we swigged vigorously from the chilled longnecks.

"So when do you leave?" Dante asked.

"I don't know."

"It's tough when your parents die," he said.

I realized at that moment I had no idea about his parents. Were they alive? Dead?

"Mine are both gone," he answered my unasked questions as if he could read my mind. "It's weird because it's like they're a line of defense between you and the Great Unknown. And then when they're gone, you can't help but feel like you're next."

I nodded sullenly in agreement. "I was worried about my future. Now I'm just worried about staying alive."

"It'll get better." My sarcasm had always eluded him.

"What happened to your parents?" I asked.

"Car crash."

"I'm sorry."

"It was right after graduation. You were up in New York."

"I kind of lost touch with this place."

"You should lose touch again as fast you can," he urged. "Go back."

"Why?"

"Because, man. You made it out. Of everyone I've known growing up here at the edge of nowhere, you have the best chance to make it, to do something big. Don't let your dad's passing change things. You were on your way. You're successful. I read the article in *The Herald* about your art show in New York, the one about La Virgen in the tree. You were a big hit."

I drank the cold beer, savoring its bitter flavor. "Things aren't always as they seem, Dante."

We sipped in silence beneath the flickering lights as we watched the cars whiz by at speeds dangerously beyond the limit.

C

RECAPPING

I spent my days languishing on the dilapidated couch, watching reruns on TV. From there, I studiously watched my mother perform her daily duties, getting Rubén ready for school, escorting him out onto the front porch when the short yellow school bus blared its horn. Through the shabby blinds, I observed as the bus driver helped Rubén climb the stairs. The bus was equipped with a wheelchair lift, but Rubén had been making strides and didn't even own a wheelchair anymore. His walker sufficed. Once Rubén had departed, I listened to my mother's movements as she churned through the house like a whirlwind, cleaning fastidiously before heading to Grandma Fina's to collaborate on the day's catering orders. After a mind-numbing succession of '70s shows, the bus returned, Rubén slowly stepping down with assistance and then using his walker to cross the front yard toward the house. My mother materialized on cue to receive him, helping him labor up the stairs. They soon became so accustomed to my horizontal sprawl in the living room that they barely glanced at me as they shuffled past me toward the kitchen, where Rubén ate an after-school snack and recounted the mundane events of his day. Speech therapy. Occupational therapy. Basic reading and math. Lunch in the cafeteria. Arts and crafts. He was fifteen years old and half-orphaned like me. Also like me, he was a Porter Cowboy, but he was allowed to learn at his own pace in the special ed classroom. It appeared from the worksheets he brought home that maybe he was currently somewhere between the first and second grade level.

In the evenings, after dinner, my mom and Rubén would head over to Grandma Fina's, joining her and a cluster of neighbors in praying the rosary. They said they were praying for our father's soul, inviting me to join. But I demurred, insisting that I must watch the prime-time TV shows as a refreshing break from the monotony and outdated propriety of the day's diet of stale reruns.

As I stagnated there, day after day, I grew a mustache and beard, not because I had planned a change in appearance but simply because I was too unmotivated to shave. My hair grew shaggy and long. My mom washed my clothes and hung them up to dry on clotheslines in the back-yard, just like Grandma Fina did at her home. At least that much was clean, even if I forgot to shower.

After countless weeks of this uninspiring routine, my mother surprised me one morning after sending Rubén to school. She stood over me, somewhat menacingly, a pile of dirty clothes under one of her arms and an incongruous spatula in the other. Did she aim to beat me and then smother me with the laundry?

"Ramón, you can't go on like this," she complained.

"I'm depressed."

"López men don't get depressed," she objected. "When did you ever see your dad lying on a couch? When did you ever see him spend a day in bed? Even when he was sick, he woke up before all of us and worked."

"Yeah, and look where it got him? An early grave."

She frowned disapprovingly. "I have a feeling this is about more than your father."

I stared past her at the black-and-white TV screen. An episode of *Leave It To Beaver* was playing on TBS. Beaver reminded me of myself back when I'd been an inventive little kid with a knack for getting into trouble with nuns.

"Ramón?" she pressed.

"Yes?"

"Did something go wrong in New York?"

I grunted noncommittally.

"When I couldn't find you and I finally reached Clara, she seemed very uneasy. And you haven't talked to her on the phone once since you've been down here. And what about your work? Aren't people waiting for you back in New York? Didn't you have a job, a gallery where you were showing your art?"

I stared at her as if she was speaking a language I failed to comprehend.

"I can't let you carry on like this," she continued, her face a fiery red chile piquín. "Your whole life you had lofty dreams and I supported you, even when your ever-optimistic dad doubted that they could be made into reality. Then when you left to go north, your dad blamed me, said it was my fault we'd lost you. And now this is how you show your thanks? By lying on the sofa day in and day out? Is that what you worked so hard for, and earned that degree for? To feel sorry for yourself and watch TV all day? What happened to your dreams?"

My dreams were as dead as my dad, but I wasn't about to admit it out loud.

"If you're not going to get back to your life," she waved the spatula adamantly, "then I'm going to have to assign you chores. I can't watch a grown man do nothing while the rest of us struggle to get on with our lives and pay the bills."

"Chores? What chores?" The mere thought repulsed me. It was a mighty fall, plummeting from dreams to chores within the span of the same conversation.

"Someone needs to go down to your father's tire shop and assess the situation."

"What is there to assess?" I asked. There were sure to be bald tires in need of vulcanizing. Giant silver molds hulking in their old places, same as years ago, when I'd run about there, getting underfoot. What would I find but a pile of unpaid bills and no rubber with which to operate, per my dad's final update?

"Well, we can't just let it sit there forever until it rusts and crumbles or gets stolen. It's an asset. Aside from the worthless piece of land in México your dad insisted on calling a ranch, it's the only asset he owned. We need to either put it to work or see if we can sell it."

"He probably owed rent to the landlord," I answered, my eyes wavering back over the TV. I was missing the jokes. Eddie Haskell was visiting Beaver's house and flirting with Mrs. Cleaver, which was always the most amusing part of the formulaic script. "Maybe the landlord would just take it off our hands in exchange for whatever the debt is."

"No. I spoke with the landlord and the place had been abandoned all those years your dad had the plant in Matamoros. So he made a special deal with your dad that he could put the plant there and start paying him rent once he had it up and running."

"That's a good deal."

"Yes. I was pleasantly surprised when he told me about it."

"Who? Dad?"

"No, the landlord. Your dad never told me anything about his business."

I sighed, reluctantly extinguishing the TV. "Fine. I'll go take a look, but I can't make any promises. Dad's assets tended to be more like liabilities."

"Don't disrespect your father's memory." My mom made the sign of the cross and looked up at the ceiling like he might be suspended up there as a chandelier.

I shook my head. It was hard to envision myself ever getting back to New York, but it was equally difficult imagining how I might survive here long-term.

As she left the room, my mom shot me a withering look. "And what is it about you López men that you don't want to ever talk about what's going on inside your heads? That's probably what killed your dad. He kept everything bottled up inside. I hope you don't turn out like him."

With that, she stomped off to complete her morning tasks. Slowly sitting up, my joints felt stiff and my limbs were sore. I even felt a bit lightheaded. My heart was likely no longer accustomed to pumping the blood upward—fighting gravity—to nourish my clouded brain. What if I did end up just like my dad? A jolt of fear flashed through my mind, spurring my heart rate. Had that final admonishment from my mom been as disrespectful to his memory as my own dread of ending up in his shoes?

———

Entering the tire shop was like stepping into a makeshift, shoestring-budget museum dedicated to my dad's life. The building still sagged next to the train tracks, the "Joe's Tire Shop" sign dangling askew by the road. Inside, the plant was just as I remembered it from my childhood. Three large steel molds painted silver occupied the long, narrow space. The roof was constructed of corrugated metal, and there was no insulation. In the summer, the heat was diabolical. Every door and window had to be kept open, large industrial fans blowing air through the place so its human inhabitants didn't bake alongside the tires. In the winter, if the molds were not in use, the oversized tin shed became a chilly icebox. The floor was made of raw cement covered in countless layers of soot and dust. Against the long back wall, a tall wide rack contained a wide assortment of molds, varied patterns gracing the insides of the massive metal rings. Toward the rear, there was a storage area for tires as well as space for the boxes of rubber my dad ordered from Akron, Ohio. Out back, protected by a tall chain-link fence crowned by rolls of barbed wire, sat stacks and stacks of bald tires waiting to be recapped. The longer they lingered there, the more rainwater they collected in their hollow innards, the thicker the swarms of voracious mosquitos one had to confront while dragging casings into the plant.

Finally, a tiny office occupied the far corner. Stacks of papers smothered a metal desk. I sat in the torn green vinyl seat of the office chair my dad had used throughout his entire career as a tire man. Here he had sat for at least two decades, running his hands through his wavy black hair, fretting over insurmountable invoices, scribbling endless cash flow calculations, strategizing different ways to squeeze more profit from his cash-strapped operation, juggling vendor payments along with the bare necessities for his family. Being in his tire plant without him yet envisioning him there in the days prior to his death, I felt overwhelmed by grief. Brushing tears from my eyes, I leafed through the papers. Most of what I saw made no sense to me, the misguided projections of a man who subsisted precariously on the ever-narrowing brink between delusion and desperation. That shrinking foothold had—at some point—become a precipice, and my father had finally teetered off it. I wondered exactly where on the plant floor that customer had found his fallen body. My eyes landed on the archaic beige phone. It still featured a rotary dial. The man had probably used that same phone to try and save my dad's life. I picked it up to see if it had a dial tone. Surprisingly, it still did. However, judging by the pile of phone bills I'd discovered in the mailbox and on the desk, that line might go silent at any moment. Placing the receiver down. I scanned the open mail, letters that my father had probably read in the days before his passing. One of them was a rejection from a life insurance company. The letter cryptically stated that due to the results of his health exam, specifically his EKG, they were unable to provide coverage at this time. He had to have known, I thought. He must have felt something was wrong with his heart. Why hadn't he gone to a doctor? Had his lack of health insurance made him resign himself to whatever his fate might bring? Had he simply gone into denial? Perhaps he had resorted to the venerated Mexican tradition of accepting "lo que Dios mande," whatever God may send. Regardless, even though he'd dragged Rubén to countless appointments over the years, he clearly hadn't taken care of himself. Now, what would become of Rubén and our mother? He'd left them alone before his time. Sorting through the papers, I found the most recent bank statement for the business. He was overdrawn by twenty-five dollars and ten cents. The overdraft amount was due to a fee for a check he'd written with non-sufficient funds. The returned check was included in the envelope. It had been a payment for $2,000 to the rubber company in Ohio. Quickly, I shuffled through more papers and found a cost estimate for boxes of rubber on the same company's letterhead. It was for the same amount. Had he died because he couldn't scrape together the money to get the plant up and running? I scratched my chin in consternation. The last thing my dad had ever signed was a hot check. The realization rendered me even more despondent. Tears flowed freely from eyes. I had to step outside the plant for a while to catch my breath and clear my mind. There was something suffocating about the air in the plant. It reeked of spent rubber, of dirty and frayed tires that had left their mark on thousands of miles of highways all over North America only to end up here—clinging to their last chance at a second life—in a shack by the side of the railroad tracks in Brownsville, Texas.

I circled back to the fenced-in area and counted tires. There must have been about a hundred of them waiting to be resurrected. If I recalled my dad's mathematical ruminations at the dinner table correctly, he could recap a tire for $20 in hard rubber costs and then turn around and sell the retread at $100 a pop. I hurried back into the office, focusing in on one of his sheets of calculations, and his plan started to come together before my fuzzy eyes. He'd needed that $2,000 shipment of rubber to recap the 100 tires sitting in the holding pen. Once he sold those tires, he'd make a cool $8,000 profit and have ten grand total in his pocket. Plenty with which to cover the higher living costs now that they had moved to Brownsville while also reinvesting in building up the business. He'd been close, I thought. So close he could taste it. I could picture his eyes glowing with excitement at the prospects, and then dimming forever as those aspirations faded away due to a frustrating lack of resources.

I was far from sure what my future held, but—for the moment—I had an idea. I sat back in the creaky office chair, leafed through the phone book, and picked up the telephone just as I'd seen my dad do numerous times over the years. I felt a long-forgotten but distinctly familiar excitement stirring inside me as the phone rang on the other end. I hadn't felt this way since my days selling chile powder in fifth grade.

———

Dante eyed me suspiciously from behind the counter at the Pronto mart. "You don't really want a job here," he assured me.

"I need to raise some money," I explained. "It won't be permanent."

"That's what I told myself when I started working here over four years ago." He leaned in and whispered as if the store might overhear and wreak some form of retribution on him, "The only thing that's 'pronto' about this place is that it quickly crushes your dreams."

"You said you were here for me," I pressured him.

"I meant physically here, like if you needed to find me and wanted to have a beer and talk."

"Just think about it. Talk to your boss."

"If you get a job here, your legend will be ruined. Everyone in town will think you didn't make it in New York. They'll call you a loser. Trust me, I know. After high school, no one's afraid of getting beat up by a former football player."

"I don't care about my reputation, Dante. All I care about is getting my hands on some cash."

"Okay," he reluctantly acquiesced. "But please, if the owner hires you, put the money to good use. Get the hell out of here. Go back to New York."

"I thought you liked having me around." I grinned, buoyed by the possibilities.

"I do, but not forever. I know you can do better."

———

The following week, I was back at the tire plant, where'd I'd been spending my days cleaning and straightening, as well as—admittedly—snooping through all of my dad's personal belongings—his old yearbooks, boxes overflowing with correspondence, photo albums of his childhood. I burst into tears yet again when I came across my dog-eared childhood journal. He had saved it all these years. It was open to the page where I had first started sketching limes. Why hadn't he kept these things at home? Why had he been so determined that my mother never fully know and understand him?

My dad had been a packrat when it came to receipts. It was as if he needed to hang on to physical evidence of where his hard-earned money had all gone so that he could reassure himself that his herculean efforts had not been completely squandered. The receipts were organized in cardboard boxes labeled by year. Within each box there were specific files for certain subjects, like rubber, rent, food, Rubén's medical bills, the money he wired me in New York.

While rifling through one of the boxes, I came across a thick file labeled simply: "Rancho." Oddly, instead of receipts for livestock feed or fence posts, the manila folder was stuffed with medical invoices. At the back, I also found a photo of a teenage girl. She had smooth, dark skin, long black hair, and dark eyes. I recognized her immediately as the girl that had attended my dad's wake alongside her mother, the weather-beaten woman with the bright gray eyes.

Why were they so familiar to me? Who where they? Why had my dad been paying for all of these medical bills while barely staying afloat himself? Could this be the elusive second family of which my mom had heard persistent rumors throughout my upbringing? My heart pounded so hard it rattled my chest. I dreaded discovering something about my father that I'd rather never know about.

The picture was attached by a paper clip to a letter. Tentatively, I flipped the photo over, reading the name "Emilia" on the back. Emilia! Now I realized who this young woman was. She was the baby my dad and I had smuggled across the border so many years ago. The letter's penmanship and grammar were those of a child, but it quickly became clear to me that it had been written not by Emilia but by her mother. In the letter, she thanked my father for all the support he had provided to help Emilia over the years with her range of health issues. According to Señora Fernandez:

Don José: Emilia was born with many problems. She would have never survived without the help of you and your son that day you took us across the river to the hospital. Over the years, as her illnesses persisted, you were always there for us, to arrange our papers so she could cross back and forth to the doctors' visits, to help pay for the medicines she needed to stay alive. My husband and I thank you for helping our daughter. She is our young- est, and without her we would be all alone and quite sad. We are forever in your debt. May God bless you. Sincerely, María Mendoza de Fernandez.

I hated myself for having doubted my father. Even now that he was dead, all I could do was think less of him than what he actually was worth. My whole life, all I had obsessed about—and focused on accomplishing—were my selfish, materialistic goals. All I had yearned for—and strived for—was a superficial American Dream wrapped up in financial success and public recognition. I had mistakenly believed that my father was fixated on the same kind of shallow objectives, but suddenly—as I found myself surrounded by boxes of receipts for all of the bills he'd paid to provide for others—I understood that my father had worked relentlessly not for himself, but for those who depended on him. His life had not been devoted to creating personal glory, but to serving those he loved, as well as those who had no means to produce on their own account. Those boxes crammed full of receipts, arrayed all about me now, contained my father's parting lesson to me. *For once, Ramón,* the papers whispered in a chorus of hushed cardboard tones, *think beyond yourself.*

Dumbfounded, I idled in the ripped green chair for an immeasurable span of time, staring vacantly at the photo of Emilia, my eyes blurring over her mother's rudimentary handwriting, until my reverie was disrupted by the shrill ringing of the beige phone on the desk.

When I picked up the phone, Dante immediately blurted out the good news. "You're hired. There's just one catch."

"What's that?"

"The hours are horrible. The owner's been thinking of trying to stay open all night, so you'd be working the shift after mine, midnight to 8 a.m."

"I'll take it."

"You could get killed, man. That's when convenience stores get robbed most often."

"I'll take my chances."

"You've lost your mind."

"Maybe," I thought about it. "Probably. We'll see." I wouldn't be the first López walking the fine line between unbridled optimism and certifiable insanity.

Night after night, I showed up at the Pronto a bit before midnight. Dante and I chugged a ritual beer together and then I worked my graveyard shift, occasionally contending politely with shocked customers who had last heard about me in a local newspaper article raving about my artistic success in New York. It was amusing to witness their quick journey through the stages of grief. First, they couldn't believe it was me, standing behind the counter at Pronto. Next came the anger. They felt betrayed by my failure, like I owed them something for their misplaced faith. They invariably bargained with my future, trying to convince themselves and me that there might yet be hope for me to get back to New York. Then, disappointment dawned on them. My success had been their success, the notion that someone from these parts could measure up in Manhattan fueling an ember of hope that their lives too could still miraculously become extraordinary. And at last, by the time I handed them their receipt, came their acceptance and pity. But I assured them I would be fine. Working at Pronto was by no means a terminal disease.

In the mornings, I'd go to the house and sleep while my mom and Rubén were off at work and school. In the afternoons, I would drive to the tire shop and continue my efforts to enhance it through the kind of elbow grease I'd never seen my dad take an interest in. I repainted the exterior in its original white and red colors. I fashioned a new sign and fixed it so it would not hang at a dismal angle. I pulled the weeds from the front parking lot. I swept and mopped the floors until I could see the gray cement. I cleaned and polished the steel molds. I replaced and added light bulbs so that the shop shone fresh and sharp, the silver paint of the vulcanizing furnaces gleaming brightly. I threw out reams of old papers and boxes of unnecessary detritus. I organized the tires into neat stacks and covered them with tarps so that the rainwater would not pool inside of them. I sprayed them so the mosquitos would stop feasting upon me when I came to work. I even staked out a space at the heart of the plant for a drop cloth, an easel, and some canvases in case artistic inspiration ever struck again.

As the weeks passed, I diligently deposited my paychecks from the Pronto into the tire shop's bank account, replacing my dad as the signatory by showing the banker his death certificate. The nearer I got to amassing the $2,000, the more I gravitated toward the blank canvas perched on the easel in the tire shop. I stared at it for hours, setting a rigid metal chair in front of it. But nothing came to me except numbers. The inventory codes for the rubber I needed to order. The street address and phone number of the company in Akron, Ohio. I could hardly contain my desire to call them and place the order, triumphantly redeeming Joe's Tire Shop in their eyes. The different sums I'd allocate from the profits to various needs, from helping my mom with the rent, to paying the landlord, to reinvesting in more rubber, to purchasing bald tires. Maybe I could someday bid on a lot from the State, just like my dad had done years earlier only to be stumped by Uncle Bobby's untimely larceny.

Instead of painting a picture, I dabbed my brush into globs of blue and yellow paint and used the canvas as a giant notepad. I used the blue for revenues that would come in and the yellow for expense that would flow out. My method was not as efficient and concise as the notepads my dad had used, but I found it therapeutic to paint again, even if my product was just an odd jumble of mathematical calculations.

Noticing the improved state of the tire shop from the road, some of my dad's old customers began to stop by to see what was going on. They were pleasantly surprised to find me there, a few of them remembering me as a kid. I told them soon I'd have the plant running, and they left me their phone numbers and notes on how many tires they needed. Invariably, they walked over to my canvases covered in numbers, which now lined a wall of the building. "You're the artist," they'd remark, their memory stirred. "You're the one that was up in New York for a while. Your dad always talked about you."

I'd smile modestly and assure them I was a tire man now.

Early on a Sunday morning, after my shift at Pronto ended, I decided to vary my routine. I swung by Señor Donut, where Perla still reigned supreme behind the counter, her hair gray now, her pink uniform tighter around her ever-expanding midriff, tugging menacingly at the buttons. We reminisced about my father as she filled a box with assorted donuts.

"I'm going out to see Emilia and her parents," I told her.

"Ay," she replied. "How sweet of you. That Emilia is a survivor. Your dad never stopped looking after them. I'm glad to see you have a lot of him in you."

I smiled as I waved goodbye and drove my dad's red Ford pickup over the desolate bridge at dawn, the river a silver snake twisting toward the Gulf beneath the changing sky. I hadn't made this pilgrimage to the ranch in about eight or nine years, not since my parents had moved to Matamoros and I had stayed at Grandma Fina's house. Still, I knew my way from memory.

Nestled behind the row of familiar trees, the ranch looked the same. But instead of a crowd of children exploding out of the cinder-block hut, only Primo Fernandez, his wife, and Emilia came out to greet me. They smiled wistfully as they saw the glossy orange box from Señor Donut I carried in my hands. We sat around their crudely made wooden table, drank coffee, ate donuts, and shared stories about my father.

"Where are all the kids?" I asked.

"They did what kids do," Fernandez explained. "They've all grown up and gone off to work. It's just us three now."

The women nodded. Emilia peered at me shyly from behind her chocolate donut, her large black eyes flitting away when I looked at her.

"Thank you for coming to my father's rosary," I told them.

"I'm sorry I couldn't make it," Fernandez said. "I work in the city in the evenings. Besides, I don't think I could have seen your father . . . like that. He was always so full of life. I'd rather always remember him that way."

I nodded in agreement, wishing I could do the same.

"Why did you stop coming to the ranch with your father?" Señora Fernandez asked.

"I thought we had our differences," I confessed. "Now I wish I could do it all over again. I wish I could have those Sundays with him back."

We all stared solemnly into our coffee cups as the dark liquid grew cold.

"We must be thankful for what we have," Primo Fernandez concluded. "Even if it's not exactly what we want."

I nodded, wishing I'd been more grateful when I'd had the chance.

"Your father was always a generous man, even when he had little to give," Primo Fernandez said. "He let us stay out here on the ranch, even when—as times got tough and he had to sell off the cattle—there wasn't much for us to do. He couldn't pay me a wage anymore, but in exchange for letting us live here, we have watched over the place, mended the fences when they've needed it . . ." His voice snagged. Hesitating, he glanced worriedly at his wife before continuing. "We understand that you might need to sell the ranch or maybe you have different plans for it?"

I shook my head, "No, this land is not meant to be sold. It is meant to be preserved as a piece of who we are. That is what my father would have wanted. If it's okay with you, I would like to continue working together in the same way."

Fernandez and his wife both sighed in relief.

"Who knows, maybe someday we'll see cattle roam across these fields again," I continued. "And you can call me at the tire plant if you or Emilia need help with anything medical. I'll do whatever I can."

"Gracias, m'ijo," they said together.

When we finished our coffee, they walked me out to the truck. We shook hands and I told them I'd be back in a few weeks. At the last second, as I was about to climb into the truck, Emilia rushed from her mother's side and gave me a hug. She didn't say a word, but I knew she was thinking of my father, and all I could do was remember her as the tiny baby that stopped crying when she was placed in my arms.

———

It took about three months for me to finally gather enough money from my Pronto paychecks so that all the bills were caught up and the bank balance exceeded the amount required for the rubber. That day, I gleefully ended my brief stint as a convenience store employee. Nobody was happier for me than Dante, who sent me off with a free beer and a round of applause.

At home over dinner, I rambled to my mom and Grandma Fina about the conversation I'd had on the phone with the man in Akron about the rubber. "They agreed to let me pay COD. That's Cash On Delivery. The rubber should be here in three days!" I scribbled some numbers on my napkin as my mom and Grandma Fina gawked at me like they'd seen a ghost. They sat speechless, their tacos hovering en route to their open mouths.

"You sound like Dad," Rubén drawled.

I paused mid-math exercise and looked up at him, smiling. "You know what, Rubén? You're right. And you know what else? For once, I'm okay with that."

———

When the freight truck carrying the rubber finally arrived at the plant, I was so eager I helped the grizzly deliveryman roll the cardboard cartons inside, using the extra dolly my dad had kept on hand for such momentous occasions. Working together, we stacked the boxes neatly in the storage area. When we were done and I had signed the papers and provided payment, he paused to puzzle at the cryptic blue and yellow canvases leaning against the wall. He didn't ask any questions. As he exited, he shook his head and muttered, "Now I've really seen it all."

I cut open the first container and got to work, just like my father had taught me as a child. I rolled in three tractor-trailer tires, one for each furnace, all of which were already outfitted with molds to retread the tires. I used a wide paintbrush to coat the tires' bald surfaces with a clear adhesive. Then I wrapped them with the rubber, which was encased in a thin blue film. As I waited for the adhesive to dry and the rubber to set, I stared hungrily at the large blank canvas I'd recently placed on the easel. When the bell rang on the alarm clock to alert me it was time to insert the tires into the furnaces, I carefully hooked them one by one to the cranes that hoisted them into place. As a kid, I had watched Pedro do this hundreds of times. Climbing up over the sides of the molds, I pushed and prodded the tires into their spots, lowered the lids over them, and spun the wheels to screw the lids tight, just like my dad had taught me when I'd been in high school. Now it was time for the ultimate test, igniting the furnaces. I threw the switches and watched the temperature and pressure gauges flutter to life as the round metal ovens heated up. I set the alarm clock to notify me when the baking process was completed, which should be in about three hours. I scanned the projections I'd painted on one of the canvases. It took two hours to set up the molds and three hours to cook the tires. If I did two shifts a day, toiling for ten hours, I could recap six tires per day. At that rate it would take me sixteen days to renovate the current tire inventory. I already had commitments from customers for all one hundred. I was aware it would actually take seventeen days, but—like my father—I preferred to round in the direction that was most beneficial to rendering rosy projections. I smiled as I gazed at that particular assemblage of numbers. Essentially, in two weeks I'd have ten thousand dollars. I didn't know what I was going to do with them, although I had laid out various possible directions in which I could go, all of which were represented by their own collections of numbers on the different canvases I'd hung. I could take the money and run back to New York, use it to start over, and give my art career another shot. Or I could stay here and build Joe's Tire Shop into the business I always dreamed it could become, had my father not insisted on squandering his profits on fool's errands like the legendary lime business that broke him more than once. I could even recruit Dante as an assistant, just like my dad had relied on Pedro, the human pinball, to increase the plant's productivity. Reinvestment was the key, I had pontificated at the dinner table just a few nights earlier, causing my mom to nearly choke on her picadillo con papas.

The plant grew hot quickly. As I scrambled to open windows and doors, firing up fans, I sensed a presence that stopped me in my tracks. I had forgotten to turn on the lights and failed to notice night falling outside. The plant had rapidly descended into dusky darkness during my frenzied labor. The molds hissed and spewed steam into the air, along with the sharp stench of baking rubber. I could imagine the recapped tires' lifeblood boiling like black lava inside the pressurized molds, merging with the bald shells and oozing into the shapes and patterns into which they were pressed. I scanned the room, my heart thundering in my chest. The presence I felt was as familiar as the sight of swirling steam and the sounds of clanging metal and hissing vapor. It was the "Joe" in "Joe's Tire Shop." It was the spirit of my father.

My eyes searched through the shadows but could discern nothing but the outlines of the molds in the dim light filtering through the windows, the steam rising toward the rafters. Surely, it was my overactive artist's imagination, I assured myself, flipping on the overhead lights and balking before the canvas I'd stared at blankly for days. Cocking my head sideways, I examined it. In one fluid motion, I swept it off the easel, flung it to the floor, and crouched over it, palette and brush in hand. Falling into a trancelike state, I worked the brush rhythmically over the canvas. At first, I found myself regurgitating numbers in blue and yellow, just as I had for months. But then, I was using my bare hands, rubbing soot and grime from the rubber over the canvas in a primal way. I didn't have an image in mind, I was simply moving across the canvas, directed by an unseen energy, an indescribable and uncontainable force that was channeling through me as never before. As the tires baked, I painted. And as I painted, I thought about my father. And when I thought about my father, I also thought about my hometown and about the border on which it had risen. My father had moved constantly, restlessly even, back and forth across that border throughout the course of his life. Maybe I too could straddle it. Not just the boundary between two nations, but rather the border of things. As much as I'd always complained about Brownsville, there was something magical about it. After all, my best ideas had all sprung from here. Maybe my choices weren't exclusively between being an artist in New York or being a tire man in Brownsville. Maybe I could paint and work to make a living right here where I'd been born, where I'd been forged into who I was, into the child I'd been, into the man I was still in the process of becoming. Maybe I could be my own person, yet still be a contributing member of my family, using some of the proceeds from the plant to help my mom and Rubén, and the Fernandez family out on the ranch. Maybe I could stand with one foot on either side of the river and not lose my balance, not be swept by its treacherous waters out to the drowning sea. It seemed that the closer

I got to the border, the more it blurred, until it disappeared. Who knew what I would do, but I was here now and I could create and I could re-cycle. And I could reconnect.

Suddenly, I paused mid-thought, my brush hovering over the canvas. And I witnessed the presence I suspected of inhabiting the steam-shrouded room. There, on the canvas, stepping forth from a sea of blue and yellow numbers in the background, emerging from black smoke and smeared grime, my father's smoldering eyes gazed intensely at me through the steam and mist. Somehow, we had found a way to momentarily permeate the eternal border between us. As tears flowed from my eyes onto the canvas, I dropped the brush and used my fingers to make smudges with the salty fluid, tenderly smoothing out the hard angles, adding nuance and shadows to his face, to his powerful figure, to the Stetson hat that crowned his head. As I wept and worked, I heard his voice urging me to never surrender. Never relent. Never stop cross-ing the boundaries before me.

When the bell rang, I stood back from my painting. It was the best work I'd ever done. I found myself making the sign of the cross and thanking my father for not abandoning me. Hurrying to the furnaces, I spun the wheels and raised the lids. Steam flooded out, swirling upward through the light. As I'd been taught long ago, I wielded a heavy crow-bar to pry the recapped tires out of their molds. I reattached the cranes and swung the tires to the floor, carefully examining their newly man-ufactured grooves. They were perfect, like freshly made donuts straight from the oven. Releasing them from their chains, I lined them up next to my canvases.

I placed my new painting back on the easel, angling it toward the wall so that my father could admire our work. Tomorrow, the recapped tires—renewed and reinvented—would roll again, as would I.

ACKNOWLEDGMENTS

I have dedicated this novel to mi familia. And I am grateful to the three families that helped me bring this novel to life.

The family I was born into provided inspiration for many of the characters, events, and settings in the book, especially my father, Rodolfo Cisneros Ruiz, my mother, Lilia Zolezzi Ruiz, my brothers Raul and Jerry Ruiz, my grandmother Ninfa Cisneros Ruiz, my cousin David Alex Ruiz, and my uncle Bobby Ruiz. The family I grew up with is comprised of more fascinating characters than I could ever mention. I appreciate the entire Ruiz Cisneros clan for being who they are: larger than life and unforgettable.

The family my wife, Heather, and I have built together has always encouraged and embraced my passion for writing. Thank you to Heather, Paloma, and Lorenzo for their constant love and support. This novel began with a childhood story my children would frequently ask me to recount. They would chant, "Tell us the chile story again, Dad." Eventually, they spurred me to write it. As I did so, I realized how I could fictionalize many experiences and observations from my upbringing on the border into a tale that might capture the imagination of readers, perhaps reshaping how they feel about the border and the people who cross it as an essential function of their lives. Lorenzo would read each new story the moment I finished the first draft. His eagerness and excitement coupled with his positive feedback fueled my desire to continue fleshing out Ramón López's perilous journey from childhood to adulthood. Paloma urged me to submit the stories to literary journals, and Heather cheered me on every step of the long, winding way. From the writing of the first chapter in 2008 to the publication of the completed novel, the entire process took sixteen years. In that time, not only did Ramón grow up but so did my own children. So, thank you to my beloved family for sharing—and cherishing—this deeply personal odyssey with me.

Finally, I am grateful to my writing family. My agent Laura Strachan first reached out to me upon reading "That Boy Could Run" when it received the 2017 Gulf Coast Prize in Fiction. Her guidance has been instrumental in my writing career. Laura brought me together with the wonderful team at Blackstone Publishing, a family of their own, and one to which I'm honored to belong. Special thanks to my editors Marilyn Kretzer and Toni Kirkpatrick. And, lastly but very importantly, I must acknowledge that one of the most rewarding surprises of being an author has been the camaraderie with fellow writers and those who champion our work. Thank you to these early readers and friends: Nora Comstock de Hoyos, Rubén Degollado, Bruce Ferber, Guadalupe Garcia McCall, Jenn Givhan, Sergio Troncoso, and James Wade. It is an honor to write alongside you, in sincere hope that our larger family of readers will welcome and embrace our heartfelt thoughts and words. May our writing help shape a kinder and more forgiving world for all those young, aspiring Ramón López's precariously balancing on borders throughout our world.

AUTHOR'S NOTE

The following stories originally appeared in the same or slightly different form in the following publications:

"Ports of Entry"—*New Texas*, 2018

"Bending the Laws of Motion"—*Seven for the Revolution*, Winner of four International Latino Book Awards, 2014

"That Boy Could Run"—*Gulf Coast*, Winner of the Gulf Coast Prize in Fiction, 2017

"Allegiance"—*Dillydoun Review*, Honorable Mention in Dillydoun Review International Short Story Prize, Finalist for Texas Institute of Letters Best Short Story Award, 2022

"The Limes"—*New Texas*, Finalist for Texas Institute of Letters Best Short Story Award, 2019

"Coffee Port Road"—*New Texas*, 2020